RED RIGHT HAND

RED RIGHT HAND

CHRIS HOLM

MULHOLLAND
BOOKS
HODDER

First published in Great Britain in 2016 by Mulholland Books
An imprint of Hodder & Stoughton
An Hachette UK company

1

A CIP catalogue record for this title is available from the British Library

Trade Paperback ISBN 978 1 473 60620 3
eBook ISBN 978 1 473 60618 0

The author is grateful for permission to reprint lines from "Red RightHand,"
written by Nick Cave and published by Mute Song Limited.

Printed and bound by Clays Ltd, St Ives plc

Hodder & Stoughton policy is to use papers that are natural, renewable
and recyclable products and made from wood grown in sustainable
forests. The logging and manufacturing processes are expected to
conform to the environmental regulations of the country of origin.

Hodder & Stoughton Ltd
Carmelite House
50 Victoria Embankment
London EC4Y 0DZ

www.hodder.co.uk

Steve—thanks for the push

What if the breath that kindl'd those grim fires
Awak'd should blow them into sevenfold rage
And plunge us in the flames? or from above
Should intermitted vengeance arm again
His red right hand to plague us?

—John Milton, *Paradise Lost*

You're one microscopic cog
In his catastrophic plan
Designed and directed by
His red right hand

—Nick Cave and the Bad Seeds, "Red Right Hand"

SEVEN YEARS AGO

THE MAN STAGGERED into the lobby of the Albuquerque field office shortly after three a.m. His hair, black streaked with gray, was matted down by rain. His face was dusted with stubble and deeply lined. Tattered clothing clung to his lithe frame. His feet were bare and bleeding. Water, tinged red, pooled beneath him.

Special Agent Charlie Thompson glanced up from her paperwork in surprise. He hadn't shown up on any of the building's exterior surveillance cameras. If it weren't for the sudden roar of the storm through the open door, she might not have noticed him come in.

Thompson had graduated from Quantico only a month before, but somehow she'd already managed to piss off her new boss. Yancey had her pulling overnights on the front desk all week. Truthfully, she didn't mind. The odd phone call aside—conspiracy nuts, usually, too tangled up in their delusions to sleep—the graveyard shift was pretty quiet.

Tonight, though, a thunderstorm had blown in like the wrath of God. Lightning forked across the sky. Rolling thunder shook the building. Sheets of rain reduced the streetlights to blurry smears.

Poor guy's probably just a vagrant trying to get out of the rain, Thompson thought—although for some reason, she didn't quite believe it.

"Can I help you?" she asked.

Pale blue eyes regarded Thompson from bruised sockets. The man opened his mouth to speak, but all that came out was a dry croak. He swallowed hard, wincing, and limped across the lobby toward her. As he approached, she realized his knuckles were scraped raw. She flashed him a smile intended to disarm and surreptitiously thumbed the emergency-alert button on the two-way radio clipped to her belt.

When he reached the desk, he tried again. "I…need to talk to the special agent in charge." The words came out thick and wrong. Dried blood was caked in the creases at the corners of his mouth, and his jawline was misshapen, as if he'd recently had teeth removed, and not consensually.

"What's this regarding?" Thompson asked.

He fixed her with his cold, unblinking gaze. A crack of thunder rattled the windows. "I think it's better for the both of us"—he breathed deeply—"if I save that information for the special agent in charge."

"It's late, sir. SAIC Yancey left hours ago. He's probably asleep by now."

"Then pick up the fucking phone and wake him up!"

He banged a fist on the front desk to accentuate his point—and only then noticed the security guards.

There were four of them. They'd come running when they heard Thompson's distress signal via their walkies. Three fanned out to flank him, guns drawn. One attempted to approach him from behind, his hand resting on his holstered weapon, but froze when the man wheeled on him.

"Don't move," one of the guards shouted. "Hands in the air!"

The stranger crouched into a forward fighting stance, his eyes darting from one guard to the next. Despite his age and his disheveled appearance, he was corded with lean muscle like a middleweight boxer. The guards tensed, their fingers tightening on their triggers.

"I'm not playing, asshole! Get on the ground—now!"

Thompson stood and put her hands up, palms out—a calming gesture. "Whoa! Easy, guys. Everyone just take a breath. I'm sure we can sort this out."

In that moment, lightning struck the building. The thunder that accompanied it was immediate, deafening. The lobby plunged into darkness.

And the stranger made his move.

He lunged at the nearby guard, his left hand extended. A flash of gunfire lit the room—blinding Thompson momentarily—as one of the other guards discharged his weapon. The bullet zipped through the space he'd just vacated and dimpled the far wall. Then the web between the man's thumb and forefinger connected with his quarry's throat. The guard gurgled sickeningly as his airway collapsed. He would have fallen had the man not grabbed his trachea in a pinch grip and yanked, twisting his wrist so that the guard's back wound up pressed to his chest—a gasping, wheezing human shield.

The man drew the guard's sidearm and opened fire.

Thompson saw the rest unfold in freeze-frames, the darkness punctuated by lightning and muzzle flashes. One guard's knee exploded, and he went down screaming. Another took rounds to the shoulder, the wrist, the hip. The last guard standing rushed the man and tried to tackle him. The man released his human shield—who slumped, unconscious, to the floor—sidestepped the assault, grabbed his would-be attacker by the hair, and drove his knee into the man's nose. Then he yanked the guard upright—blood spraying in an arc from both nostrils—and tossed him through a glass display case.

Less than thirty seconds had elapsed since the storm had knocked out the building's power. Thompson clutched her shiny new sidearm in trembling hands and waited for the lightning to reveal her target.

The emergency backup lights kicked in, illuminating the fallen guards. Their assailant was nowhere in sight. Thompson, feeling suddenly exposed, took cover in the foot well of the desk.

For a long while, nothing happened. The only sounds she heard were the static hiss of rain against the windows and her own shallow, panicked breathing. Eventually, she mustered up the courage to climb out from beneath the desk and look around.

But when she emerged, she felt a gun barrel, still warm from firing, press against the back of her head.

"Put your weapon on the ground and get up slow."

She did as he instructed, her hands raised, her heart-beat a manic drumroll in her chest.

"Listen very carefully," he said. "I don't give a flying fuck what time it is. Get your goddamn boss on the line and tell him that the Devil's Red Right Hand would like a word with him."

TODAY

1.

J AKE RESTON'S GAZE traveled from the yellowed photo in his hand to the squat brick structure of Fort Point jutting into San Francisco Bay and the Golden Gate Bridge looming above it. Then he frowned and shook his head.

His wife, Emily, sighed. "Still no good?" Their youngest squirmed in her arms and let out a cry. Emily rocked her idly to settle her. "Sophia's hungry. She's going to get cranky if I don't feed her soon."

"We're getting closer," Jake replied. "Looks like we're maybe ten yards off—twenty at most."

"You said that half an hour ago," Emily said wearily. She looked as tired as she sounded. Her face was pale and drawn. Dark circles framed her eyes. She'd been averaging an hour or two of shut-eye a night since they left home a week ago. Apparently Sophia didn't sleep well in hotels—which meant neither did Emily.

"I know. I'm sorry. This time, I mean it."

Emily pursed her lips but said nothing. Hannah—their eldest, at thirteen—rolled her eyes and plucked her cell phone from her pocket. Jake struggled to tamp down his frustration at their lack of enthusiasm. He couldn't blame them, really; this was taking way longer than he'd anticipated. At least their middle child, Aidan—who was, at present, twirling in place with his arms out while making airplane noises—seemed content to let his dad fritter away the last Saturday of summer vacation.

"Just a little longer, guys—I promise."

"Uh-huh," said Hannah without looking up from her phone.

"You know," he said, gesturing toward the crowded overlook behind them, "some people actually come here of their own accord."

"They're probably just waiting to see somebody jump," Hannah muttered.

Aidan stopped spinning. His face lit up with glee. "They let you jump off the bridge into the water?"

"No!" Jake and Emily said in unison, a moment of parental telepathy.

"Your sister was just kidding," Emily added, flashing Hannah a stern look.

"No, I'm not." She waved her cell phone at her mother. "Says here sixteen hundred people have leaped off it to their deaths since it first opened. A record forty-six in 2013 alone."

Aidan's expression turned worried. "Wait—the people who jumped *died?*"

"Don't listen to her, buddy—she's just messing with you. Hannah, stop being morbid. C'mon," Jake said, heading farther down the path, "I think the photo was taken over here somewhere."

The photo was of Jake's parents—Jake's favorite picture of them, in fact. Forty years ago next month, they'd driven down the coast from Eugene on their honeymoon and asked a passerby to snap the shot. Over time, the colors had washed out, lending the photo a slightly magical quality, and their pose—his father's hands thrust into the pockets of his jeans, his mother clinging to his arm, their hair mussed by the breeze— exuded effortless cool. The photo felt like a secret window to a foreign land, and the people in it were so young and hip, Jake had trouble reconciling them with the hopeless squares who'd raised him. Looking at it, he couldn't help but wonder how he must appear to his own children.

Jake thought it would be cute to stop off on their way home from Disneyland and re-create the photo as a video to wish his parents a happy anniversary, but it had proved harder than anticipated. First, they got stuck in the Bay Area's brutal traffic. Then the city was socked in with morning fog. Once the fog burned off, Jake had trouble finding the right spot. It was no wonder Emily's patience was wearing thin.

Now, though, things were looking up. The day was clear and bright. The sky behind the bridge was a field of blue, unbroken save for the gulls that circled overhead. A lone tugboat chugged across the choppy bay. The temperate ocean breeze blunted the sun's rays and dashed the surf against the rocks. Sea spray filled the air with saline and cast fleeting rainbows at the water's edge. It looked like a postcard come to life.

Jake raised a hand to halt his family and checked the view against the photo again. This time, he smiled.

"Gather up, guys—we're here!"

"Finally," Hannah said.

"Hannah!" her mother chastised, more out of reflex than disagreement.

"What? We've been walking forever."

Jake patted his pockets, looking for his phone. It wasn't there. He cursed under his breath.

Emily shot him a look that could have stopped a city bus. "Don't tell me you left it in the car."

"Okay," he said, flashing her a crooked grin. "I won't tell you." Normally, she found his goofy sense of humor charming. Today, though, she didn't seem amused.

Hannah held her cell phone out. "Here, use mine. Your camera app sucks anyway."

"Thanks, kiddo," Jake said—not remembering until her expression darkened that she'd asked him not to call her that anymore. It seemed like only yesterday that she was greeting him at the door when he came home from work with a squealed "Daddy!" and a knee-height hug.

He opened her camera app and toggled it to video. Then he took a big step backward, trying to fit everyone into the shot. "Aidan, squeeze in closer to your mom. Em, Sophia's got her fingers in her nose again. Hannah, no bunny ears, okay? Once I start recording, I'll count down from three, and we'll all yell *happy anniversary!*"

"Dad," Aidan said, "aren't you going to get in here with us?"

"I'd love to, buddy, but somebody's got to work the camera!"

"But Nan and Papa had a stranger take *their* picture."

You know, Jake thought, the kid had a point. He looked around for someone to hit up, but his prospects were slim. A trio of cyclists rode past, headed toward the bridge. A teenage couple sat hand in hand to one side of the trail, staring moonily into each other's eyes. A woman jogged by in a blur of neon green, her face flushed, her exposed skin gleaming with sweat. None of them looked as if they'd welcome the interruption.

Then Jake spotted an older gentleman moving their way. His face was pallid, his gait halting. Despite the day's warmth, he wore a tweed driving cap and khaki trousers, an argyle sweater over a collared shirt. His clothes hung baggily around his scrawny frame, like dry-cleaning on a wire hanger. Jake thought he looked lonely—the kind of guy who might feed pigeons in the park.

"Excuse me, sir? Would you mind holding my daughter's phone so my family can record an anniversary message for my parents? It'll only take a second, I swear."

The man looked at the phone and then at Jake. His eyes were the pale blue of faded denim. "Sorry," he said, "but I ain't much for gadgets. I got no idea how to work that thing."

"That's fine—I can press record. All you'll have to do is point it." He thumbed the button on the screen and held the phone out to the man.

The man hesitated for a moment, as if searching for some way to decline politely. Then he shrugged and shuffled over. When he took Hannah's ridiculous, bedazzled phone from Jake, he did so gingerly, as if it might break.

Jake trotted over to his family. Tousled Aidan's hair. Turned to face the camera. Put his arms around Hannah and Emily. "Are we all in the shot?"

15

The old man peered into the phone's camera lens as if it were a viewfinder. "I dunno," he said, "I can't see shit."

Aidan giggled. Emily reddened and gave Jake a gentle elbow to the ribs. Jake forced a smile and said, "I think you're holding it backward."

"What? Oh, hell." He turned the phone around. "There you are. Wait—does that mean I'm on your video now?"

"Don't worry—we can cut that bit when we get home. Ready, guys?"

One by one, all save the baby murmured their assent.

"Three... two... one..."

But they never did record their message.

Because that's when the tugboat slammed into the bridge's south tower and exploded.

2.

Michael Hendricks tossed back his drink and slammed the shot glass onto the dark-stained bar. "Hey, barkeep: another whiskey."

The young woman to whom he'd spoken looked up from the table she was wiping clean and replied, "I'm not a barkeep—I'm a waitress."

He squinted dubiously at her. She was in her late teens or early twenties. Her freckled face was free of makeup, and her brown hair was pulled back into a ponytail. She wore a heather-gray T-shirt with the restaurant's logo on it, and jeans cuffed high enough above her ballet flats to show her ankles. "You've been pouring me drinks all afternoon, haven't you?"

"Yes."

He yawned and scratched idly at the scruff on his jawline. It'd been weeks since he'd last shaved. "Then I fail to see the difference."

"The difference is, I'm not a barkeep—I'm a waitress. I'm just covering the bar until our real bartender comes in at five."

Hendricks peered around the dining room. Its walls were adorned with lobster traps and colorfully painted buoys, lacquered stripers, and woven fishnets dyed green-brown by use. The tables were empty. A few still needed tidying, but most were reset for dinner already—flatware wrapped in white cloth napkins, clean water goblets waiting to be filled. The lunch rush, if you could call twenty-odd patrons that, had cleared out hours ago. "I'm sorry—is my drink order pulling you away from all your other customers?"

"Nope. I'm just saying drinks aren't really my area."

"Ain't like shots of whiskey are difficult to make."

"Apparently, they're easy enough to drink."

Her sarcasm wasn't lost on Hendricks. "Ah. I see. You think I'm hitting the sauce a little hard."

"Not my business," she replied.

"No disagreement there."

"I mean, it's a little early, is all. Most folks aren't even off work yet."

Hendricks went to check his watch, only to discover that he wasn't wearing one. His eyebrows gathered in obvious puzzlement. "Yeah, well, I'm retired."

"Retired from what?"

From running false-flag missions for the U.S. government, he thought. From killing hitmen for a living once he got back home. "From giving a shit about what anybody thinks of me getting drunk in the middle of the day," he said.

She sighed and changed tactics. "How about a bite

to eat, at least?" Her tone was solicitous and optimistic. Hendricks pegged her for a chronic overachiever, unaccustomed to failure.

"How about you pour me another goddamn whiskey?"

"Fine." She ducked behind the bar, fetched a bottle of Early Times from the well, and refilled Hendricks's shot glass. Then she poured him a cup of coffee from the thermal carafe beside the register. "On the house," she said.

"Look, kid—"

"Cameron," she said.

"Look, *Cameron*," he corrected himself, "I appreciate the effort. But you don't know me, and you couldn't begin to understand the shit I've been through. You've got no idea why I'm here or what I've lost."

"I've also got no idea how you're still upright. Just take the coffee, okay?"

Hendricks picked up the coffee and took a sip. It was lukewarm and tasted of plastic. He made a face and set it back down. Then he raised the brimming shot glass in Cameron's direction.

"Cheers," he said. But before he brought the drink to his lips, she shook her head and stormed away.

He watched her round the corner at the far end of the bar and disappear from sight. Seconds later, he heard the kitchen's swinging double doors bang open. Once they'd clacked shut behind her, leaving Hendricks certain she couldn't return without him hearing, he dumped the shot into the potted ficus tree beside him.

He'd been coming to the Salty Dog—a quaint, clapboard-sided seafood joint overlooking Long Island's Port Jefferson Harbor—for three weeks, always parking his ass on the same stool from noon to closing. In that time, the ficus had been outdrinking him three to one. He was amazed he hadn't killed the thing by now. Every once in a while, he made a show of spilling a shot across the bar, in part to establish himself as a sloppy drunk, and in part to explain the smell this corner had taken on. It must've worked, because no one in the place had said five words to him until today, when the new girl decided to take pity on him—and even *she'd* been here a week before she gathered the nerve.

Hendricks figured she was just some overzealous undergrad, bright-eyed and idealistic, who'd yet to learn that the broken people of the world rarely wanted to be fixed. And although he was plenty broken, it was a life of violence—not booze—that was to blame.

The shot disposed of, the waitress gone, Hendricks watched the anchored sailboats bob like seabirds on the bay. He was happy for the momentary quiet. It didn't last.

A shadow fell across the restaurant's storefront. Hendricks swiveled in his stool and saw a black Range Rover roll to a stop at the curb. A spray-tanned side of beef in wraparound sunglasses climbed out of the backseat. Then he pushed open the Salty Dog's front door and stepped inside.

He wore a polo shirt two sizes too small for him and a pair of garish madras shorts. Canvas loafers, each the size of a rowboat, encased his feet. If his getup was intended to help him blend in with the yacht-club set, it fell well short of that goal. His nose was misshapen; his ears were cauliflowered. There was no doubt in Hendricks's mind that he was hired muscle.

The man took off his sunglasses and looked around the restaurant. Hendricks feigned indifference, swaying drunkenly atop his stool and idly spinning his empty shot glass on the bar like a top. The man eyed Hendricks in his frayed khaki shorts, rumpled button-down, and sweat-stained Titleist ball cap and apparently dismissed him. Hendricks looked like half the drunks in every ritzy-zip-code bar from here to Hilton Head.

The man flipped the sign in the front window to CLOSED, shut the curtains, and took up a position by the door. Another guy of the same make and model entered and headed toward the kitchen without a word. Along the way, he rapped on the restroom doors and checked inside. When he entered the kitchen, Hendricks heard the chef's surprised tone quickly give way to friendly recognition. They conversed a moment—Hendricks couldn't make out the exact words, but by the sound of it, the chef was intro-ducing him to the new girl—and then he returned to the dining room and gave his buddy a nod.

The man beside the door parted the curtain slightly and gestured to someone outside. The door swung open once more. Hendricks half expected another spray-tanned goon, but instead in walked a handsome thirty-something man in a linen shirt, seersucker shorts, and leather flip-flops. His complexion had a Mediterranean cast, and his high cheekbones, tousled hair, and cultivated stubble made him look as if he'd stepped out of a men's magazine. Once the door closed behind him, the Range Rover pulled away.

"Good afternoon," he said to Hendricks. "My name is Nick Pappas."

"James Dalton," Hendricks lied. "But my friends call me Jimmy." He'd taken the name from Patrick Swayze's character in *Road House* as a nod to an old friend. Hendricks never used to put much effort into coming up with aliases, but his buddy—and former partner in crime— Lester had always taken great pride in it. Every one of 'em was an in-joke, a reference.

Lester had been murdered almost a year ago. Keeping the tradition going was one way Hendricks chose to honor him. Waiting in this upscale tourist trap for Pappas was another.

"And what should I call you," Pappas asked, "James or Jimmy?"

"The jury's still out on that," Hendricks said. "After all, we just met. But I've got to hand it to you, Nick, you make one hell of an entrance."

Nick laughed. "Not everywhere, I'm afraid. Here I can afford to, because I own the place."

Hendricks knew that, strictly speaking, that wasn't true. On paper, the Salty Dog was one of many restaurants owned by a company called Aegeus Unlimited, which had a PO box in Delaware, a bank account in the Caymans, and a board composed entirely of people who'd died before they reached majority—at least, if the Social Security numbers on the articles of incorporation were to be believed. But then, there were loads of reasons the head of the Pappas crime family might like to keep his name off the paperwork.

Hendricks looked from Pappas to his goons and back. "I gotta ask—am I in some kind of trouble? 'Cause if your waitress wanted to cut me off, all she had to do was say so—she didn't have to bring you all this way."

Pappas smiled, showing teeth of gleaming white. "Not at all. My arrival here has nothing whatsoever to do with you. The fact is, James—and, understand, I'm not saying this to brag—I'm a very wealthy man, with business interests around the globe. Hotels. Restaurants. Construction. Waste management. As such, my schedule can be quite demanding. From time to time, I need a break—a few hours spent consuming good food and drink in good company. It affords me the opportunity to decompress. Today is one of those days."

"You always close down the place when you come in?"

"I do. I find it discourages unwanted interruptions."

Unwanted interruptions was a funny way of saying *People trying to kill me,* Hendricks thought.

Even among criminals, Nick Pappas was legendarily paranoid. Hendricks supposed he would have been too if his family were as fucked up as Nick's was. Until recently, the Pappas crime family was small potatoes—ignored by the larger New York outfits because their business interests were limited to Astoria's Greek community—but their reputation for infighting was positively Shakespearean.

Nick's uncle Theo had assumed control of the family business eleven years ago after Nick's grandfather took a tumble down the stairs of his Crescent Street town house and broke his neck. It was Theo who discovered the body and called it in.

A year later, Nick's father, Spiro, took over when Theo was found facedown in his morning yogurt, a bullet in his head. Though there were six people in the house at the time—family members all—and to a one, they claimed to've neither seen nor heard a thing.

Spiro had ruled until three years ago, when a hit-and-run left him in a persistent vegetative state. Nick and his five siblings spent months after his so-called accident jockeying for control of the family. By the time Nick claimed the throne, one of his brothers was dead, and his little sister had fled to points unknown.

Hendricks imagined Pappas family holidays were pretty tense.

Jealousy aside, Nick's remaining siblings had little to complain about; they'd profited mightily with him at the helm. His business acumen had expanded their empire exponentially and elevated the Pappas clan from small-time crooks to major players on the national scene.

Pappas's meteoric rise didn't go unnoticed by New York's other crime families. Some threatened war, but most saw him as a kindred spirit, which was how he'd wound up the youngest voting member in the history of the Council.

The Council was a group of representatives from each of the major criminal outfits operating in the United States. Though their organizations were often rivals, Council members convened whenever their respective or-ganizations' interests aligned.

Killing Hendricks was one such interest.

Hendricks's business model was...unconventional. When someone was marked for death, Hendricks would make sure that person's would-be killer wound up in the ground instead—so long as the intended victim paid up, that is. Ten times the price on the client's head was his go-ing rate. Always up front, nonnegotiable.

His buddy Lester, with whom he'd served in Afghanistan, was the operation's tech guy. He ID'd the clients and gathered intel on their targets. Hendricks han-dled the wetwork. For a while, business was booming. Then the Council caught wise and sent a hitman to hit him back. The man they sent—Alexander Engelmann—

was tenacious, sadistic, and hard to kill. Hendricks managed to do it, barely, but not before the bastard tortured Lester to death. Ever since, Hendricks had dedicated every waking moment to determining who, exactly, was on the Council so he could take them down.

But without Lester's computer chops to rely on, Hendricks was forced to resort to old-fashioned detective work, and leads were scarce. Council members ran tight ships. Their street-level employees were largely kept in the dark, and those in their inner circles knew better than to run their mouths. Those who did usually wound up dead.

Thankfully, Pappas's crew was new to this and not as disciplined as they should be. Thirty-six hours into a meth bender, one of his lieutenants blabbed to a call girl he was sweet on. Hendricks had saved that call girl's life once— she and her first pimp didn't part on the best of terms, so he'd paid a guy five hundred bucks to take her out—which meant she was more than happy to pass along what she had learned.

"I guess this is my cue to leave," Hendricks said to Pappas, knowing damn well that it wasn't. He'd been watching Pappas for months, trying to figure out how to get close to him. Pappas never went anywhere without his personal security detail. He had several properties he split his time among—a penthouse in midtown Manhattan, the family home in Astoria, freestanding houses in Guilford and Oyster Bay—none of which had his name on the paperwork, and each of which had its own dedicated security staff. He varied his daily routine to avoid ambushes. He wasn't married. He had no children. His girlfriends were under constant lock and key.

But a few times a month, he liked to pop into one of his restaurants for a lavish meal.

Even then, though, Pappas was careful. He showed up at odd hours and never called ahead. When he arrived, he locked the doors behind him and picked up the tab for everyone already inside. Hendricks had figured the best way to get close to Pappas was to be inside one of his restaurants when he got there—and soft-pedaling his interest in staying would get him closer still.

"Not at all!" Pappas said. "Have you eaten?"

Hendricks feigned confusion at Pappas's interest. "I haven't," he said.

"Then I insist you stay. We're having one of everything sent out. Would you care for a drink while we wait?"

"I wouldn't turn one down."

"Excellent. What's your poison?"

"Whatever gets the job done. Today I'm drinking whiskey."

"Milos," Pappas said, "do me a favor and fetch our new friend James a drink."

One of Pappas's men ducked behind the bar, reached up, and grabbed an unopened bottle of Johnnie Walker Blue from the top shelf. The pistol he wore at the small of his back showed as he did. When he cracked the seal and poured Hendricks three fingers—a hundred bucks' worth at most establishments—Hendricks licked his lips with exaggerated anticipation.

"Please," Hendricks said to Pappas, "call me Jimmy."

Pappas beamed. His men smiled too and appeared as at ease as hired goons could ever be while on the job. That was good, helpful.

They wouldn't look so happy when the night was through.

3.

Special Agent Charlie Thompson hovered awkwardly on the threshold of her parents' kitchen. The dangly earrings her mother had gotten her for Christmas tugged uncomfortably at her ears. Pots bubbled on the stove. The air was warm and humid and redolent with spice.

"There must be *something* I can do to help," she said.

"Don't be silly," her mother replied. "Kate and I have this well in hand. Why don't you go bring your father a beer?"

Thompson's face creased with worry as she watched Kathryn O'Brien mangle the onion she was trying to dice. "You sure you're up to this?"

O'Brien cocked an eyebrow at Thompson and smiled. "You heard your mother," she said. "Beat it!"

Thompson shrugged and grabbed two cans of Narragansett from the fridge. Then she headed out to the garage.

The overhead door was open, the cars, as ever, in the driveway. A workbench took up half the narrow space, and tools hung from pegboards above it. Thompson's father crouched over a partially disassembled lawn mower, his hands blackened by grease.

Thompson popped the top on both beers and handed one to him without a word. Foam gathered on his mustache when he drank.

"You gotta work on this right now, Pop?"

"Is there something else I oughta be doing? Ain't like your mother wants me in the kitchen."

"Join the club—she just threw me out too. Asked Kate to stay, though."

"You don't look pleased."

"A little leery, is all."

"Why?" he snapped. "You think your mother's gonna say something inappropriate and embarrass you?"

"No," Thompson said carefully, "I'm worried Kate's gonna take off a finger. Her knife skills leave a bit to be desired."

"Oh." He looked chastened. "I'm sure your mother will watch out for her."

Thompson's parents were Catholic. When she came out, they'd been as supportive of her as their faith allowed— but she'd never brought a woman home before. She'd been worried how her parents would react to O'Brien ever since they got serious last fall. It's why she'd postponed the meet-the-parents trip three times already. It's why she'd nearly canceled when the alarm went off this morning and then twice more on the drive from DC to Hartford.

She sipped her beer and watched her father tinker with the lawn mower. "You talk to Jess lately?" she asked.

Jess was Thompson's baby sister. Four years out of college and trying to make it as an artist, whatever that meant. Near as Thompson could tell, it mostly meant couch surfing, binge drinking, and emotional breakdowns.

"Not since she and the new guy—Tree? River?"

"Leaf."

"Leaf. Right. Not since they left for Costa Rica. You?"

"I Facebook-messaged her the other day. She said she'd be back in time to see us this weekend. Guess she was mistaken."

"You know Jess," he said gruffly. "Never been so good with schedules." He removed the hex nut from the mounting bolts and yanked the mower's carburetor free. Fuel puddled on the floor. "Son of a whore!"

"Something bothering you, Pop?"

"Yeah—I forgot to clamp the goddamn fuel line." He rectified the error and pushed the mess around with a rag.

"Seriously, what's wrong?" It wasn't like him to lose his temper. "Is this about me and Kate?"

Her father wiped his hands off on his pants. "It's not my place to say."

"Pop, I'm asking. What is it?"

"She's your goddamn *boss*, Charlie, that's what!"

Ah. There it was. She should have known.

Thompson's dad was a captain with the Hartford PD. A real nose-to-the-grindstone kind of guy. He'd joined the force straight out of high school. Climbed the ranks from lowly beat cop to head of precinct. To him, chain of command was sacrosanct.

"What're you saying? You think your daughter's fucking her way to the top?"

"*I'm* not saying it, but you're a fool if you think others aren't."

"Let them talk. I honestly don't give a shit."

"No? You should. Some of them hold your career in their hands. And speaking of, you ever stop to think what happens when the two of you break up? She holds all the cards, Charlie. Odds are, you'll wind up pushing paper in some shitty basement office in East Bumfuck."

"That's not gonna happen, Pop."

"Yeah? How the hell do you know?"

"Because, goddamn it, Kate and I are getting married! So whatever you really think of her—of *me*—you could at least pretend to get on board."

She hadn't meant to snap. Hadn't meant to tell him that way.

And she certainly hadn't meant for Kate to overhear.

O'Brien stood in the doorway to the garage, one hand still on the knob. It was clear by the look on her face that she'd been there awhile.

Thompson struggled for words. A blotchy flush crawled up her father's neck.

"Kate, I—"

"Later," O'Brien said. "I just got a call from HQ. Something's happened in San Francisco. We have to go."

4.

Jake Reston forced himself onto his hands and knees. His vision was blurry, his thoughts a muddle. He couldn't hear a thing over the ringing in his ears.

He struggled to recall where he was, and why. The back of his neck was hot and tight, like he'd been out in the sun too long. Ditto the portions of his arms and legs his T-shirt and shorts failed to cover. When he was nineteen, he'd spent his summer break from college laying pavement with a road crew. Shoveling hot-mix asphalt for ten-hour stretches in the August heat, fumes rising off the molten sludge, proved a recipe for heat exhaustion, and despite his best efforts to stay hydrated, it had leveled Jake more than once. This felt similar, which led Jake to wonder if heat exhaustion was what had caused him to collapse today—but oddly, given his apparent sunburn, it wasn't all that warm outside.

As Jake's vision cleared, he noticed a mangled bike frame beside him on the trail. Its paint was blistered. Its seat and back wheel were missing. Its front wheel spun lazily on its axle, the bare rim clotted here and there with chunks of smoldering rubber. He couldn't help but wonder what had happened to the bike's rider.

The dirt beneath Jake was spattered red. He raised a hand to his face. When he touched his nose, a jolt of pain made him recoil. He probed again more gingerly; it seemed to be crooked. A sticky gash caked with dirt and clotting blood ran across it. Blood seeped from both his nostrils.

Jake brushed the loose dirt from his face and hands. He ran his tongue over his upper teeth and spat out grit. The fog in his head lifted some, and flashes of memory returned. He tried to piece them together, but important bits were missing and they didn't quite line up right, like the fragments of a broken glass. They were on their way home from Disneyland, he remembered, when they'd stopped off to re-create his parents' honeymoon photo, and then…and then…

Wait. *They.* He and Emily and the kids.

Adrenaline surged through his system and brought his thoughts back to the here and now. They'd found the spot. Posed to record the video. Then something hit him from behind. And then blackness. And then this.

Fear twisted Jake's guts. He looked around. The effort made his head pound, his vision swim. There wasn't much to see, anyway—the air was choked with thick dark smoke that seared his lungs with every breath.

Jake tried to stand. The world seemed to wobble around him, and he was forced back to his knees. "Hannah! Aidan! Emily!" he shouted, his voice a dry croak, loud enough to strain his vocal cords, yet so faint that he could barely hear it.

There was no reply. He crawled upslope a ways and tried again. This time, he heard something. His name. High-pitched, frightened, questioning. Emily, he realized.

Jake scrabbled toward her on all fours. Put his hand in something sticky. Recoiled when he realized it was a rivulet of blood.

He followed it back to its source. It wasn't Emily, but a woman clad in neon-green gym clothes. Jake vaguely recalled seeing her jog by before whatever happened had happened. Her exposed flesh was red and angry. A twisted hunk of metal jutted from the back of her head, charred black at the edges, bloody hair matted all around.

"Emily!" he screamed. "Where are you? Talk to me— are the kids with you? Are you okay?" It occurred to him he ought to hear Sophia crying. His heart tapped out a brittle rat-a-tat against his rib cage.

"I'm over here! I, uh, think I fell." She sounded dazed, rattled, not herself. "Sophia's here with me!"

"Where are Hannah and Aidan?"

"I—I don't know!"

Jake crawled toward the sound of his wife's voice, limbs protesting the whole way. He found her hovering over Sophia, who lay silent and unmoving atop Emily's windbreaker. Emily's forehead was sliced open and bled freely into her eyes.

"Oh God. Is she…" He couldn't bring himself to finish the sentence lest uttering the words might make them so.

"She's breathing," Emily answered, her voice high and

tremulous from worry, "but unconscious, and she's got a goose egg on the back of her head. I...I must have landed on top of her when I fell." Her chin quivered. Grief warped her features. "I know I shouldn't have moved her, but I couldn't leave her lying in the dirt."

He put his hands on her face, palms to cheeks. "Look at me. This isn't your fault. Whatever happened leveled all of us. And I promise you, Sophia's going to be just fine." Emily nodded. Blinked back tears. Put on a brave face. He wondered if her bravery felt as hollow as his did.

Jake knelt over Sophia. Placed a hand against her tiny chest and took heart in its steady rise and fall. Patted her cheek gently and said, "C'mon, little one—wake up for us, okay?"

Sophia didn't stir. He patted her cheek once more, harder, and when that didn't work, he shook her gently. He was about to try again when Emily placed her hands on his to still them and shook her head. "Careful," she said, and only then did he realize he'd been on the verge of going too far, of shaking her too hard—his panic taking over.

And then, by some miracle, Sophia opened her eyes and began to cry.

Jake had never heard a sound so beautiful in all his life.

But his relief was short-lived. With Sophia awake and responsive, his priorities shifted.

"Em, think back. When you fell, did you see Hannah and Aidan?"

She frowned as she struggled to remember. "No. I don't think so. They weren't with you?"

He shook his head. "No. We got separated somehow, and when I came to—I—I don't know. Help me up. I'm going to go find them." She grabbed his elbow, and with her support, Jake found his feet. "Hannah!" he bellowed, fighting the urge to cough. "Aidan! Tell me where you are!"

"Dad!" It was Hannah, strong and clear. "Dad, we're over here!"

He stumbled toward them, a smile breaking across his filthy, bloodied face when he saw shapes in the smoke resolve themselves into his children's forms. Hannah sat with Aidan's head in her lap, stroking his hair as he wept. They'd bickered the whole drive here, he recalled, but now she was there for him when he needed her. For a moment, Jake was overcome with pride; he felt as if he'd just been offered a glimpse of the amazing woman Hannah would become.

"Are you two all right?" he asked. Aidan shook his head, his tears carving arroyos in the dirt and ash that caked his face.

"I'm okay," Hannah said, though she was scraped up pretty good, "but Aidan's leg is broken. I don't think we can move him without help."

She was right, Jake realized. Aidan's leg extended away from his body in an unnatural zigzag. Bone, jagged and gore-streaked, protruded from his shin.

"Where are Mom and Sophia?" Hannah asked.

"Back that way."

"Are they..."

"They're fine. We're all going to be just fine," he said, putting a hand on his son's shoulder. "You hear me, buddy?" Aidan nodded, and his sobbing abated some.

Jake knew Aidan needed medical attention, but he was worried that if he left to get help, he'd never find his way back here. Reflexively, he reached for the pocket where he normally kept his cell phone, but it wasn't there. *Right,* he thought, *I left the damn thing in the car, and Hannah had to lend me hers to take the video. It couldn't have gone far.*

He looked around—the ocean breeze taking mercy on him and dispersing the haze some—and spotted it lying a few feet from them at the path's edge, its bedazzled edges sparkling, its screen a dark reflection of the sky.

He ran to it. Dialed 911. The phone rang twice, and then the call was dropped.

Jake tried again, muttering, "C'mon, c'mon, c'mon," as it began to ring. This time, an operator answered. "Oh, thank God," he said. "My family and I are on the trails just up the hill from Fort Point, overlooking the Golden Gate Bridge. There was some kind of explosion."

"We're aware of the situation, sir," the operator said. From the tension in her voice and the clamor behind her, it sounded like half of San Francisco had called it in. "Are any of you hurt?"

"My son's leg is badly broken. I think he's going to need a stretcher."

"Are you in immediate danger?"

Jake looked around. The nearby trees were scorched bare. Ash rained lazily from the sky. "I...I don't *think* so."

"Okay. Just stay put, then. Help is on the way."

"Thank you," he said. "Thank you so much."

Jake trotted back to Emily, who held Sophia close and tried to calm her. Brought them over to where Aidan lay and told Emily the EMTs were coming. Jake was so overcome by everything that had transpired—and so relieved his kids were safe—he never stopped to wonder where the gaunt old man who'd been holding Hannah's phone had gone.

5.

So HE SAYS, 'Nicky, I'd like to introduce you to my uncle.'
And I reply, 'Your uncle? Thank Christ—I thought that
was your mother!'"

The table erupted with laughter. One of Pappas's hench-
men, Milos, slammed his palm down on the dark-stained
wood so hard, their plates jumped. The other, Dimitris, just
chuckled and shook his head. The two of them looked so
alike that, for a time, Hendricks couldn't tell them apart.
Eventually, though, he was able to keep them straight,
partly because Milos was by far the more gregarious of the
two, his wide eyes dopey and inattentive while Dimitris's
were sly and watchful, and partly because Dimitris had an
ugly scar that snaked around his right biceps and disappeared into his shirtsleeve. Hendricks had seen his share of
scars like that during his black ops days. It was a shrapnel
wound—which meant Dimitris was ex-military.

They'd been sitting here for nearly two hours, the table littered with picked-over plates of steamed mussels and fried calamari, grilled shrimp and baked stuffed lobster—even the remnants of a salt-crusted sea bass, roasted whole and filleted at the table by the chef. Bottles littered the table too. Ouzo for Dimitris—Barbayanni, a brand that Hendricks had never heard of before today. Cruzan Rum for Milos, who drank it straight—wincing every time—once his compatriots teased him for cutting it with Diet Coke. Johnnie Walker Blue for Hendricks. A bottle of an unpronounceable Greek red wine for Pappas.

Pappas's goons seemed to have no compunction about getting drunk so long as Hendricks was too—in fact, their boss encouraged them—but Pappas chose to nurse his wine. He was shrewd and watchful even among friends, a trait Hendricks might've admired if he didn't despise everything about the man.

"Another drink, Mr. Dalton?"

"I told you, Nick—please call me Jimmy. And I'm not even done with the last one yet!"

Pappas flashed Hendricks an impish grin. "Then I suggest you rectify that presently."

Hendricks smiled back. "Hey, who am I to argue? You're the boss."

He blinked hard, reached clumsily for his drink, and knocked it over. Amber liquid spilled across the table. Hendricks frowned and blotted at it with a cloth napkin.

"On second thought," he slurred, "I think I may've hit my limit."

The chef—a scraggly tattooed guy named Noah who turned out to be a genius in the kitchen—came over to the table bearing a platter piled high with cheeses, fruit, and local honeycomb. He and Cameron were the only two working—Pappas had instructed Noah to give the rest of the dinner-shift staff the night off, and he'd slipped Cameron and the chef a thousand bucks apiece for their trouble.

"Noah!" shouted Milos. "Sit and have a drink with us." Milos's cheeks were flushed. His forehead gleamed with sweat. His smile was broad and guileless.

Noah looked uncertainly at Pappas, who gestured toward an empty chair. "By all means, Noah—join us."

Noah sat down. Milos sloshed some rum into a dirty glass for him and poured another for himself. Dimitris poured a fresh drink too. The three men clinked and drank.

Milos slammed his empty glass on the table and stood, teetering slightly. "Dimitris," he said, clapping Noah on the back, "pour this man another round. I gotta see a horse about a piss."

"Yeah," said Hendricks, rising unsteadily to his feet and staggering after Milos. "What he said."

Hendricks had been waiting all afternoon for the right time to make his move. He wasn't carrying any weapons because he'd had no way of knowing whether Pappas's goons would pat him down when they arrived. That made taking on two armed thugs at once a risky proposition— riskier still if Pappas was also carrying. Plus, he wanted to keep the waitress and the chef out of the line of fire, if possible.

Once they rounded the corner to the restroom, Hendricks put on speed so that he and Milos reached the door at the same time. With Milos zigzagging drunkenly down the hall, it wasn't hard for Hendricks to catch up. After a moment's stop-start awkwardness, Hendricks pushed open the door and gestured for Milos to go first.

"Thanks, pal," the big man said, his eyes glassy, that goofy smile still pasted on his face.

As Milos stepped across the threshold, Hendricks tripped him with an outstretched foot. Milos pitched forward. Hendricks followed him into the restroom, grabbed the back of Milos's head as he went down, and slammed it into the sink. The porcelain cracked. Milos shuddered involuntarily, and then his limbs went loose. He was out before he hit the floor, head dented, blood oozing across the tiles.

Hendricks emptied Milos's pockets. Found a wallet. A cell phone. Half a pack of gum. A tiny ball of plastic wrap knotted at one end and filled with white powder, likely cocaine. He ground his heel into the phone until it broke and left the rest of Milos's pocket litter beside it. Then he relieved Milos of his pistol, a compact semiautomatic .22 rimfire he wore at the small of his back.

Shit. He should've figured. It seemed like big guys always carried little firearms. Hendricks thought it was because they put too much faith in their own strength, or maybe they believed that they looked bigger by comparison. Whatever the reason, it meant he'd be taking on Dimitris with a glorified cap gun.

At least it was loaded to capacity. A round in the chamber. Nine more in the magazine. He thumbed the safety off. Opened the restroom door a hair and listened. Milos had gone down so hard, Hendricks worried someone might've heard, but the merriment in the dining room continued unabated.

He slipped into the hall, eased the door closed behind

him, and pushed through the swinging double doors to the kitchen. Cameron was standing at a stainless-steel prep station scarfing down a hodgepodge plate of leftovers.

"What are you..." she began. Her eyes widened when she saw the gun. Hendricks put a finger to his lips, and she fell silent. Then he gestured with his barrel toward the walk-in.

"But—"

"No buts. Go."

When she reached the walk-in door, he jerked it open and gestured for her to get inside.

"And if I don't?"

"You really want to find out?"

She glanced toward the kitchen door and the dining room beyond it. "I could scream."

"You could—but you seem like a bright kid, so I'm betting you won't."

She eyed him for a moment and then stepped inside. "All the way," he said. She sighed and headed for the back. "Good. Now sit."

"Why?"

So I can close the door without you rushing it, he thought. "Because I said so," he said.

She reluctantly complied, sitting down atop a stack of produce boxes. Her breath plumed. Gooseflesh sprung up on her bare arms.

"For what it's worth," he said as he swung the door shut, "this is for your own good."

She said something in reply, but her voice was barely audible, blunted by the walk-in's insulated walls.

Hendricks wedged a wooden spoon into the hole intended for a padlock and strode with purpose into the dining room, no longer bothering to feign drunkenness. For a moment, the three men at the table paid him little mind. But that changed when he shot Dimitris in the face.

It was nothing personal. A head shot was simply the quickest way to put a target down. Or, at least, it *would* have been if Hendricks had had a real gun to work with instead of this rinky-dink .22.

Dimitris took the shot just below his left eye, but it didn't penetrate his cheekbone; it just deflected off it and furrowed his flesh from cheek to ear. There was a crash of plates and glass as Pappas upended the table and took shelter behind it. The chef, Noah, scurried after him.

Hendricks had hoped Dimitris would go down, but instead he growled in pain and rage and then charged. Hendricks fired again as Dimitris closed the gap. Caught him in the left biceps. But Dimitris just kept coming.

Hendricks tried to sidestep Dimitris, but there was a lot of him to sidestep. Dimitris swiped at Hendricks with one meaty fist. Hendricks blocked it with an outward sweep of his left forearm, his elbow a right angle. Dimitris countered with a vicious uppercut. The punch caught Hendricks in the jaw. His head snapped back. His knees buckled.

As Hendricks toppled, Dimitris went for his piece. Hendricks fired off a wild shot as he fell. It struck Dimitris in the side, but he still didn't go down.

Hendricks landed on his back. The wind rushed out of him. Dimitris raised his weapon, a .22, just like his buddy's. Hendricks put three rounds into his chest. Dimitris lost his grip on his gun at the impact, and it sailed across the room. He took a halting step toward Hendricks, and then finally collapsed, falling forward so that his weight pinned Hendricks to the floor.

A crack of gunfire, and Dimitris's corpse bucked as if electrocuted. Another, and a floorboard three inches from Hendricks's head kicked up splinters. Pappas was firing at him blindly around the table.

Hendricks rolled, heaving Dimitris's body off him and using it for cover. Pappas hit his dead henchman in the leg, the back, the neck—none of the shots, thankfully, a through-and-through. Hendricks waited for a lull in the shooting, and then he put two rounds through the table Pappas hid behind. A .22 might not have much stopping power, but its slender rounds could sure as hell punch through a half an inch of lacquered wood. Pappas screamed, and his gun clattered to the floor.

Hendricks climbed to his feet and circled the table, the .22 held ready. When he came even with the table's edge, he saw Pappas frantically applying pressure to a wound in his thigh. Noah sat wide-eyed and trembling beside him, face spattered with Pappas's blood. As Hendricks approached, Noah crab-walked backward through the rubble from the upturned table and began to cry.

"Relax," Hendricks said to him. "I'm not here for you—it's Pappas that I want. Don't cause any trouble, and I promise you'll come out of this unharmed. Understand?"

Noah swallowed hard and nodded.

"Good."

Hendricks knelt, his gun trained on Pappas, and pocketed the man's dropped pistol—a .45. Its caliber explained the lack of through-and-throughs; fatter rounds spread out more when they hit, which in turn slows them down. That meant the .45 had more stopping power than Milos's .22, but Hendricks didn't trust any gun he hadn't had the chance to inspect.

"What are you after?" Pappas asked through gritted teeth. "Money? Name your sum and I'll gladly hand it over, provided you let me go."

"I don't want your fucking money."

"What, then? Revenge? If so, let's not waste time. Pull the trigger and be done with it."

"Don't worry—we'll get to that, once you tell me everything I need to know. But first, you and I are going for a little trip to someplace where we won't be bothered. Someplace where nobody will hear you scream. I set it up weeks ago for this very occasion. And I promise, once I get you there, you *will* talk."

Pappas spat. "The fuck I will."

Hendricks smiled. "You have no idea who I am, do you?"

"Should I?"

"I don't know. I thought you might."

"Why's that?"

"Last year, the Council paid a man named Engelmann to have me killed."

The gunshot had rendered Pappas's sun-kissed countenance pale. Hendricks's words made him go paler still. "Wait—you're the guy who's been whacking our hitters?"

Hendricks said nothing.

"Look, you've got to understand, that wasn't my call. I was on the Council for all of a week when they decided to sic that guy on you."

Hendricks stepped on the hand Pappas held to the bullet wound in his thigh. Pappas screamed and writhed in pain. "Is that supposed to make me feel better?" Hendricks said. "My best friend is dead."

Hendricks lifted his foot. Pappas's screaming ceased.

"So, what," he said between gasps, "you plan to take down the Council single-handedly?"

"Of course not. You're going to help me."

"You're out of your goddamn mind—particularly if you think I'm going to talk."

"It's not a matter of if. Just when. To be clear, I plan to kill you either way, but you get to decide how quick and painless your death will be."

Pappas flashed a manic smile that teetered between terror and bravado. "Gee, thanks."

"Don't blame me. It's the Council that put you in this position. If you'd like to return the favor, you'll tell me everything I want to know."

"You don't understand. If I talk, they'll kill my family."

"What do you care? Half your family wants you dead."

"That doesn't mean that I don't love them," he said. "Listen, you're a businessman. Let's talk about this. I'm sure we can reach some kind of agreement."

"We're done talking for now. There'll be plenty of time for us to chat once we get to where we're going. I've got a car out front. Get up, or I will get you up."

As Hendricks turned toward the door, Pappas shouted, "Wait!"

That's when Hendricks realized that Pappas had been stalling for time all along.

Too late, he wheeled and saw Noah lunging toward him, the fillet knife from the upturned table in his hand.

Goddamn it.

Hendricks tried to bring the .22 around, but there was neither time nor space. The knife slid into his side as Noah slammed into him. Its blade, still specked with salt crust, felt like it was on fire.

Noah drove the knife forward with all his weight. Hendricks dropped his gun, wrapped his hands around Noah's wrists, and tried desperately to halt the blade's progress as they fell, limbs tangled, to the floor.

Noah had gravity on his side. Hendricks had momentum on his. Rather than halt the blade's forward progress, Hendricks wrenched Noah's wrists sideways, angling the blade away from his vital organs. The blade glanced off a rib, parting skin and stinging like a motherfucker, and then wedged itself in the floorboards. Hendricks landed right beside it, but Noah's forward motion sent him tumbling. Hendricks kept hold of Noah's wrists, and Noah somersaulted over him and slammed hard into the floor. He sounded like a sack of flour when he hit. Hendricks yanked out the knife, scrabbled to his feet, and buried it in Noah's chest. Noah's chef's whites blossomed red. His eyelids fluttered, then stilled.

Fool me once, Hendricks thought.

He held his left arm to his side as he rose, trying to stanch the flow of blood from his wound, and looked for the .22.

Then he spotted it—in Pappas's hand. He was aiming it at Hendricks's head.

Pappas stood a few feet away, his weight on his good leg, his thigh wound seeping. "You piece of shit," he said. "These men were family to me. I promise yours will pay for what you've done."

"I've got no family left," Hendricks replied. "The Council took them from me. That's why I'm here."

The statement was true enough, if intentionally misleading. When Engelmann came after Hendricks, he did so by targeting the only two people in the world that Hendricks cared about: his partner, Lester, and his former fiancée, Evie. Engelmann tortured Lester to death, extracting Evie's location from him in the process. But Lester held on long enough to tip Hendricks off and afford him the advantage he needed to kill Engelmann. Afterward, Evie and her husband, Stuart, entered witness protection. Hendricks had no idea where they were or how to find them.

Evie had been pregnant when Hendricks last laid eyes on her. By now, she must've had the baby, which meant there were again two people in the world that he cared about.

Hendricks's hand crept toward the gun he'd pocketed. Pappas slowly shook his head, a teasing gesture. "You'll never get to it in time."

Pappas was probably right, but Hendricks didn't have a better play to make.

He went for the gun. His wound made him clumsy. Dulled his reflexes. The hammer snagged on his pocket, which gave Pappas time to react. A shot rang out. Hendricks's eyes clenched shut as he braced for the bullet's impact—a useless reflex.

But the impact never came.

Then Pappas hit the floor.

Hendricks opened his eyes. Wobbled a little from blood loss. Saw the waitress in a textbook shooting stance a few feet away. Her face was pale. Her eyes were wide. Her hands were white-knuckled around the grip of Dimitris's gun.

Hendricks's thoughts were a jumble. "What…who… how the hell did you get out?"

"The walk-in's interior is equipped with a safety release so employees don't freeze to death. You can lock people out, but you can't lock anybody in. Next time, barricade the door. If I weren't on your side, you'd be fucked."

"But—"

"Shhh." She tilted her head and squinted as if straining to hear something. A second later, he heard it too.

Sirens.

"We have to leave," she said. *"Now."*

6.

T HE HEELS OF Kathryn O'Brien's sandals clacked against
the polished tile floor as she strode purposefully across
the bustling lobby. Her capri-length chinos and sleeveless
blouse looked out of place in a building dominated by
men in somber business suits, but the crowd parted defer-
entially around her nonetheless. Thompson—who felt
woefully underdressed in shorts and a V-neck T-shirt—
wasn't sure whether that was because they recognized
O'Brien or because her every movement exuded authority, but either way, it was something to see.

The FBI's New Haven, Connecticut, field office was
a modern red-brick building occupying a full city block
a short walk from Yale's campus. It was indistinguishable
from most office buildings in the area but for the fact
that it was set back from the road and encircled by
a fence of galvanized steel painted black to look like

49

wrought iron. Small, unobtrusive NO TRESPASSING signs were posted here and there along the fence, and all entrances, automotive and pedestrian, were gated. The building's clean lines and manicured lawn lent the property a serene air. Inside—today, at least—the mood was anything but.

At forty miles away from Thompson's parents' house, the New Haven field office was the nearest FBI facility in the area. Thompson and O'Brien had made it there in under half an hour. In the car, Thompson tried to apologize for her dad's harsh reaction to their visit. O'Brien shrugged it off—said it wasn't fair to hold Thompson responsible for what her father thought—but Thompson could tell that it bothered her.

When they reached the front desk, O'Brien said, "What's the situation?"

"Ma'am?" The kid behind the desk was wide-eyed, overwhelmed.

"The situation. I'll need a briefing, the sooner the better." O'Brien noted his confusion. "Someone told you I was coming, right?"

"Uh…" It was clear he had no idea what was going on. Thompson felt a pang of sympathy for him. He was a baby agent thrown into the deep end, and she remembered all too well what that felt like.

"Director O'Brien!" A forty-something black man in a polo shirt and khaki shorts trotted over to them, tennis shoes squeaking, and stuck out his hand. "Ty Russell— special agent in charge of the New Haven field office."

The agent behind the front desk blanched when he realized the woman standing before him was the ranking officer on-site, and he shrunk a little in his seat.

"Good to meet you, Ty. Please, call me Kathryn. This is Charlie Thompson. She's with me."

Russell's handshake was firm and cool. "Sorry about the mix-up here," he said to O'Brien. "It's not every day we get a visit from the head of CID. And things have been a little nuts this afternoon, as you might imagine. I got here only ten minutes ago myself—I was at my niece's birthday party when I heard."

"What can you tell me about what happened?"

Russell looked pained. "Not much more than what the news is carrying, I'm afraid. I haven't been briefed yet, so I can't even say for sure whether the explosion was intentional, although obviously the Bureau and Homeland Security are proceeding as though it was. I had a conference room set up for you with a secure link to DC, as you requested. I'm sure they can fill in some of the blanks."

He led them to an elevator and up two floors. The doors slid open to reveal a bullpen crackling with nervous energy. A dozen people on phones, all talking at once. Countless e-mails, texts, and faxes coming in. Every face drawn tight with stress.

"As you can see," he said, "we're doing what we can. Sifting through chatter. Liaising with our West Coast offices. But there's only so much we can do from three thousand miles away. Ah, here we are."

Russell ushered them into a conference room and closed the door behind him. A large cherry-laminate table dominated the room. Faux leather office chairs surrounded it. An equipment tech ran wires from one of two laptops to the flat-screen television on the wall. "Dan Nakamura, meet Assistant Director Kathryn O'Brien and, uh, Charlie Thompson. Dan will be assisting you with anything you need."

"Were you able to get in touch with anybody from NSB?" O'Brien asked.

"Yes, ma'am," Nakamura replied. "Special Agent Sarah Klingenberg is waiting on me to dial in as we speak."

"Then, please, don't let me stop you."

Nakamura got to work while O'Brien remote-desktopped into her Bureau computer.

"You know this Klingenberg?" she asked Thompson under her breath.

"A bit," Thompson replied. "We were at Quantico together. She's a bit of a striver, always looking toward the next rung on the ladder. It's served her well, I hear—word is, she's become Osterman's go-to gal." James Osterman was the assistant director in charge of the FBI's Counterterrorism Division. "But she's a solid agent, and her heart's in the right place. Honestly, we could do worse."

O'Brien nodded. "Good," she said. "The last thing we need right now is for this to devolve into a pissing contest."

O'Brien—like Osterman—was an assistant director, though she was in charge of the Bureau's Criminal Investigative Division, or CID. The CID fell under the Criminal, Cyber, Response, and Services Branch, or CCRSB, and was responsible for policing everything from violent crime to major thefts. The Counterterrorism Division fell under the National Security Branch, or NSB. The NSB was founded in 2005 in response to a presidential directive to consolidate the counterterrorism, counterintelligence, weapons of mass destruction, and intelligence resources of the Bureau under a single senior Bureau official, and most of its resources were siphoned directly from the CID. They lost a lot of good agents and over a quarter of their budget in the restructuring and had been playing second fiddle ever since. The result was an intra-agency rivalry as heated as it was counterproductive.

Thompson fished a pair of earbuds from her purse and plugged them into her loaner laptop. She placed one earbud in and let the other dangle. Then she opened an array of tabs in the laptop's browser: CNN, NPR, the *San Francisco Chronicle*, the *LA Times*, Twitter. Counterterrorism wasn't Thompson's bailiwick any more than it was O'Brien's—Thompson worked for the FBI's Organized Crime Section, which fell under the umbrella of the CID—but she knew the Bureau well enough to realize O'Brien's official briefing would be sanitized and out-of-date. She wanted to get a sense of what was going on in real time.

The television at the head of the room came to life, displaying a Windows desktop and a buffering chat window. Nakamura gave O'Brien a wireless keyboard and mouse. "You should be good to go," he said.

"You're not staying?" O'Brien asked.

Thompson smiled. O'Brien was something of a technophobe. She couldn't even work the volume on their television once they'd routed it through Thompson's receiver.

"Pretty sure this conversation's above my clearance level," he replied.

As the door closed behind him, the chat window glitched, displaying horizontal rainbow stripes, and then a woman appeared on the screen, her blond hair pulled through the back of her FBI ball cap.

"Special Agent Klingenberg? This is AD O'Brien, can you hear me?"

A brief delay, during which O'Brien's voice echoed back at her, and then Klingenberg nodded. "Yes, ma'am. I've been told to bring you up to speed. How much do you know so far?"

"Assume I know nothing."

"Copy that. At a little after noon Pacific time, a tugboat collided with the Golden Gate's south support tower and exploded. Given the size of the blast, it's unlikely it was accidental. The bridge is still standing, thank God, but several of the support cables have snapped. Portions of the bridge are canting dangerously, and the roadway is impassable. First responders are coordinating with FEMA and the Army Corps of Engineers to figure out a plan of action to evacuate the bridge. It's unclear how badly the structural integrity has been compromised or how many casualties were incurred."

"Do we know how many people were on the bridge at the time of the blast?"

"No. We're still waiting on the data from the tollbooths. Early DOT estimates put the number of cars on the bridge at the time of the explosion at anywhere between four and eight hundred, but again, that's cars, not people. And those estimates count the bridge's full span—one point seven miles of roadway, six lanes wide. Most people on the bridge were well outside the blast radius, but the ensuing panic caused a pile-up north of the crash when they tried to flee."

"And the investigation?"

"We're still in the early stages, ma'am. And the nature of the incident has made collection of physical evidence impossible thus far. But the fact that the bridge is a major landmark works to our advantage. Analysis of cell-phone pictures uploaded to social media just prior to the blast indicates the tugboat's markings were painted over, which suggests whoever did this might've stolen it or at least wanted to obscure its point of origin. The bay below the bridge is still on fire, as I'm sure you've seen from the news coverage. U.S. Park Police are locking down the primary scene, triaging the wounded, and detaining witnesses for questioning."

"U.S. Park Police?"

"Yeah. The bridge's southern span cuts through the Presidio, which falls under their jurisdiction."

"Ah. Of course. What about water traffic?"

"All commercial and recreational boating in the area has been suspended, and vessels already on the water have been instructed to drop anchor until the Coast Guard can inspect them and clear them to dock. The San Francisco field office is coordinating with local PD and Homeland Security to search every inch of the waterfront to determine where the tugboat came from and who was piloting it. We're talking hundreds of vessels and nearly eight miles of waterfront, though, so it's going to take some time. I'll be wheels-up soon to oversee the effort—although I'm going to have to hitch a ride on a military flight, because commercial air, rail, and bus transportation to and from the Bay Area is on lockdown."

"Has anybody taken credit yet?"

"Yeah. The usual suspects, mostly—with one notable exception."

"Yeah? Who?"

"A group calling themselves the True Islamic Caliphate. They released a detailed statement within seconds of the blast, which sets them apart from the rest of the nut brigade."

"Who are these guys? I've never heard of them."

"Join the club. The truth is, they seemed like small potatoes until today, with little influence outside their native Syria. State tells me the TIC has historically been more a militia than a terror group; until today, their primary focus was on overthrowing the Assad regime. We're still trying to determine how—or even if—they could've pulled this off."

"Was their statement written or video?"

"Video. Grainy, indoors, a dirty sheet as a backdrop. In English, although it's clear the man reading it—who we're working to identify—is not a native speaker. They e-mailed it to all the major news outlets as well as the White House. I'm told they tried to put it up on YouTube shortly thereafter, but by then the administration had already been in contact with Google, who owns YouTube, and they blocked its upload."

"I wonder what that little favor cost the president," O'Brien mused aloud. "What did the statement say?"

"The bulk of it was pretty boilerplate—your basic 'Death to America!' type stuff. But they specifically referenced a tugboat striking the southern tower of the bridge. Since the time stamp on the e-mail indicates it was sent less than a minute after the explosion, we're taking it seriously."

"As well you should. How come it hasn't hit the airwaves yet?"

Klingenberg hesitated. "The video…included threats of further violence. Said the attack on the Golden Gate is just the beginning. We've asked the press to sit on it until we can confirm their involvement so it doesn't cause undue panic. It's anybody's guess how long the embargo's going to hold."

"Anything CID can do to help? We're happy to pitch in wherever we're needed."

"Thank you. I'll convey that to my AD and get back to you." Then her mask slipped for a moment, and O'Brien caught a glimpse of the impossible strain she was under. "Between you and me, ma'am, San Francisco is a lawless mess right now. The city's locked down. Its citizens are panicking. The police are overwhelmed. Several businesses that serve the Muslim community have been vandalized already. If the video leaks, it's going to get a whole lot worse. Anything your people can do to keep the peace would be appreciated."

"We'll do what we can."

O'Brien signed off and closed the window. Then she heaved a sigh and turned her attention to Thompson. "That went better than expected," she said. "Do the talking heads have anything interesting to say?"

"Nah," Thompson said. "Facts are thin on the ground, so they're mostly in the bullshit scaremongering phase. I swear, it's like they—"

Thompson's expression changed. She put a finger to the earbud she was wearing. "Hang on," she said. "CNN's breaking in with something. They claim they've got video."

"Of the TIC taking credit?"

"No, of the attack itself."

Thompson unplugged her headphones, and the laptop's tinny speakers cut in. "...if legitimate, this home movie—which was uploaded only minutes ago and has since gone viral—appears to show the moment of impact. We're presenting it unedited in its entirety. Obviously, its content may be unsuitable for some viewers."

The screen went black. Then there was the sound of wind and rustling followed by shaky cell-phone footage of a dirt footpath lined with low, dry scrub.

An old man's face appeared—blurry, but oddly familiar, Thompson thought, although she couldn't place him— and immediately filled the screen. He had one eye closed, like he was peering through the viewfinder of a camera. His open eye was icy blue.

"Are we all in the shot?" came the faint voice of a man from off camera.

"I dunno," the old man replied—too loud, thanks to his proximity to the microphone. "I can't see shit."

A child giggled. "I think you're holding it backward," said the man off camera.

"What? Oh, hell." The old man turned the phone around. A handsome family—mother, father, and three children ranging in age from baby to teenager—swung into view at the north edge of the trail. The Golden Gate Bridge was so close, it loomed impossibly tall behind them. A tugboat chugged across the bay toward the south tower. From this distance, its progress seemed unhurried, lackadaisical. With foreknowledge of what was to come, the cheery banality of the scene took on a perverse air. Thompson felt like she was watching a snuff film, or a car crash in slow motion. "There you are. Wait—does that mean I'm on your video now?"

"Don't worry—we can cut that bit when we get home. Ready, guys?"

His wife and children muttered noncommittally.

"Three...two...one..."

The image jerked slightly as the tugboat hit, as if the old man had realized at the last second what was happening and recoiled. The screen went white, then tumbled end over end in a blur of sky and fire and dirt.

When the CNN anchor reappeared, Thompson rewound the feed and played it again. Then O'Brien called Nakamura back in and had him put it up on the big screen.

They watched it through a second time, people from the bullpen drifting through the open conference-room door to watch, their faces slack with horror. When it finished, O'Brien said, "Is it possible to watch it frame by frame?"

"Sure," Nakamura replied. He dragged the video's progress bar back to the beginning and began advancing manually. "This is gonna take forever," he said. "You want me to skip ahead?"

"Yes," said O'Brien, but at the same time, Thompson shouted, "No!"

Everybody in the room looked at her. Thompson felt her face go red. Her heart sped up like she'd just mainlined a double espresso. The physical reactions were due not to embarrassment but the thrill of discovery.

"Back it up a bit," she said. "One frame at a time, just like you were doing before."

Nakamura complied.

"Slower," she instructed. "Slower. *There!*"

In the frame Nakamura'd stopped on, the old man's face was plainly visible. He was rawboned and deeply lined. His pale blue eyes glinted in the sunlight. O'Brien looked at him, then at Thompson, who was clearly impatient for her to see what she had seen.

When O'Brien looked at the screen again, it clicked.

"Jesus Christ," she said. "It can't be."

"It *is*," Thompson insisted. "I'd know him anywhere."

"Who is he?" asked SAIC Russell, who'd come in while the video was playing.

"That," Thompson said, "is Frank Segreti."

7.

FRANK SEGRETI WAS running blind. Damn near literally, thanks to that bomb blast. Fucking thing must've gone off at least a half an hour ago, and still the afterimage remained, an amorphous blob of green at the center of his vision, obscuring the world around him and forcing him to rely on his peripheral vision. It reminded him of that bank job back in '82 when he'd tried to cut through the vault door without a welding mask. His crew got the cash out okay, but when the cops showed up and everybody scattered, he nearly got pinched because he couldn't see a thing and tried to climb into the wrong fucking car.

At least he'd had a moment's warning before the tugboat detonated. He knew something was hinky when he noticed it was picking up speed the closer it got to the bridge support. At the moment of impact, he flinched, so his forearms were protecting his face when the bomb went off—which was probably the only reason he could see anything at all. The shock wave knocked him off his feet and into the brush that bordered the trail. If those hadn't cushioned his fall, he almost certainly would've broken something. When he came to, smoke tinted the sky the oily brown of an old sepia photograph. Ash rained down from above, gray-white and guttering red. Those poor young lovebirds who'd been perched at the far edge of the trail overlooking the bridge were shredded by debris, and the family who'd stopped him lay unconscious on the trail. Frank wanted to help them, but there was nothing he could do without risking capture, so he fled. He hoped they were okay.

Could the bomb have been meant for him? Frank was unable to discount the idea. If his enemies realized their previous attempt to blow him to kingdom come had failed, they might find a certain pleasing symmetry in another bomb attack. But it didn't strike him as likely. As far as anybody knew, Frank Segreti was long dead—and anyway, an attack like this was awfully imprecise. No, he thought, if they'd found him, they woulda probably popped him from afar with a high-powered rifle or grabbed him off the street and tossed him into a panel van to drive him someplace remote so they could work on him awhile in peace.

If the attack had nothing to do with him, that meant he had a chance—albeit slim—of getting out of this alive.

"Sir! *Sir!*"

The voice came from somewhere behind him. Male, tinny, distant. It took a moment for Frank to realize it was aimed at him.

Frank spun, head swimming as he did. A man in a U.S.

Park Police uniform was standing a few feet behind him. How he'd escaped Frank's notice before, Frank had no idea. He didn't realize until this moment how profoundly the blast had affected him. His ears rang. His equilibrium was shot. His head was cloudy and slow to process information. Concussion, probably. Not Frank's first.

The officer placed a hand on Frank's shoulder. "Are you all right?" he asked. It sounded as if he were shouting from the end of a railroad tunnel. Consonants were lost. Meaning dulled. Frank mostly discerned his words based on the movement of his lips.

"I'm fine." His own words also sounded muffled to his ears, but the cop recoiled as if he'd shouted. The effort it took to speak set him coughing, a hoarse jag that ended with him spitting a wad of phlegm onto the path. "I'm fine," he repeated, quieter, once his coughing subsided.

"We need to get you checked out. First responders are setting up a triage area in Crissy Field. Come with me— I'll take you."

"No!" Frank said, alarmed. If he were held, counted, and cataloged, he was as good as dead. He eyed the man's sidearm. Handicapped the odds of wresting it free of its holster in his addled state. Decided they weren't in his favor. "I mean—you can't. There's a family down the path from here," he said. "Two parents and three kids. They were closer to the blast than I was. I think they're hurt."

The cop looked torn. It was clear to Frank he'd been instructed to bring anybody he encountered back for processing. But then he nodded. "Okay. I'll go check on them. See if they're all right. But you stay put until I get back."

"Sure thing, Officer," Frank said. "I ain't going any-where."

The cop took off down the path. As soon as he disap-peared from sight, Frank fled.

Eager to avoid other first responders lest he be forced to do something he'd regret, he ignored the footpath, in-stead ducking into the scraggly underbrush and pushing upslope through the branches.

Small fires licked at trees where embers had caught. Debris littered the ground: Chunks of asphalt the size of Frank's fist. Twisted bits of metal in glossy automotive fin-ishes. A single tasseled loafer. As soon as Frank identified the last, he looked away; he didn't want to know if any-thing was still inside.

Once he could no longer see the footpath, he felt as though he were in a forest that could easily stretch miles rather than in a narrow swath of trees boxed in by roads. But sirens wailed all around, competing with the ringing in his ears and belying his apparent isolation.

His aging muscles protested. His bum knee ached. His lungs burned. Now and then, he was racked with coughing fits, which forced him to stop until they subsided. Frank was only sixty-three—a decade younger than anyone who met him might've guessed—but they'd been sixty-three hard years. He'd spent a good forty of them drinking, smoking, and whoring around like he was still that young punk from Hoboken with something to prove to the big dogs across the Hudson in New York. Now he was paying the price for those transgressions—and it turned out the interest was steep.

Frank had been coming to the Presidio ever since he'd settled in San Francisco six years ago. A former U.S. Army base now designated as a national park—albeit an unusual one, given its location within an urban center and the fact that people lived and worked within its boundaries—the Presidio, with its rolling hills and half-wild campus, provided a welcome respite from the densely populated city that surrounded it. He liked to walk the footpaths through the forest groves or the dunes along the water's edge. He'd sit for hours on his favorite bench and watch the sailboats tack across the glimmering bay. It beat staring at the walls of his overpriced efficiency apartment on Nob Hill and made the life he'd left behind seem as distant and ephemeral as the hazy outline of Alcatraz in the distance.

Today, though, the Presidio might prove just as inescapable as that legendary prison—and as Frank's own past.

Frank was well versed in law enforcement procedures. He'd spent his life studying them so that he could exploit their weaknesses. No doubt the authorities were in the process of setting up a perimeter around the park; limiting access to and from the site so they could assist the wounded, process evidence, and sift for suspects among the witnesses made sense. But the place was huge—a little over 2.3 square miles—so there was no way they could have fully locked it down yet. If he could escape before they did that, there was a chance that he might live.

Frank came to a chain-link fence topped with barbed wire. On the other side, a narrow roadway was cut into the overgrown slope. He heard a crunch of tires. A siren growing louder. He cursed and hit the ground. A white Dodge Charger with a blue stripe raced by, its light bar splashing red and blue across him. More Park Police, he thought, though the Feds were no doubt close behind.

Once the Charger passed, he rose clumsily, bracing himself on the chain link for support. Then he stripped off his argyle sweater and threw it over the barbed wire to protect him. His button-down snagged as he struggled over the sweater-draped fence. As he attempted to unhook it, a barb sank into the palm of his right hand. He gritted his teeth and fought the urge to howl in pain. A groan escaped him as he yanked his hand free and climbed back down. Blood pooled in the hollow of his palm. He wiped it on his shirt and made a fist to stanch the bleeding. Red seeped between his fingers and dripped onto the roadway.

Another car approached, its engine roaring. Frank crossed the road as quickly as his bum knee would allow, ducking out of sight a fraction of a second before the car sped by. Then he scurried once more upslope through the underbrush.

Not bad, old man, he told himself. *Not bad. Just keep it up, and no one will ever know you were here.*

8.

IN A DUSTY corner of a sprawling English Tudor home in Clinton, New York—a quiet college town not far from the decaying industrial city of Utica—a phone began to ring.

Sal Lombino frowned. His daughter, Isabella, stopped plunking at the piano and looked at him. "Can I get it, Daddy?"

"Not this time, honey. What'd Ms. Malpica tell you?"

She rolled her eyes and said, "That I had to practice at least half an hour every day."

"And how long's it been?"

She shrugged. "I dunno. Twenty minutes?" The sheepish smile on her face made it clear she knew damn well it hadn't been but was hoping her old man was too big a softie to call her on it.

"Try again," he said, smiling himself. Sal hoped that

Izzie never got any better at lying than she was today, midway through her seventh year. But he knew better. Lying was in her DNA. Her hateful bitch of a mother did it for sport. Sal did it for a living.

"It's been five minutes," she singsonged low and melancholy, her face an exaggerated pout.

"That's more like it. Seems to me you should keep playing, then, and leave the phone to me."

"Okay," she said reluctantly and resumed clanking out her tune—a meandering version of "Twinkle, Twinkle, Little Star" with more wrong notes than right.

Truthfully, Sal didn't much care if she practiced—the lessons were his ex-wife's idea, no doubt intended to waste Sal's money and drive him batty when it was his weekend to take Izzie—but the phone ringing was not the house's primary line. It was his business line, the one that rarely rang, the one he never let his daughter answer.

Sal worked for the Council. He was, in fact, its only full-time employee. Council business was typically carried out by freelancers or members of its constituent organizations, but because those organizations were often rivals, the Council required someone unaffiliated with any of them to act as go-between.

That man was Sal. He was solely responsible for executing Council orders and looking after Council interests worldwide. It was a position that commanded fear and respect. He had no formal title, because he had no need of one—but thanks to his predecessor, who'd originated the role, those who whispered about him in dark corners of the underworld referred to him as the Devil's Red Right Hand.

Personally, Sal had never much cared for the sobriquet.

For one, he'd been an altar boy growing up and didn't like the implication he was playing for the wrong team. For two, it was a little arch. And for three, it made him wonder if there was a counterpart on God's side who'd one day punish Sal for everything he'd done.

Sal's office was a cliché of a gentleman's study. Mahogany paneling. Built-in floor-to-ceiling shelves lined with books he'd never read. A hinged, hand-painted globe that doubled as a bar cart. Burnished-leather armchairs. Banker's lamps. An antique Wooton desk on which sat a phone, a leather blotter, and a computer.

Sal walked by it without a glance. His office was for show. A rodeo clown, intended to distract. He never conducted any business of real import in it.

The ringing phone was in his second guest room, which was tucked behind the kitchen. The third floor of Sal's house comprised a guest suite—bedroom, bathroom, and sitting room—and that was where visitors typically stayed. Consequently, this bedroom was rarely used, and everything about it appeared to be an afterthought: The simple, metal-framed twin bed. The cheap floral comforter. The empty dresser. The prefab particleboard nightstand, upon which sat a lamp, a box of tissues, and an old rotary phone.

The phone wasn't registered in Sal's name. In fact, the line used to be connected to his neighbor's teenage daughter's room. When their house was foreclosed on years ago during the recession, he had surreptitiously had it rerouted and set the bill to auto-deduct from an online checking account opened for just that purpose. The former was a simple matter of redirecting a single wire; the latter, snatching a bill from his neighbor's mailbox and calling the phone company to update the payment method. Committing fraud to get money out of major corporations is a tricky business, but committing fraud to *give* them money is easy, because they never think to question getting paid.

Sal stepped into the bedroom and shut the door, muffling Izzie's halting notes but not silencing them entirely. The phone continued to ring, as he knew it would until he picked it up. He fished around inside the tissue box on the nightstand and pulled out a small electronic device the size of two stacked decks of cards: an audio jammer. Its textured black plastic surface was perforated at one end to accommodate an internal speaker, and its controls consisted of a single on/off/volume knob on the side. It was powered by a nine-volt battery and had cost him a little over a hundred bucks—from Amazon, if you can believe it.

He turned it on and cranked the volume up. The sound of static filled the room, not so loud as to be intolerable but loud enough to render useless any listening devices within a hundred and fifty feet. Then, finally, he picked up the receiver. "Yeah?"

"Sal, it's Bobby V. We gotta talk." Bobby V. was the Council rep for the Ventura crime family.

"This better be fucking good, Bobby," Sal replied. "It's my weekend with Izzie."

"Ah. I take it you haven't seen, then."

"Seen what?"

"If you'd seen, you wouldn't have to ask—you'd know. Turn on your TV."

"What station?"

"Doesn't matter. Any of 'em."

"Hang on."

He grabbed the remote from the nightstand drawer and turned on the tiny flat-screen atop the dresser. The cable box defaulted to the local NBC affiliate. Under a BREAKING NEWS banner was an aerial shot of the Golden Gate Bridge, thick smoke billowing from beneath it. The portion of the bridge directly above the smoke was hard to see, but it appeared to be canting, and several of the vertical support cables swung free, their ends frayed. The span on either side was littered with overturned cars.

"Jesus Christ," Sal muttered.

"Yeah, it don't look good."

Sal cleared his throat. "Do they have any idea what happened yet?"

"If they do, they sure ain't saying, but it looks to me like a big-ass bomb went off."

"Bobby, I hope you're not calling to ask if we had anything to do with it."

Bobby scoffed. "Course not! I'm sure it was ISIS or some shit."

"Then why'd you call? I assume you have a reason beyond torpedoing my fucking weekend."

"They playing the video yet?"

"What video?"

"They got cell-phone video of the blast. Smiling family. Big boom."

"No."

"Keep watching. They will. And when they do, pay attention to the ugly mug that kicks the whole thing off."

Sal sighed with frustration. "Listen, why don't you just cut the bullshit and tell me what this is all about?"

"Because some things gotta be seen to be believed."

Sal kept watching. As promised, the aerial footage cut

71

to a shaky cell-phone video, first of a footpath, then of an old man's blurry face. Sal tilted his head and squinted. "Holy shit. That's Frank Segreti."

"Oh, thank God—you see it too. When he popped up on my TV, I thought I was losing my goddamn mind."

"He looks like hell."

"You think? I'd say he looks pretty fucking good for a dead man."

"This doesn't make any sense. We blew up Segreti's ass seven years ago."

"Did we?"

"C'mon, Bobby. The safe house the Feds stashed him in was leveled by the blast—no one coulda made it outta there alive. And besides, they found his DNA when they processed the wreckage, it said so in their report."

"Yeah, well, that video tells a different story," Bobby said. "We need to convene the Council and hold a vote to authorize the funds to send a hitter after Segreti."

Sal's brow furrowed as he weighed his options. It'd take a couple days at least to organize a meeting, and even then, there was no guarantee they'd vote in favor of offing Segreti; they'd been reluctant to take action ever since the Engelmann job had gone sideways last year. "No. There isn't time. Every second we wait, Segreti gets a little farther away."

"I hate to break it to you, Sal, but you don't have the clout to authorize an op without Council approval."

"Of course I don't," Sal snapped. "And neither do you. There's only one man who does."

"You saying you're gonna take this to the chairman?"

"I don't see any other choice."

"Do me a favor, then, and leave my name out of it."

"Why, Bobby, you sound scared."

"Scared? Hell, no. It's just—you know how he's been since the Feds announced Engelmann's death. Communicating by dead drop. Voting by proxy. A different burner twice a week whether he used the last one or not. He's goddamn paranoid, and for good reason. If Council business were ever linked to him, he—and everything we've been working toward—would be ruined. The last thing I need is to wind up on his bad side just because I put a bug in your ear."

"How the fuck do you think I feel? I'm the one who hired Engelmann. The chairman blames me for his failure."

"Aw, c'mon. You're his handpicked guy. He can't stay pissed at you forever. Hell, maybe putting Segreti in the ground will get you back into the chairman's good graces."

"Maybe. But first, I gotta be the guy to tell him the shitheel's still alive. One thing's for sure, though."

"What's that?"

"This time, I'm not leaving anything to chance. I wanna see him die with my own eyes. It's the only way we'll know that this time, the motherfucker stays dead."

9.

HENDRICKS LEANED HEAVILY on Cameron's shoulder as she helped him from the car, the wound in his side stamping her T-shirt red with every step. "C'mon," she said. "My apartment's upstairs. Let's get you in before someone sees you."

She struggled to support his weight as they crossed the patchy lawn. "Wait," he said, trying to wriggle from her grasp and turn around. "The car."

Cameron eyed his eight-year-old Accord—four-door, silver, nondescript. She'd driven it two miles inland from the restaurant while Hendricks lay in the backseat applying pressure to stanch the bleeding and cursing every time she hit a pothole. Now it was parked at the curb in front of an ugly prewar home that had been converted, shabbily, some decades ago into multiple apartment units. "Is stolen, I'm guessing."

Who *was* this girl? he wondered. "Nah. It's clean. I bought it from a private seller and paid in cash. But it doesn't matter now. If anybody saw us leave the Salty Dog, it will lead the cops right to your door. We need to ditch it."

"What we *need* is to get you inside. You're barely upright. You're covered in blood."

"Damn it, kid, this isn't a negotiation. The car has to go."

"Look—there's a strip mall a half a mile from here. Let me take you upstairs and get you situated. Once you're safely off the street, I'll come back down and move it to their lot, okay?"

His gaze traveled from the car to his blood-soaked shirt. Realized that of the two, the latter was more likely to be noticed. "Okay," he conceded.

They scaled the concrete steps to the porch. Hendricks braced himself with his free hand on the rust-flecked pipe railing. Up close, he could see the house's aluminum siding was dingy, and the nearest downstairs window's bottom pane was split by a diagonal crack. Several mailboxes hung crookedly beside the door, each marked with peel-and-stick reflective letters, *A* to *E*, and handwritten names scrawled on masking tape. Hendricks scanned them as he went by: Ndiaye. Williamson. Goldenstern. Samuels. Karasiewicz. "Which one's you?" he asked.

Cameron chuffed as if to say, *Nice try*. "None of them. I never peeled the old name off when I moved in."

The front door was unlocked. Inside was a narrow hallway that smelled of cigarettes. The brown indoor/outdoor carpet was worn bare. They bypassed two doors labeled *A* and *B*, respectively, and headed up the rickety stairs.

The wound in Hendricks's side flexed excruciatingly as they ascended. He was breathing heavily by the time they reached the second floor.

"Sorry," Cameron said, "but I'm in E. We've got one more flight to go."

Hendricks set his jaw, and they pressed on.

The top floor was narrower than the first two because it was essentially attic space, tucked into the pitch of the roof. It was hotter up here by a good fifteen degrees. There was no hallway, just a small landing with one door. As they neared it, a dog inside went apeshit.

"You failed to mention you have a dog," Hendricks said.

"Oh, don't sweat it. That's just Cujo."

Claws scrabbling on hardwood. Snarls punctuated by a snapping jaw. "Sure, a pissed-off dog named Cujo—what's to sweat?"

"No, I'm serious," she said, swinging the door open with a flourish. The barking trebled in volume. Hendricks tensed, but inside, there was no dog—just a motion sensor jury-rigged to an off-brand MP3 player that was plugged into a speaker dock. "It's the actual Cujo...you know, from the movie? My landlord's a sketchball. This keeps him from prying. On the upside, he takes cash and didn't ask a lot of questions when I moved in."

She reached down and shut the barking off. Then she helped him to her futon. Hendricks collapsed atop it, panting.

She disappeared into the bathroom and returned with a towel. "Lemme see your side," she said.

Hendricks peeled off his ruined shirt. Cameron blanched when she saw the jagged gash across his rib cage.

She took a steadying breath, then folded up the towel and pressed it to the wound.

"Hold this a sec."

He complied. She stripped off her belt—military-style, canvas—and wrapped it around his chest, over the towel. Then she yanked it tight to hold the towel in place.

Hendricks sucked air through clenched teeth.

"Sorry," she said. "But we need to keep applying pressure until the bleeding stops."

"I could've just *held* it."

"Maybe, but I don't trust you not to pass out while I'm gone."

"I'll be fine. This isn't the first time I've been stabbed."

Cameron eyed his naked torso, taut and riddled with scars. "Yeah. Guess not."

"Okay, I did as you asked—I came inside without a fight. Now go move the car."

"All right, all right, I'm going."

She crossed the room to the dresser. Grabbed a fresh shirt from the drawer. Turned her back to him. Hesitated briefly, then pulled her bloody top up over her head and tossed it to the floor. Hendricks saw a flash of lower back, lean and sun-freckled, but looked away before she exposed her bra.

When she reached the front door, she paused and turned. "Don't die on me, okay? I won't be long."

Hendricks nodded, grimacing at the effort, and reluctantly, she took off down the stairs.

As soon as the door swung shut behind her, Hendricks rose shakily from the futon and began ransacking her apartment. He was hobbled by the wound and knew he didn't have long, but luckily the place wasn't very big—maybe one hundred and fifty square feet, bathroom included. And, thankfully, it was nearly bare of furniture, just a futon, a dresser, and a papasan chair, all of which—if the patterns on the sun-bleached floorboards when he moved them were any indication—had come with the place.

He removed drawers and overturned them. Rifled through their contents and checked to see if anything was taped to their undersides. He checked inside the futon's cushion and the papasan's too. Ditto the toilet tank and minifridge.

Every time he twisted, lifted, or bent, the knife wound tore a little—but it wasn't deep, and the towel had slowed his bleeding significantly. His jaw clicked when he moved it, thanks to the punch Dimitris had landed, but he was pretty sure it wasn't broken.

He was furious that he'd allowed Pappas to get the drop on him, and while he was grateful to Cameron—or whatever her real name was—for saving his life, he had no idea who she worked for, so he couldn't discount the possibility that she had shot Pappas to silence him. If she was working for the Council, though, why hadn't she just put him down when she'd had the chance?

Fine, then. Maybe she was on his side—but why? And who the hell was she? Hendricks didn't know, but he aimed to find out.

Twenty minutes later, Cameron returned. As she pushed open the door and stepped inside, she said, "Don't worry—it's just me." Puzzlement flickered across her face when she saw her belongings in piles on the floor. Then she noticed that Hendricks was sitting on her futon, the .45 he'd taken from Pappas aimed squarely at her gut. "Uh, did I do something wrong? Or are you delirious from blood loss? I saved your life, re-member?"

"I remember," he said. "But I think it's time that you and I got to know each other better."

"Fine by me," she said, the quaver in her voice putting the lie to her casual bravado, "but do you really think you need to point a gun at me to do that? I'm one of the good guys."

"Who says *I* am?" He gestured to the papasan chair with his gun barrel, its cushion bare, its slipcover lying on the floor beside it.

"I do," she replied, moving slowly toward it with her hands up halfheartedly and then sitting down. "But we can play it your way."

He glanced at the laptop that sat beside him on the futon, a tricked-out custom job with more ports than Hendricks knew what to do with and a seventeen-inch screen. "I found your computer," he said.

"Good for you. I wasn't hiding it."

"It's a serious piece of hardware."

"For a waitress who lives in a total dump, you mean."

"For anybody," he said. "Care to explain to me what I found on it?"

"Sure," she said. "I think the word you're looking for is *nothing.*"

"Come again?"

"I built that thing myself. It's encrypted six ways from Sunday and requires a USB passkey to log on. That passkey is in my pocket. I could give it to you, if you'd like to boot it up and poke around."

Hendricks frowned. "Later, maybe. First, let's talk about the dossier you've got on me."

"What, the one in the dresser?"

"That's right."

"Oh, I'd hardly call that a *dossier,*" she said with exaggerated snootiness, as if mocking his word choice. "It's just some clippings, really, of stuff I couldn't find online and haven't had time to scan yet. If you really wanna see what I can do, you should check out what's on that baby," she said, nodding toward the computer. "I've got a virtual corkboard of news pieces stretching back four years. Same with crime-scene photos and coroner's reports. And then there's the juicy stuff. I'm talking real-time data collection on every criminal organization in the country from a half a dozen federal databases—and Interpol too, obviously. Five separate regression analyses, both parametric and non-, that all feed into a weighted model designed to treat each according to its accuracy in predicting prior known movements—"

"Whoa. Slow down. *Whose* prior known movements?"

She looked at him like he was the kid in class who couldn't be trusted with the paste. "Well, *yours.*"

"So you admit that you've been tracking me?"

"Yes, of course!"

"For how long?"

"I dunno...a few months now? But like I said, my data stretches back way farther than that."

"Who do you work for?"

"Nobody right now. That's why I'm here."

"I don't follow."

Cameron cocked her head and regarded him quizzically. "You really don't remember me, do you?"

"Should I?"

"I dunno. Four years ago, you saved my mother's life. I thought maybe you'd recognize me."

"I've saved a lot of people. Killed a lot of people too. You're going to have to give me more to go on."

"Cameron's not my first name, it's my last."

It took a few beats, but eventually, it clicked. "Jesus. You're Dana Cameron's kid."

When Hendricks met Dana Cameron, she was the head of bioinformatics for Veridian Laboratories. Dana was a brilliant programmer and had been a rising star in the male-dominated world of Silicon Valley before the pharmaceutical giant poached her to run its nascent division, which aimed to use rapid genotyping and next-gen computer modeling to tailor its promising new cancer drug to individual patients. The corporation's executives pledged to give her a billion dollars to use however she wished in order to reach that goal.

When Veridian made the announcement, their stock soared. The scientific community heralded the decision as revolutionary. Bill Gates wrote in his annual Gates Foundation letter that the partnership could reduce cancer mortality by 80 percent in the next decade.

But the honeymoon was short-lived.

Six months into her new job, Dana discovered that the results of several in-house studies of Veridian's new drug had been suppressed—studies that indicated the drug increased patients' risk of stroke and cardiac arrest more than twentyfold. She made the mistake of giving her company's CEO, Gavin Lockley, the chance to make things right and take the information public before she did. If the world found out about the studies, Lockley and Verid-

81

ian stood to lose tens if not hundreds of billions, so he'd responded the way any shrewd businessman would: he'd hired someone to kill her. That's how Hendricks wound up in her employ.

He remembered the job well, in part because the man Lockley had hired to kill Dana was a seasoned pro who'd nearly succeeded in his task before Hendricks finally finished him off, and in part because his clients were rarely as decent and principled as she was.

Hendricks set down his gun and smiled. "You were just a knobby-kneed kid with braces back then."

"I wasn't *that* young—I was sixteen!"

Hendricks was thirty-one. He didn't have the heart to tell her that from where he was sitting, sixteen qualified as *that young.* "I seem to recall your parents called you Rosie."

"Yeah. My first name's Rosalind. My parents named me after Rosalind Franklin, the scientist whose research Watson and Crick ripped off to write their paper on the helical structure of DNA. Mom always said it was her way of reminding me that if I wanted something in this world, I had to fight for it. Dad used to joke that he went along with it because he thought that an old-lady name would scare off potential suitors."

"How are they? Your parents, I mean."

"Mom's good, I guess. She's in Geneva, working for the World Health Organization."

"And your dad?"

"Wrapped his Benz around a tree on the way home from a bar last Christmas Eve."

"I'm sorry."

"Thanks. Me too. It's not like I didn't see it coming, though. He fell apart after the attempt on Mom's life.

Took a leave of absence from his law firm. Started hitting the bottle pretty hard. Thanks to Mom's testimony at Lockley's trial, Veridian's stock plummeted, and Mom became the poster child for corporate transparency. She wanted to use her newfound fame to help people. Dad just wanted it to go away. They fought a lot. One night—after he'd downed half a bottle of Canadian Club—he got physical, so she threw him out. When the cops called to tell me he'd..." She swallowed hard and cleared her throat. "I hadn't seen him in a year."

"Cameron, what are you doing here?"

"What do you mean?"

"You know what I mean. What do you want with me?"

"I want to *help* you."

"Help me what?"

"You know...do what you do."

"Kill people?"

"Stop bad guys," she corrected. "Look, in my research, I've learned everything there is to know about your operation. You were sloppy when you began. Reckless. Then, for a few years—starting around the time you saved my mom—you got careful, savvy. Lately, your MO's changed. You're playing offense, not defense, and you've become reckless again. My guess is you had backup for a while—someone who helped you identify clients and watched your back—and now you don't. And given your recent hate-on for this Council or whatever, I'm guessing that that someone's dead."

Hendricks's mouth became a thin sharp line, his expression as dark as his thoughts. "His name was Lester. He was a good man. A good friend."

"I'm sorry. I didn't mean to be glib. I just think that I

could be of assistance to you, is all—and from what I can tell, you could use the hand."

"I'm not exactly looking for an intern," he said.

"And I'm not looking to be one. You're a field guy—I get that. But it seems to me you might need a little tech support. An eye in the sky. A voice in your ear. A ghost in the machine."

"Does your mother know you're here?"

"Does yours?"

At that, Hendricks smiled wanly. He was an orphan who'd never known his mother. He took some comfort in the fact that Cameron didn't know that about him, at least.

"Look," he said, "my last tech guy, Lester, was a soldier, a warrior, and I still managed to get him killed. It'd be ridiculous—immoral, even—to take you on."

"Immoral?"

"Damn right. You're a kid."

"I'm twenty."

"Like I said."

"Don't give me that ageist bullshit. If your buddy was a soldier, I'm guessing you were too. It fits my profile. How old were you when you first enlisted?"

"Eighteen," he said, "and if I'd had any idea what I was signing on for, I would have run screaming the other way."

"I know what I'm signing on for."

"No, you don't. And I can't afford to babysit you until you realize this isn't the life for you."

"No one's asking you to babysit me. I can take care of myself. Just ask Nick Pappas."

"That was a lucky shot," he said.

"The hell it was. Thanks to Lockley, Mom made sure I knew my way around a firearm."

"You ever aim one at a person before today?" She opened her mouth to reply, but nothing came out. "That's what I thought. Pappas is dead, you know. You *killed* him. How's that sit with you?"

"It was him or you. I didn't kill him so much as exchange one death for another, the net result of which will be fewer innocent people hurt. My conscience is clear."

"Yeah? Then why are your hands shaking?"

Cameron looked down at her hands and seemed surprised to discover he was right. She balled them into fists to still them. "They're not. I'm fine."

"No, you're not. Taking a life isn't like balancing a spreadsheet. Every time you kill someone, justifiably or not, it takes a toll—the first one more than most. You've probably been coasting on adrenaline ever since. But when the crash comes, once the adrenaline abandons you, it comes hard."

"Don't tell me how I'm supposed to feel."

"I'm not. I'm just saying I've been there. In my case, the shakes were just the beginning. Next thing I knew, I broke out in a cold sweat, and my throat constricted until I felt like I couldn't breathe. Then my mouth filled with saliva—"

But by then, Cameron was already on her feet and halfway to the bathroom. Hendricks followed her wordlessly. Knelt down beside her. Held her hair back when the sickness came. Her stomach clenched. Tears streamed down her cheeks. She retched until there was nothing left for her to bring up and then a little while longer.

He felt bad for pushing her toward this. There was a chance she wouldn't have wound up puking if he hadn't. But he needed her to understand that this wasn't a game.

When she finally ran out of steam, he fetched her a glass of water from the sink. It smelled like old pipes. "Here. Drink this."

She took a big gulp. Rivulets of water spilled from the corners of her mouth and ran down her chin.

"Easy," he said, "or it'll come back up."

She slowed down. Sipped carefully. When the glass was empty, he fetched her another.

"You okay?" he asked.

"Getting there," she said, her voice like sandpaper.

"You understand that I can't take you on, right?"

Tears brimmed in her eyes again. "But I saved your life."

"Which is already more than I deserve."

"So that's it, then?"

"Oh, you won't be getting rid of me that easily," he said. Cameron laughed; it sounded forced and weak but was better than nothing. "Far as I'm concerned, you and me are in this together until I know for sure we got away clean. Which means you're going to need to patch me up. After that, we'll lie low for a little while and rest. Then we'll get out of here together. But once Long Island and this Pappas mess are in our rearview, we'll go our separate ways. Deal?"

"Deal," she said, reluctantly. "Hey, can I ask you something?"

"Sure."

"There's one data point I couldn't find, no matter how hard I tried. If anybody knows it, it's locked down so tight even I couldn't get my hands on it."

"What's that?"

"Your name. You never gave one when you saved my mom."

Hendricks mentally scrolled through his many aliases and then thought, *Fuck it—she's earned this much at least.*

"My name is Michael," he said.

10.

CHARLIE THOMPSON PACED outside the conference room, nervy from anticipation. O'Brien was inside, on a call with the director. She'd been in there for nearly an hour.

Forty minutes ago, some Podunk online news site blew the embargo on the TIC's recorded statement taking credit for the bombing and threatening further attacks, no doubt garnering millions of clicks before the major outlets could follow suit. Since then, the airwaves had become a feeding frenzy, and the Bureau's phones rang off the hook—panicked citizens jumping at shadows, mostly.

The conference-room door opened. O'Brien stepped out, looking tired and drawn. Thompson froze midstride and stared at her, eyes avid.

"Well?" Thompson asked.

"I'm sorry. The answer's no."

"What do you mean, no?"

"Oh, come on, Charlie, you can't really be surprised. We're in the midst of a national security crisis. We know next to nothing about these TIC whack jobs, which means we're behind the eight ball already, and we have no idea what they might do next. The last thing we need's another 9/11 on our hands. Now that the video's out there, the world's eyes are on us. We need to do this by the book, no mission creep, no side projects. We simply don't have the resources to go after Segreti right now—if, in fact, that man was even him."

"*If?* Are you kidding me? You know damn well that was Segreti."

"Sure, it *looked* like him, but we have overwhelming evidence that suggests he died in federal custody."

"We *had* overwhelming evidence," Thompson corrected. "It went out the window the second Segreti showed up on tape. As far as I'm concerned, we owe it to this guy to protect him. We already failed him once. And remember, he walked in of his own accord."

"Yeah, and put four federal agents in the hospital. Three of them were so badly injured, they were deemed unfit for duty. One will never walk right again."

"You weren't there, Kate. I was. Segreti was a mess when he walked in. He felt cornered, threatened. If he'd wanted to kill us, he easily could have. But he didn't. He held back. Then he surrendered his weapon and offered Organized Crime Section its biggest collar in thirty years."

"Oh, c'mon. That's speculative at best. We don't even know for sure what Segreti can give us. You have to admit, the story he was peddling sounded a little too good to be true."

"Sure, except we hadn't even finished debriefing him

before the safe house we'd stashed him in blew sky-high. You ask me, that does wonders for his credibility."

"Maybe so, Charlie, but either way, it doesn't matter. The Bureau can't afford to be distracted by Segreti right now."

"Just send me, then. I'll go alone. Work the trail. See if I can bring him in. Surely the director can't object to that."

O'Brien frowned. Said nothing. Thompson's eyes widened in understanding.

"This isn't coming from the director, is it? This is *you.* You're the one making the call not to go get him."

"Listen, Charlie—"

"Why should I? It's clear you haven't been listening to me."

O'Brien's face showed hurt and anger. "You'd do well to take a breath and remember who you're talking to. Right now, *fiancée* has to take a backseat to *commanding officer.*"

"Fine. As my commanding officer, you need to let me do my goddamn job. Tell me, did you even ask the director? When you were on the conference call, did you even bring Segreti up?"

"What do you want me to say? No, I didn't fucking bring him up. The country is under attack. You really think I ought to tell my boss and every AD in the Bureau that we should divert time and effort from hunting down the TIC because the employee I'm sleeping with has a bee in her bonnet?"

"So now I'm just some office lay with a head full of silly notions?"

"Of course not. But as hurtful as he was, your father was right about one thing: we need to look at this objectively, to think about how others in the Bureau would see it."

"And here I thought they'd see it as an opportunity to rectify one of the biggest blunders in Bureau history. But then, you never gave them the chance."

"Believe me, Charlie. I did you a favor. If I pitched your pet project today of all days, neither of us would be taken seriously again."

"Fine. Then let me go get him."

"I can't. You *know* I can't."

"Just give me seventy-two hours—that's all I ask."

"I'm sorry. There's too much work to do. The director's ordered both of us to return to DC as soon as possible. I'm going to get us on the next flight. We can have one of the staffers here drive your car back down."

"You know what? I think I'll save them the trouble and drive it back myself. I could use a few hours to cool off."

11.

SAL LOMBINO TOOK a breath to steady himself and plucked the handset from its cradle. He dialed the number of the chairman's latest burner from memory. Sal had a head for figures. It used to come in handy when he had to calculate the vig back in his loan-shark days.

The phone rang seven times before the chairman answered, the voice mail, as ever, disabled.

"You've got a lot of nerve calling me today. Don't you watch the news?"

"I do, Mr. Chairman," Sal replied. "In fact, that's why I'm calling."

"I'm afraid I don't follow."

"That old guy on the cell-phone video they been showing every ten seconds? That's Frank Segreti. As in—"

"I know who he is," the chairman snapped, irritated

that Sal had broken his cardinal rule: never use a name when talking on an unsecured phone line.

"Then you know the damage he could do to all our efforts if he were to resurface. Which means we need to find him and ensure he never does."

"Then convene a meeting. Take a vote. And leave me out of it."

"There isn't time, and even if there were, there's no guarantee that the vote would go our way."

"So, what, then? You want my approval to spend Council funds to go after him? You've got it."

"Thank you, sir. But I'm afraid I need more than money."

"Like what?"

"We've got an asset in our pocket who stands to lose at least as much as we do if the, uh, gentleman in question reappears. But right now, he's otherwise occupied, so I wouldn't dare call on him without your say-so."

"Are you kidding me? Do you realize what you're asking? We need him to stay on task. If he's burned now, a key component of our endgame will be compromised."

"I'm aware of that, sir. And I won't lie—it's a possibility. But our endgame's in jeopardy either way if we don't neutralize this threat. Besides, under the circumstances, I'd say he owes us big."

"On that, we are agreed—but are you sure that he's the right man for the job? You know what a goddamn mess he made the last time, and apparently, he still managed to miss his fucking target."

Sal knew all too well. He'd seen the coroner's reports. Limbs torn from bodies. Flesh and hair reduced to ash. Shattered fragments of tooth and bone picked out of ceiling joists. "I don't think we have much choice—but this time, I'll insist on video confirmation."

There was a long pause on the chairman's end. "Fine. Do it. And leave me out of this from here on in. I don't want to hear another peep from you until Segre—until the matter is settled," he said carefully. "Am I understood?"

"Yes, Mr. Chairman."

"Good. Because your continued…employment… depends on it."

The chairman disconnected. Sal sat there for a moment listening to the hiss of the dead line. Then he returned the phone's receiver to its cradle and let out a ragged sigh.

"Who was that, Daddy?"

Sal looked up to see his daughter, Izzie, in the doorway. He'd left her finger-painting in the kitchen, her reward for half an hour's piano practice. Her hands were smeared with paint in every color of the rainbow. There was a dot of glossy green on her nose.

"Nobody, sweetheart. A wrong number. C'mon, let's get you washed up."

12.

"YOU READY?" Cameron asked.

Hendricks checked to be sure the bedsheet they'd used to tie his ankles to the far end of the futon frame was secure, and he looped his arms around the metal armrest that currently served as its headboard. He rolled his neck, eliciting a crack, and exhaled deeply, willing himself to relax. Then he nodded. He was unable to speak because Cameron's belt was clenched between his teeth.

"Good. That makes one of us." She uncapped the bottle of rubbing alcohol she was holding and then placed a hand on the towel resting against Hendricks's knife wound. Until recently, her belt had held it in place. "Hold on tight—this is gonna suck."

She peeled back the towel. Clotted blood caused Hendricks's skin to stick to it for a moment before releasing. When raw wound met open air, he drew a sharp breath and bit down harder on the belt. Cameron recoiled at the sight of his parted flesh striated pink and red. Then, with obvious reluctance, she doused it liberally with alcohol.

Every muscle in Hendricks body tensed at once. He lurched uncontrollably on the futon, his neck corded, his face red and then purple. His entire body broke out in a sheen of acrid sweat. A hex nut loosened by his thrashing shook free, and the support strut on the futon frame gave out. It banged against the floor, and the mattress canted precariously.

Eventually, Hendricks's agony subsided. His muscles relaxed, and he released the armrest. He collapsed atop the tilted mattress, limbs quivering, and gulped air while he marshaled his wits.

That's when he noticed a sharp rapping—from the door, he thought at first, visions of an approaching SWAT team dancing through his head. But then he realized it was coming from the floor.

Cameron noted Hendricks's narrowed eyes, his calculating expression, and said, "Don't worry. That's just my downstairs neighbor, Wayne." Then, toward the floor, she shouted, "You can stop anytime now, Wayne! I'm not making noise anymore!"

The rapping stopped. Hendricks looked from the floor to Cameron. "Do we have to worry about him?" he asked.

"Worry how?"

"That he'll get suspicious. That he'll call the cops."

Cameron laughed. "Oh, he's plenty suspicious already. But unless he stopped dealing weed since I left for work this morning, I think we're okay."

"Good," he said. He didn't relish the thought of being forced to silence a civilian. "On to step two."

"You sure about this?"

"Nope. Never done it for a wound this big before. But it's not like we have much choice. And remember: If I pass out, just keep going. It'll probably be better for the both of us."

Cameron swallowed hard. Poured alcohol over the paper towel on which her instruments rested: A pair of tweezers. A spool of thread. A sewing needle bent as best they could into a semicircle. All three were still damp from the last time she'd disinfected them.

Threading the needle was more difficult than she'd expected, but eventually she managed. She rested it against Hendricks's side, flesh dimpling beneath it, and let out a deep breath before beginning. When the needle pierced his skin, his stomach muscles tightened reflexively and he let out a growl.

"Sorry," Cameron said, pausing.

"Don't be," he replied, his voice low and strained. "And for God's sake, keep going. You're just doing as I've asked. As much as this sucks, I'm better off with you doing it than me."

"Why?" she asked, twisting the needle through until the tip showed on the other side of the wound and then grabbing it with the tweezers. "You think because I'm a girl, I must know how to sew?"

Hendricks's cheeks colored. "No! I—"

"Jesus." She pulled the needle clear, thread trailing, and began a second loop. "I was *kidding.*"

"Anybody ever tell you you've got lousy comedic timing?"

"And here I thought that I was helping you relax."

"I'll relax when I'm all stitched up," he said, although

in truth, he doubted it. He'd be jumping at shadows until they were far enough away from Long Island that the likelihood that anyone would connect them to the Pappas mess was nil. And he wouldn't *fully* relax until he'd tracked down every sitting member of the Council and put them in the ground.

"I wish I had some booze to offer you. I should've thought to swipe a bottle of vodka from the Salty Dog."

"I've had quite enough today already."

"Speaking of, I must've poured you eight shots this afternoon. How the hell'd you manage to stay sober?"

Hendricks, despite his pain, managed a weak smile. The kid had good instincts; she was trying to distract him so the stitches didn't hurt so much. "A little sleight of hand and a strategically placed ficus."

"So *that's* why your corner of the bar always reeked of whiskey. I just figured it was you. No offense."

"None taken," he said. "That was kind of the idea."

"Sorry I pushed that coffee on you. At the time, I worried…" She trailed off, lost in thought.

"Don't sweat it," he replied.

They fell silent for a while. Cameron concentrated on her stitching. Hendricks tried not to squirm. As the pain intensified, he decided he did better with the distraction.

"I told you my secret to staying sober," he said through gritted teeth. "Now it's my turn to ask you something,"

"Shoot."

"Did you get yourself hired on at the Salty Dog just so you could keep an eye on me?"

"Yeah," she said.

"That was a ballsy play."

"Well, I'm nothing if not ballsy," she replied.

"You didn't give them your real name, did you?"

"I'm not *stupid*. I gave 'em a fake Social under the name of Cameron Franklin and rigged a trick license so the photo blurred out when they tried to photocopy it."

"A trick license?"

"Yeah. All it takes is a little clear reflective paint. You know, the stuff that makes signs glow in the dark? It's available at any hardware store. Anyway, you dip your paintbrush into it, wait until it gets a little tacky, and then flick some onto the photo—the address too, if that's also made up. Not enough to cover them entirely, just a spatter here and there. Then, when they photocopy it, the paint reflects the copier light, and whatever's behind it is obscured. If you do it right, it just looks like there was a defect in the copier's glass plate, but no matter how many times they try to move it and get a better copy, the result's the same."

"Impressive," he said, and he meant it. Even Lester hadn't known about that technique.

"Just one of the many talents I'll bring to the table if you decide to take me on."

Hendricks sighed. "I thought we settled this already."

"Not to my satisfaction."

"What makes you think that you're cut out for this kind of work?"

"What makes you think I'm not? You think unless a chick's got a nose ring and a neck tattoo, she doesn't know her way around a computer?"

"It's not your computer chops I'm worried about," he said. "Lord knows you found me easily enough. But now that you mention it, a pair of chunky glasses wouldn't hurt."

She feigned surprise. "Wait, was that a joke? Is the big bad action hero trying to grow a sense of humor?"

Much to Hendricks's surprise, it *was* a joke. He hadn't intended to crack wise just then—he scarcely had since Lester died. Sometimes, he was so focused on avenging Lester's death, he forgot how much he missed the man's company, or any friendly human's, for that matter.

"All kidding aside," he said, "you must realize I can't possibly take you on. My job—my life—is just too dangerous. I wouldn't be able to live with myself if I lost someone else."

"Look, I get it. Your job is scary. But you *choose* to do it, just like I *chose* to seek you out. The risk is mine to take. And, I might add, you're damn lucky I did, because if I hadn't, you'd be dead."

"Maybe so, but why on earth would you *want* to choose this life? You're a kid, for God's sake. You should be in school, not stitching up hitmen in some dump of an apartment."

"Hit*man*," she said. "Not hit*men*, plural. And *I'm not a fucking kid*. Besides, I tried the college thing; it didn't take."

"What do you mean, it didn't take? What happened? You don't strike me as the type to wash out."

Cameron pursed her lips as if she was weighing whether or not to tell him. "My first day at school, all the RAs in the freshman dorm broke us up into groups. Typical orientation-week bullshit, I guess. They made us sit in a circle and introduce ourselves. Asked us each to tell a story about an event that made us who we are. Most of the answers were pretty boilerplate and calibrated to impress. A game-winning slap shot in the state championship. That weekend spent volunteering with Habitat for Humanity. How a cousin's peanut allergy inspired them to become an immunologist or whatever. It was excruciating, like sitting through a live reading of everybody's college-application essays.

"Then the girl before me went. She'd been quiet until her turn, barely making eye contact with the rest of the group, but she came alive when she began to talk. About the nagging sense she had when she was young that something was fundamentally wrong with her. About the struggles in school and at home because of it. About her suicide attempt at fourteen and how the counseling her parents put her in afterward gave her the strength to come out to them. To tell them that their sweet little boy didn't see himself that way. That inside, deep down, he knew he was meant to be a girl."

"Jesus."

"Yeah. Everybody in the room was shocked. The bravery it took...the matter-of-fact way that she presented it. The fact is, she didn't have to—with her parents' consent, she'd started hormone treatment early, and she looked every bit the gender she presented as. I think she came out because she wanted people to know what she'd been through. Because she wanted to be understood and accepted for who she really was."

"Wow. How'd you follow *that?*"

"I didn't! Until she told her story, I was going to do what everybody else did and puff myself up so people would like me. But once she said what she said, I realized I couldn't, so I just passed."

"Did you two end up friends?"

"You'd think so, right? I mean, that seems like where the story's going. Thing is, I was in awe of her bravery, but I was so caught up in my own freshman-year awkwardness, I didn't really know what to say to her—or how to act around her—so no. Not that I was rude to her or anything. I'd say hello when we ran into each other. But I never told her how inspiring her story was to me. I never told her how much it helped me realize my own teen angst was so much self-indulgent bullshit."

"And I'm guessing from your tone that you can't tell her now. What happened?"

"The same thing that always happens when someone has a genuine, human moment. Someone else came along to shit on it."

"How so?"

"One of the guys in our first-night group talked some smack about her to his friends. They started teasing her for sport. Next thing you know, the whole campus is in on it, and her sixth-grade picture's stapled up all over campus—only then her name was Thomas, not Rebecca. They turned her into a pariah. A sideshow attraction. And while plenty of kids spoke out publicly against it, none of them—none of *us*—had the guts to actually be a friend to her; we just made tutting noises from afar. She was a cause to us, not a person. And truthfully, I don't think anyone was too surprised when she turned up dead."

"Suicide?"

"The cops said no. Officially, her death was ruled an accidental overdose—one of four that year on campus, although the others weren't fatal. Doesn't it just fucking figure the only time anybody looked at her like she was a normal kid was when she was laid out on a slab?"

"That's awful—but it doesn't exactly explain why you left school."

"I left because of what happened after."

"What happened after?"

"That's the problem. *Nothing*—or at least, not officially. In the months she'd been at school, Becca had reported dozens of instances of harassment. Her dorm room had been vandalized, her Facebook and Twitter accounts spammed. She'd put up with catcalls, hate speech, and public ridicule. But once she was found dead, the school pretended like none of that had ever happened. They just wanted to sweep any unpleasantness under the rug and move on."

"I take it you had other plans?"

"You're damn right I did. I felt like shit for not standing up for her—for not standing *with* her—when I had the chance. When it might've mattered. When it could've saved her life. I was too self-involved. Too timid. Too afraid. But I felt sick at the thought that the people who'd made her life a living hell would get away scot-free. So I took it upon myself to make sure they didn't."

"How?"

"The only way I knew how. My interest in school was graphic art—a handy skill set for an ID forger, by the way—but my first love, and greatest talent, has always been computers. Mom raised me on them. I've been coding for as long as I've been reading, and I've been breaking into secure networks for sport for going on eight years. So I did what I do best. I hacked the dickbags who'd been harassing her online. Wrote a worm that'd infect their smartphones and look for any correspondence in which the name Becca was mentioned. Ditto the words *tranny*, *she-male*, and half a dozen other terms so awful they'd make you blush. Then I did the same for anyone who'd received those messages. In the end, I had a list of twenty-three hard-core offenders. Anyone who had just stood by while they jawed, I dropped from my list, because I figured they weren't any worse than me—all they did was not speak up."

"And what happened to those twenty-three?"

"I rigged their search history so it looked like they'd visited chat rooms of known terror groups. Added them to the no-fly list. Posted their Social Security numbers and credit card information on the dark web. Made a website for each of them that kept track of their online-porn-viewing habits and rigged the SEO so it'd be the first hit anybody who Googled them found."

"Damn. Remind me to never piss you off."

"Better to have me as an ally than an enemy," she agreed. "Anyway, I mighta bragged a little that I was behind the sites, and the administration caught wind. The dean of students didn't appreciate my efforts. It turns out one of the kids who'd been harassing Becca was a legacy whose family name was on our sports complex."

"They tossed you out?"

"Yeah. For violating school policy on bullying, of all things."

"Ouch."

"The irony wasn't lost on me," she said. Then she patted his stomach gingerly. "You're all stitched up, by the way."

Hendricks inspected her work. For someone with no medical training, she'd managed a passable suturing job. It wouldn't heal pretty, but it'd heal. *One more scar for the collection*, he thought. There'd come a day he wouldn't be able to tell this one from all the others.

"Thanks," he said. "You got anything to eat? Seems like I should replace some of the stuffing that I lost."

"Sure," she said. "You want ramen or ramen?"

Hendricks smiled. "Ramen's fine."

Cameron filled her electric kettle and turned it on.

"Shame you don't have a TV," he said. "I'd love to check the local news, see if anybody's looking for us."

She looked at him like he'd just lamented her lack of a Victrola. "What century is it again? I don't need a TV—I have a *laptop*."

"Oh," he said, chastened. "Right. Fire it up for me, would you?"

Cameron took a USB drive from her pocket, inserted it into the port on the side of her laptop, and turned the laptop on. It booted scary-fast. "Can you take it from here," she asked, "or do I need to explain to you what a browser is?"

"I'm good, thanks."

Hendricks went to Google News, but before he'd typed anything in the field, the day's top headlines caught his eye. "Ah, hell," he muttered.

"What's wrong?"

"There's been some kind of attack."

"Where?"

He clicked through to CNN. A video began to play— three talking heads blabbing at once, with a disaster scene behind them on the big screen. "San Francisco," he said. "The Golden Gate."

"Oh God," she said, crossing the room and peering over his shoulder at the screen. "I grew up just south of there, in Redwood City. Is it still standing? Is anyone hurt?"

"The bridge is still there," he said, watching shaky he-

105

licopter footage of first responders trying to rescue people trapped atop it. The faces of the stranded were filthy and slick from the spray of the fireboats below. Their expressions were a mix of hope and terror. Thick dark smoke mingled with the rising steam and periodically blocked the bridge from view. "But it looks like there were casualties."

The kettle clicked off, the water inside boiling. Neither of them moved.

They watched awhile in heartsick silence. The images of the rescue efforts were soon replaced by cell-phone footage of the attack itself, film that looked as if it was initially intended to be a cheery home movie. Then came a grainy video of a young man with a scraggly beard dressed in traditional Muslim garb. He claimed credit on behalf of a terror group whose name meant nothing to Hendricks—which was odd, he thought, given that his old unit had hunted terrorists for years—and promised there were more attacks to come. After that was a statement from the president urging calm, followed by a tirade from that blowhard Senator Wentworth, who insisted America close its borders and turn the Middle East into a parking lot. Between each segment, the talking heads parsed, speculated, stoked, argued, and divided.

Hendricks forced himself to back his browser up and search for any fallout from the Salty Dog.

"Anything?" Cameron asked.

"Nothing but a headline: 'Reports of Shots Fired at Local Eatery.' When you click through, there's no story—just a note saying the page will be updated as more facts are available."

"That's good news, right?"

"Could be. At the very least, it's not *bad* news. If I had to guess, I'd say local PD is distracted, their attentions elsewhere. Probably every cop from coast to coast is tracking down known militants. I hate to say it, but what happened in San Francisco helped us. It means we should be able to crash here tonight without much worry and then head out first thing in the morning."

"That's ghoulish."

"That's life—*my* life, at least. And it'd be yours, too, if I were to take you on."

"If?" she said hopefully.

"Poor choice of words," he said, "because it's never gonna happen."

Cameron sighed and returned to her vestigial kitchen to set the water boiling again. She unwrapped two packets of ramen and dropped the tangled noodle-bricks into two bowls. While she was otherwise occupied, Hendricks opened an incognito window in her browser and pulled up Twitter. He typed in his user name, *j_rambo1972*, and his password, *3v31yn*, and hit enter.

His account was protected; a little lock icon beside the user name indicated that only those to whom he'd given permission could see his feed, and he had only one follower. That account was also protected. Neither of them had ever tweeted. Both their avatars were Twitter's default egg.

The accounts were set up years ago by Lester as a way for them to communicate if their usual channels were compromised or otherwise rendered inaccessible. To the outside world, the accounts appeared inactive—two of the literally millions of abandoned handles on the platform. But they could be used to communicate via direct message without affecting their perfect-zero tweet count.

For the longest time, the other account had belonged to Lester. But last year—just after Lester died—Hendricks briefly saw his ex, Evie, and he'd slipped her the user name and password on a piece of paper as she squeezed his hand in good-bye. The account was intended only for emergencies, and it had sat dormant for months, but Hendricks still checked it every day.

Today, when the page loaded, he sat up ramrod straight. His stitches strained, though he hardly noticed.

Over the envelope icon in the toolbar, there was a *1*.

Hendricks had a message.

He clicked on it, pulse thrumming in his ears. A window opened.

We need to talk, it said.

Hendricks replied, *Where/when?* Then he held his breath, although he had no reason to expect the reply to be immediate.

The reply was immediate. *Roadhouse Truck Stop, I-76, PA. ASAP.*

He Googled the place. It was in the middle of nowhere. Open twenty-four hours. Approachable from the highway and two rural routes. A good place for someone on the run. A good place to spring a trap too.

As if it mattered. If it wasn't a trap, then Evie was in trouble. And if it *was* a trap, then Evie was in trouble.

He typed a quick reply as Cameron wandered over. She handed him a bowl of ramen and a spoon. Cocked an eyebrow as he hastily closed the browser window.

"Change of plans," he said, taking the bowl. "We're getting out of here tonight."

13.

FRANK CROUCHED IN the underbrush and watched the Park Police go door to door down Funston Avenue. They worked in teams of two, one conferring briefly with the residents, the other idling in a cruiser at the curb. He'd seen dozens of them doing the same throughout the Presidio as he fled inland through the woods, running parallel to the Battery East Trail until it intersected with Lincoln Boulevard and then following Lincoln southeast.

He'd hoped to leave the Presidio before they locked down the perimeter, but the park was lousy with coppers, and the scrutiny given to everyone they came across was too intense. His forged ID was convincing enough for everyday use, but it would never stand up to a database search, and although he was thought dead, his prints were doubtless still on file.

Best to hole up for a while until the investigation

shifted away from the park, he thought, and then slip out unnoticed. But finding a decent hiding place was proving harder than anticipated.

He'd spent half an hour casing the Lendrum Court town houses. They were bland midcentury beige boxes with taupe accents, situated on a terraced slope bisected by a winding drive. In most cities, units like these would be low-income housing. On the Presidio, they ran nearly five grand a month.

But as exorbitant as their rents were, the buildings were among the cheapest housing in the park, which meant they wouldn't have as much security as the luxury properties overseen by the Presidio Trust. Trees towered over the Lendrum Court complex on all sides, isolating it from the outside world, and its parking lot was half empty, which meant some units were temporarily unoccupied thanks to the lockdown.

In short, the place looked perfect—at least until a neighbor had spotted Frank prying open a corner unit's sliding-glass window and chased him off.

That was over an hour ago. He'd attempted to put some distance between himself and the angry neighbor in case the guy reported him, and he worried the Park Police might now be on the lookout for him. His progress was slowed by his injuries. His punctured palm bled every time he flexed it wrong; his bum knee crunched like gravel with every step.

Frank stuck to the woods whenever possible. It wasn't always. To cross beneath the Presidio Parkway, he'd had no choice but to take the sidewalk for a few excruciatingly exposed minutes—there wasn't cover enough beside the road to hide him until Lincoln jagged away from Highway 1.

As Frank pressed eastward through the pines, their thick canopy enclosed him. Nestled in this copse of trees, he could almost believe that the world of fire, chaos, and destruction he was fleeing was a thousand miles away. But what little of the sky he could see between the branches was ambered by the noxious smoke that continued to pour out of the wreckage of the tugboat, and the air—which scratched at Segreti's throat with his every breath, and made him cough—tasted of oil and ash. Even the peppery scent of pine resin was no match for it.

Eventually, Frank came to a break in the trees and found himself at one end of a large cemetery. He rested for a moment in the shadow of a stone obelisk, catching his breath and attempting to get his bearings. The headstones all around made somber dotted lines that seemed, by a trick of perspective, to converge on his position. The implication troubled him. When he ducked back into the forest, he left behind a bloody handprint on the granite where he'd leaned.

When he hit the edge of the Main Post, he froze. The Main Post was essentially the Presidio's downtown. From Mexico's handoff of the base to the U.S. Army in 1848 until its closure by Congress in 1989, the Main Post had been the center of the Presidio's administrative and social life. Now its historic brick buildings were home to museums, businesses, and tourist attractions.

Today, its massive central lawn was set up as a staging area—tents, personnel, and heavy equipment everywhere. Dozens, maybe hundreds, of police and first responders flitted back and forth across it, their clothes and faces blackened with soot. Armed men in riot gear stood guard at regular intervals. Frank felt like he'd just put his foot through the papery scrim of a wasp's nest.

He hunkered down and watched awhile as afternoon marched toward evening. He was trying to discern pattern, logic, strategy, but the scene was too chaotic. He gave up and slowly made his way around the perimeter of the Main Post—always watchful, always just inside the tree line. That's when he spotted the perfect house in which to hide.

It was a gorgeous Queen Anne–style home with off-white clapboard siding and a red roof. Three stories, with a front-facing gable and a wraparound porch, a portion of which was glassed in. Simple wooden struts added historical accents to the roof and deck posts. A set of concrete stairs led upward from the sidewalk to its front path. A narrow border of succulents and drought-faded wildflowers rimmed the house on all sides.

The rear of the house abutted the woods, so Frank had a straight shot to the back door without much fear of being seen. And he watched the Park Police knock for several minutes straight without answer—they'd clearly taken the sleek blue Jaguar F-Type in the driveway as a sign someone was home—so he knew he'd have the place to himself.

He waited for the cops to disappear around the corner. Then he burst from the trees and ran, stiff-limbed and creaky, to the house. As he traversed the yard, he felt naked and exposed, but once he reached the door, he breathed a sigh of relief. He was tucked comfortably out of sight of the neighbors and of the street.

The door had an inlaid window, three panes by three panes. He needed something he could use to bust the pane nearest the doorknob and then he'd be inside. But as he looked around for a rock, a garden gnome, whatever, he heard something that stopped him short: a low growl from just behind the door.

His head jerked toward the window, but the dog was too short for him to see. What he *did* see was a woman watching him wide-eyed through the glass.

For a moment, Frank froze, and the two of them stared at each other. In another context, he might have found her striking. She was a light-skinned black woman a few inches shorter than he, slender in a manner that suggested activity rather than diet or vanity, with high cheekbones and brown eyes flecked with gold. She wore white cotton pajamas with pink piping and pink roses small enough to look like dots all over them. She looked to be in her sixties, and her hair— steely gray—fell in tight natural curls. The ends were wet, as if she'd just been sitting in a bath. Her pajamas clung to her breasts and hips, dampness bleeding through.

It looked to Frank like she'd been crying. Her eyes were glassy and red-rimmed, the skin beneath them dark as bruises. That was understandable, given the day. Her city was injured. Frank knew how deep that ache could be. As a young punk running small-time rackets on the streets of Hoboken, Frank used to eye the gleaming city across the Hudson with almost romantic longing. That longing metastasized and he'd succumbed to Manhattan's siren song, to life as a made guy. When the towers fell, they took some secret part of him with them, something no new construction, no matter how ambitious, could re-place. In Frank's eyes, the New York skyline was a key that no longer fit. What it had once opened inside him, it never would again.

Frank watched her approach the door. She moved slowly, her slippered feet scuffing along the floorboards. A goodly amount of white wine in a glass sloshed in her hand but never quite spilled over. When she reached the door, she unlocked it and swung it open wide. Beside her was a tan little ball of fur who looked as puzzled as Frank felt.

The woman turned and shuffled back the way she'd come. The dog—a Pomeranian, Frank thought—regarded him a moment, then trotted over. Frank offered it his hand, still caked with blood. The dog licked it once and solicited a head scratch. Then it followed its mistress back inside, its claws a ticking clock against the floorboards.

Frank shook his head in puzzlement and followed too, his movements as deliberate as if he were navigating a minefield. He closed the door behind him. Set the lock on the knob. Engaged the dead bolt. By the time he turned around, the woman had disappeared from sight.

He set off in the direction she'd gone and soon found himself in a kitchen of stainless steel and gleaming white. A dog bowl in one corner was heaped to overflowing with kibble. The woman was rooting around in the bottom of her refrigerator, the open door hiding her from view. A memory flickered across the fore of Frank's mind, of a mook he'd been sent to teach a lesson to who'd kept a backup piece inside his vegetable crisper. The asshole offered Frank a beer, all cool and civilized, reached into the fridge, and then damn near blew Frank's head off when he turned around. Thankfully, condensation kept the gun from firing or Frank wouldn't be alive today—and that mook still might be.

When the woman closed the refrigerator, Frank braced himself reflexively and eyed the nearby knife rack, but all she had in her hand was a half-empty bottle of chardonnay. She set it on the counter beside her wineglass and fetched a fresh one from the cupboard. Then she poured Frank a drink and topped up her own. He accepted it automatically, although in truth he had no idea what was going on, and it unnerved him.

"You're bleeding," she said, nodding at the bloodstain on his shirt. Although she didn't slur her words, they came out flat and affectless. She sounded as if she'd taken something for anxiety, Valium or Xanax, before she'd started on the chardonnay.

"I cut my hand," he said carefully. "Not badly. It's fine now." He didn't actually know if that was true—the barbed wire had been rusty, the puncture deep—but the last thing he wanted was for her to call a doctor.

She said nothing for a full minute. Just looked at him and drank. Frank met her eyes but did not lift his glass. The dog looked back and forth expectantly between them.

"I know you," she said finally.

Frank waited for her to continue. She didn't. "I don't understand," he said.

"From the TV," she replied.

Frank's guts went crawly. Gooseflesh sprung up across his skin. "I think you've got me confused with someone else."

She shook her head. Frowned slightly, as if trying to hold on to a slippery thought. Her eyes brightened somewhat, and when she next spoke, her voice was stronger, more assured. "There's a cell-phone video the networks have been showing. A smiling family. A boat hitting the bridge. I must've seen it thirty times before I turned the news off. I couldn't stand to watch any longer. It was too horrible. You took that video, didn't you?"

Shit. If his face was out there, it was only a matter of time before the Council came for him. "Yeah," he said, "I took it."

"The anchor said the family in the video survived. Apparently, their eldest child was the one who uploaded the video. But no one seemed to know what became of you."

"I'm glad they're okay," he said. "We were separated by the blast." He offered neither details about himself nor explanations of why he'd shown up at her house, which was two miles from where he'd last been seen.

Silence descended once more. The woman sipped her wine. Frank ignored his. She was trembling, Frank realized—her wedding ring clinked against her wineglass as she raised it to her lips.

"I'm not going to hurt you," he said.

She blinked at him in confusion.

"You're shaking," he added, by way of explanation.

"Oh. I'm not…It's just…" She waved her hand as if the gesture were sufficient to finish her thought, which Frank supposed it was.

"Did the people on the news ever mention my name?"

"If they did," she said, "I don't remember."

"It's Max," he said, "Max Rausch." Max Rausch was the name on all his fake IDs.

"I wish I could say it's nice to meet you, Max. I'm Lois." She raised her glass in a halfhearted toast. Frank did the same with his. Then they drank, two strangers in a quiet house—he a sip, she the entire glass.

14.

HENDRICKS WATCHED FROM his perch across the street as the big rig shuddered to life. Its runner lights flickered on. Its air brakes emitted a hydraulic hiss. Then its headlights were engaged, pushing back the dark of night, and it pulled out of the parking lot, kicking up dirt as it rumbled past. Hendricks averted his eyes and blinked away the grit.

The Roadhouse Truck Stop was situated just off the Pennsylvania Turnpike between Harrisburg and Morgantown. It was no doubt a gorgeous stretch of countryside by day, Hendricks thought, but at night it was just a desolate pool of black bisected by a thin ribbon of rarely traveled highway.

The Roadhouse was a mom-and-pop place, not part of a national chain, and it looked like a remnant of an America long forgotten. A midcentury sign topped a metal pole tall enough to be seen from the toll road. The sign's colors were faded, and the incandescent bulbs that framed it were long dead. The main building was cinder block, off white and grungy at the edges from exhaust. Fluorescent light spilled from its storefront, bathing the men out front smoking in its sickly glow. Two banks of gas pumps extended out from it, one on either side. Behind the main building was a second one, small and windowless, containing showers, and behind that was an overnight lot, a dozen eighteen-wheelers side by side. The smaller lot out front had, until now, been blocked from view by the truck that just drove off.

The Roadhouse sat at the intersection of two rural routes, a stoplight blinking yellow where they met. Across the street in one direction was a low-slung motel, its neon sign declaring VACANCY. In the other direction was a road-salt storage dome, dun brown, beside which sat a pair of idle snowplows, weeds sprouting around their tires.

It was nearly three a.m., and business was slow. The lunch counter was a quarter occupied. The booths were out of sight around a corner.

Hendricks had been watching the place for an hour. He had another hour before he was expected. Though the drive from Long Island took less than four hours, he'd told whoever had summoned him it would take six—in part because he figured he'd need some time to steal a new set of wheels, and in part because he wanted the chance to case the place before he went in.

He was wrong about the wheels. It turned out Cameron had a car stashed around the corner, a four-year-old Volvo wagon. It was clean—a hand-me-down still registered to her mom—and it had room enough for him to lie in the back and rest while Cameron drove. Hendricks was grateful she was the type to bike to work, otherwise the car would have been sitting in the Salty Dog's lot, inaccessible and useless. Now it was parked across the street from the Roadhouse in the motel's lot, Cameron hunched behind the wheel so she could case the truck stop from the other side. She'd been thrilled at the prospect of joining him. He'd told her not to get used to it, that she was to do nothing but observe, and even that was a onetime deal.

"Sure thing, boss," she'd replied.

The wind gusted, cold and clammy. The lone streetlight swayed. The sky was clear and full of stars. The heat of the day had long since bled off into space. Hendricks zipped up his new sweatshirt and crossed his arms for warmth. The stitches in his side protested. He wondered how long it had been since he'd washed down those four Advil with Gatorade in the Walmart parking lot in Hempstead, New York, trying simultaneously to dull the pain and replace the fluids he'd lost.

He watched trucks come and go from his perch atop one of the snowplows. The dirt lot in which it sat was dark. The salt dome behind him prevented anyone from seeing him in silhouette.

Walmart was where he'd gotten his new clothes: a pair of olive-drab cargo pants, a navy blue henley, a gray zip-up hooded sweatshirt. The fits were close, but not quite; since his old clothes were covered in blood, he'd made Cameron go in to get them. She'd also picked up a few other supplies: gauze pads and medical tape; a pack of disinfecting hand wipes; two pairs of pocket binoculars; ammunition for Pappas's .45; several cheap, prepaid cells (Android smartphones, to Hendricks's surprise—burners had come a long way since he'd started using them four years ago); two Bluetooth earpieces; a backpack; some snacks for the road. All told, it wasn't cheap, but the cash Pappas had slipped her at the Salty Dog more than covered the bill.

When they'd arrived at the Roadhouse, Hendricks had Cameron drive by slow a couple times, but there'd been no sign that he was walking into an ambush. There'd been no sign of Evie either, so Hendricks decided they'd set up at two vantage points, a phone line open between them, and watch the place awhile.

"Hey," she said in his ear, "can you read the license plate on that pickup now that the tractor-trailer moved?"

He raised his binoculars. Eyed the boxy old Chevy—mid-1980s, he figured, in two-tone red and white. "Yeah, I can read it."

"Pennsylvania tags?"

"Yup."

"Cool. I'm ready when you are, then."

Hendricks read the number to her. Heard her tap at her keyboard. Aimed his binoculars at her while she worked, her face lit ghostly white by the laptop screen, barely visible from this distance. He reluctantly admitted to himself that it was nice to have some backup for a change. And the kid was good. She didn't fill the line with idle chatter or complain that she was bored. She was alert and attentive, her focus unwavering. And she'd infiltrated the PennDOT database without breaking a sweat.

"Says here it's registered to a Stan Walters," she said.

Hendricks's adrenaline spiked. His palms grew sweaty. His chest felt as though someone had filled it with helium.

Stan Walters sounded awfully close to Stuart Walker. Stuart Walker was Evie's husband's name—and WITSEC liked crafting aliases their charges would answer to.

"Huh," Cameron said.

"What?"

"Well, as a matter of course, I've been cross-referencing every address we pull up running tags with local tax records."

"And?"

"And the address on Walters's registration doesn't seem to exist."

That clinches it, Hendricks thought—*Evie really* is *inside*. He hoped she was all right. He wondered how long she'd been waiting. He wondered if she was alone or if Stuart had come with her. He wondered—guilt and hope battling—if Stuart even knew she was here.

"That's the one we've been looking for," he said. "I'm going in."

"I thought you said I'd go in first to scope the place out before you risked it," she said, disappointment evident in her tone.

It's true; he had said that. Cameron made the perfect scout. No one was looking for her. No one would suspect her of working with Hendricks, because there was no obvious connection between them. But he couldn't stomach the notion of making Evie wait any longer than she already had—or of Cameron somehow spooking her.

"Yeah, well, the plan's changed."

He climbed down from the plow gingerly, stitches pulling, and flipped up the hood on his sweatshirt. Then he trudged across the road, hands thrust deep into his sweatshirt pockets, one of which contained Pappas's .45. The truckers smoking out front eyed him suspiciously when he materialized from the darkness. Hendricks nodded at them as he walked by.

Inside, the restaurant smelled of grease. The floor was institutional tile, scuffed and dulled by wear. The booths and bar stools were emerald-green vinyl. The bar and tables were a matching green veneer that was meant to look like marble but mostly looked dirty. Fox News played on the television in the corner—muted, mercifully. A live shot of the Golden Gate was green-screened in behind the talking heads. It was nearing midnight on the West Coast, but crews still struggled to quell the fires and evacuate the bridge. Plumes of smoke and steam were lit from within by fire and emergency lights.

A cook at the griddle. Neck beard, T-shirt, apron, ponytail. Two men at the bar. One fat and sagging in his stool, ass crack visible between his untucked work shirt and filthy jeans. The other all hard angles—knees, elbows, nose, and Adam's apple—a skinny leg bouncing as he hunched over his coffee. A married couple who looked as if they hauled freight together made quiet conversation over two plates of chicken-fried steak. Every one of them tense, jumpy, worry-lined.

And then he saw her.

The problem was, it was the wrong *her*.

Not Evie.

Special Agent Charlotte Thompson.

She held a cup of coffee in both hands. Her eyes were trained on Hendricks as he froze, unsure, in the middle of the dining room.

She heaved a sigh. "Relax," she said. "I'm alone." If anyone else heard her, they didn't bother to acknowledge it. He approached the booth cautiously, mindful of any hint of movement in his peripheral vision that might signal agents closing in, and remained standing.

"What the hell are *you* doing here?"

"That's a long story."

"Shorten it."

"It kinda resists shortening. Sit down—I'll buy you a cup of coffee and explain."

"Do you still work for the FBI?"

"Yes."

"Am I still on their Most Wanted list?"

"Yes."

"Then I think I'll buy my own damn coffee somewhere else, thanks."

He turned to go.

"Wait!" Thompson called. "Please."

He paused. Looked back at her over his shoulder. His instincts screamed at him to run. His knife wound just plain screamed as his torso twisted.

"Give me one good reason," Hendricks said. "One good reason why I shouldn't get as far away from here— and you—as possible."

She swallowed hard. Her brow furrowed. Hendricks thought that she seemed nervous. "Look," she said, "the Bureau doesn't know I'm here. No one does. If I were to die tonight...to disappear..."

"I have no reason to kill you," he said sharply, disgusted by her insinuation.

"I know that. I do. I just want you to understand the risk I'm taking, meeting with you. My career—my *life*—is in your hands."

"Yeah, but why? If you're so afraid of me, why come here?"

"Because I have no one else to turn to. Because I need your help."

15.

WHEN THOMPSON LEFT the New Haven field office in her Ford Escape, she'd headed south as promised, toward DC. But once she passed Trenton, New Jersey, she got off I-95 and jagged west toward Lancaster County, Pennsylvania.

Verdant fields unspooled on either side of Thompson as she sped through the twilit countryside. The sunset beckoned like a signal flare, pink fading to indigo as she drove. The sky seemed so much bigger out here than it did in DC. The tallest man-made structures were grain silos. Trees were mostly relegated to the scruffy borders between vast swaths of farmland. Hay bales cast long shadows across the fields.

Eventually, she rocked to a halt on a winding country road beside a modest ranch-style house, tidy but in need of paint. Petunias hung in baskets on the porch. A garden occupied the side yard, encircled by protective mesh. Tomato plants rustled in the evening breeze.

The house was lit, inside and out. The curtains were drawn. They parted slightly when Thompson pulled up and fell closed before she got out of the car.

She crossed the lawn—dry grass crunching underfoot— and scaled the porch steps. But before she had a chance to knock, a man behind her spoke.

"Hands where I can see them."

Thompson complied.

"Good. Now turn around real slow."

When Thompson turned, she found herself looking down the barrel of a shotgun. Its matte-gray finish gleamed dully in the glow of the porch light.

"If you mean to use that thing," she said, "you'd do well to hold it tightly to your shoulder. Loose like that against your bicep, you're likely to miss me—even at this range—and maybe break your arm in the process."

"Charlie?"

"Evening, Stuart."

He lowered the shotgun. "Jesus, Charlie, you scared the hell out of us!" Then, louder: "Evie, you can come on out—it's Charlie!"

The front door opened, and Evelyn Walker stepped outside. She looked beautiful, if harried, in a floral sundress, her hair in a haphazard bun. Her face was sun-kissed, her eyes tired. An apple-cheeked baby was propped on her hip.

Three years ago, Thompson began investigating a new hitman on the scene, one who seemed to go after only other hitters. He was talented, elusive. Always avoided or disabled surveillance cams. Never left fingerprints or

DNA. At first, her fellow agents doubted his existence and took to calling him Charlie's ghost. But eventually, the evidence Charlie amassed was undeniable.

Thompson had assumed he was working for some upstart criminal organization intent on taking out the competition. She was wrong.

Last year, their paths crossed at a casino in Kansas City. She was there tailing a hitter by the name of Leonwood. Her mystery hitman was doing the same. Neither of them realized that Leonwood was bait, intended to draw her ghost out so an assassin called Engelmann could kill him.

Thanks to Engelmann, the casino op went pear-shaped. More than thirty people were killed. Thompson would have been one of them if her ghost hadn't compromised his anonymity to save her life.

When Engelmann discovered his quarry's identity, he beelined for Hendricks's former fiancée, Evelyn Walker. Hendricks beat him to her but was forced to divulge that the report of his death was a lie and that he killed people for a living. Though he eventually dispatched Engelmann, he couldn't guarantee Evie's continued safety, so he coerced Thompson into putting Evie and her family into WITSEC.

"My goodness," Thompson said. "Is that Lucy? She's so big!"

"Eight months old next week," Evie said.

"Is she crawling yet?"

"Oh yeah. She's motoring around like a champ. Poor Abby can't keep up with her." Abigail was the Walkers' bulldog, and upon hearing her name, she toddled out onto the porch, her stubby tail wagging.

"She'll be driving in no time," Thompson said.

Evie flashed her a wan smile. "I'm guessing you didn't stop by just to check up on the baby."

"No. I didn't."

"Then maybe you should come inside and tell us what brought you all this way."

They went inside, and Evie gestured for Thompson to take a seat. Lucy fussed in Evie's arms and let out a cry. "Looks like it's past time for someone to go to bed. Stu, how about you get our guest something to drink while I put Lucy down?"

"Sure thing. What can I get you, Charlie? Coffee? Water? Iced tea?"

"Actually," Thompson replied, "I'd love a beer, if you have one."

He raised an eyebrow. "I thought agents couldn't drink on duty."

"I'm not exactly on duty."

Stuart headed to the kitchen and returned with two longneck PBRs. He handed one to Thompson. She twisted off the cap and took a sip.

"So," Evie said when she returned, "what can we do for you?"

They sat in awkward silence for a moment. Thompson drank her beer and wondered how to begin.

"First of all," she said, "you have to understand I'm not here in any official capacity. In fact, if the Bureau ever finds out I was here, I'll be out of a job—maybe even arrested."

"I don't understand," Evie said. "What exactly is this about?"

Thompson sighed. "Stuart, would you mind giving us a little privacy?"

"Me and Evie are a team. Anything you say to her, you can say to me."

Thompson looked Evie in the eye. Evie nodded almost imperceptibly.

"Evie, I need you to help me get in touch with Michael Hendricks."

Stuart's face contorted with disgust. "You mean the asshole who blew up our house and forced us into hiding?"

"Easy, Stu," said Evie. "That's not helping." Then she returned her attention to Thompson. "Why do you need to get in touch with him?"

"Have you seen the news today?"

"Yes. It's terrible. But you can't possibly think Michael had anything to do with it."

"No, of course not. But there's a cell-phone video of the attack going around, and the man who took it is in danger. Years ago, he turned state's evidence against some very dangerous and powerful criminals. They attempted to kill him before he could testify. Until today, everyone—good guys and bad—thought they'd succeeded. Now that he's resurfaced, I think they'll try to kill him again, and I can't let that happen. I need Michael to protect him."

"You're not serious," Stuart said.

"Unfortunately, I am."

"Why can't *you* do it? You're FBI, for Christ's sake."

"I've been ordered not to. The Bureau's spread too thin. Until we catch the bastards who attacked us, my hands are tied."

Evie frowned. "Even if I wanted to help you, what makes you think I have the faintest idea how?"

Thompson sighed. "Because for months, you refused to testify against Michael, and then suddenly, you agreed.

Because I happen to know he *wanted* you to accept federal protection, even if that meant cooperating with us to build our case. Because..." she began, and then she glanced at Stuart, uncertain if she should verbalize the rest. *Because despite everything, you still care about him.* But she didn't need to. Evie caught her meaning and silenced her with a glance.

"This is bullshit," Stuart said. "You can't just show up here and accuse my wife of—"

"Stu, don't. She's right. Michael and I have been in touch."

"Are you fucking kidding me? After everything he put us through?"

"It's not that simple, Stuart. He saved our lives. And whether you like it or not, he and I have a history. Besides, it's not like we've been secret pen pals. He reached out a few months ago to insist I take the deal the Feds were offering. Told me not to lie or hold back to protect him. Said it was the only way for me to keep my family safe. So I did. For Lucy. For *you.*"

"And to feed his fucking martyr complex," Stuart snapped.

"That's not fair."

"Isn't it? Sorry, Evie, but your ex-boyfriend's not some tortured soldier with a heart of gold—he's a bugfuck whackadoo who murders people for money. The sooner you come to grips with that, the better."

"Fiancé," she said.

"Excuse me?" Stuart—indignant.

"He's not my ex-boyfriend. He's my ex-*fiancé*."

Stuart shook with rage. He cocked his arm back and threw his bottle at the wall. It exploded, raining glass and suds, and Thompson's hand moved by instinct toward her gun, but Stuart was already halfway to the back door. He banged it open hard enough to shake the house and disappeared into the night.

Tears shone in Evie's eyes. Abigail cowered at her feet. Down the hall, Lucy began to cry.

"I'm sorry," Thompson said. "The last thing I wanted was to drive a wedge between you two. Believe me, if I had any other choice, I wouldn't be here."

"Don't worry about Stuart. He'll come around. He just needs time."

"I hope so," Thompson replied, because she couldn't think of anything else to say.

"Do you swear that you're not playing me? Because if you are—"

"I'm not. I swear."

"And you really think that Michael can protect this man?"

"I honestly don't know, but if anybody can, it's him."

Evie wiped her eyes and nodded.

"Okay," she said, "I'm in."

16.

HENDRICKS SLID INTO the booth opposite Thompson. She raised her mug to her lips and sipped, then set it down again but left both hands wrapped around it. It was a calculated gesture, he knew, intended to call attention to the fact that she was unarmed. Hendricks's own hands remained thrust deep into his sweatshirt pockets, his right palm sweaty against the diamond grip of his stolen .45.

"That Evie's truck out there?" he asked.

"Yeah. I thought you'd bolt if you saw my car, so I borrowed it."

"Is she okay?"

"Evie's fine. She sends her regards."

Hendricks hesitated. "And the baby?"

"Beautiful," Thompson said. "Just like her mother. Stuart says hello," she added.

"Somehow," Hendricks replied, "I think you got his message wrong."

A waitress shuffled over to take his order, her tired eyes, oily skin, and frizzy hair suggesting that she'd been on shift since dinner.

Hendricks asked for coffee, black. In his earpiece, Cameron said, "Ooh—get me some!" Truth be told, he'd forgotten she was still on the line. He reached up and tapped the button on the earpiece to terminate the call. Thompson arched an eyebrow but said nothing.

Once the waitress delivered Hendricks's coffee and retreated out of earshot, Hendricks said, "I'm listening."

"I assume you know what happened in San Francisco."

"Yeah. I saw. It's awful. How are rescue efforts going?"

"Slowly, from what I'm told. Structural damage has made clearing the debris difficult. The wrong move could be catastrophic."

"What about this True Islamic Caliphate? I confess I'd never heard of them before today. You have a bead on them yet? Any idea what else they might have planned?"

"We're pursuing a number of leads," she said—a rote response. As Thompson heard her own words, she rolled her eyes and slumped a little in her seat. "Oh, to hell with it. Who're you going to tell? Truthfully, until today's attack, those mopes were barely even on our radar. Nobody thought they had the know-how—or the stones—to pull this off. Which means we're stuck playing catch-up, and we have no idea when or where they might hit next."

"I imagine finding these bastards is the Bureau's sole priority right now," he said. Thompson nodded in assent. "Which begs the question: Why are you here talking to me?"

"Have you seen the cell-phone video the networks have been playing?"

"Of course," he replied. "Who hasn't?"

"The old man holding the camera is a former mobster by the name of Frank Segreti. Seven years ago, he walked into our Albuquerque field office, half mad and badly injured, and demanded to speak with the special agent in charge. I was manning the front desk at the time. It was late. Storming. The guy was so bedraggled, I figured he was just some crazy homeless person trying to get out of the rain. I summoned security. He incapacitated them without breaking a sweat. Then he put one of their sidearms to my head and demanded that I call my boss. Once I did, he put the gun down and surrendered."

"What did he want?"

"Revenge. Protection. An audience to hear his tale. Understand, I wasn't present when they questioned him, and his file's so locked down, I still don't have clearance to see all of it, but I got an earful when I escorted him three hours south to an FBI safe house in Las Cruces. He claimed there was a shadow organization—some kind of criminal UN, to hear him tell it—operating in secret within the United States. That every major outfit in the country had a seat at the table. That you couldn't move so much as a kilo of coke within the contiguous forty-eight without their say-so. He said he'd worked for them for years. That he was their top lieutenant. He called himself the Devil's Red Right Hand."

As Hendricks listened, his mouth went dry. As casually as he could manage, he asked, "What did he say this organization was called?"

"Understand, we've never been able to confirm his

story, but he said they called themselves the Council." She sized him up for a sec, her gaze burrowing into him. "That name mean anything to you?"

There was no point lying, he realized. She knew it did. She could see it in his body language, in the dilation of his pupils. "Yes."

Thompson pounded the table with her fist—a gesture of celebration, of vindication. Coffee sloshed everywhere. The other diners turned as one to look at them. To Hendricks, whose survival depended upon being as inconspicuous as possible in any given environment, their attention felt like the sun's rays focused through a magnifying glass. He glared witheringly at Thompson and said nothing until, one by one, the other patrons turned around and resumed their conversations.

"I shouldn't have to remind you what it would cost the both of us if we're seen talking," he said finally.

"I know. I'm sorry. But you have to understand, the Segreti Walk-In is the stuff of legend around the Bureau. Most people figure he was just puffing himself up with crazy stories, exaggerating or even outright inventing his intel so we'd agree to protect him. You can't blame them for being skeptical—the idea that an organization of that magnitude could operate without the Bureau's knowledge seems like a stretch, and the guy just walked in cold."

"You believe him, though."

"I saw firsthand what he was capable of. And once upon a time, I got it in my head there was a new hitter on the scene, someone hell-bent on wiping out his competition. The Bureau brass thought I was nuts. They said no one man could take out so many pros all by himself. Turns out I was right. I guess you could say I've learned to trust my gut."

"Your gut was wrong about me. I'm nothing like the men I killed. They were monsters, plain and simple. The world is better off without them in it."

"That's not really for you to decide, though, is it?"

Hendricks shrugged. "I stopped them when you couldn't. My conscience is clear."

"Is it?"

"About *those* deaths, yes."

They fell silent then, the ghost of Lester Meyers haunting them both. If only Hendricks hadn't brought him into his operation. If only Thompson had reached him *before* Engelmann did instead of shortly after.

Hendricks cleared his throat self-consciously and said, "So, Segreti walks in and promises you the moon. And yet," he says, nodding skyward, "there it hangs, just like it always has. What went wrong? How'd you get from there to here?"

"The safe house was compromised. Someone blew it up before we even finished debriefing him. Four Bureau agents died in there. Three U.S. Marshals. Two state's attorneys. And, we thought, Segreti. The blast reduced most everyone inside to ash, but we were able to pull his DNA from some of the remains. It matched samples taken from the gauze we'd used to bandage his wounds while he was in custody at our Albuquerque field office. We'd kept it when we changed his dressings so we could run it through CODIS and see if any relevant priors popped. At the time, we didn't know if he was legit."

"I imagine someone blowing up your safe house went a long way toward validating his story."

"Yeah, you could say that. But over the years, when we failed to turn up any evidence of Segreti's phantom organization, those who—unlike me—weren't directly involved in his case just sort of forgot about it."

"The blast…do you think you had a mole? Someone who could've ratted on you to the Council?"

"Maybe. Maybe not. It's hard to say. No one skipped their shift that day. There's no record of any outbound calls from the safe house. His security detail's cell-phone records came back clean."

"Absence of proof—"

"—isn't proof of absence," Thompson finished. "I know. But it's just as likely the Council was tracking him somehow. We know nothing about how they operate."

Hendricks thought that was a stretch. The Council trucked in loyalty and fear. They'd be more likely to lean on someone than rely on fancy gadgetry. But Thompson believed in the rule of law and in the institution for which she worked, so she was unwilling to face the fact that somebody on her side of the fence was crooked. Hendricks sympathized. Once, as a young soldier, he'd felt the same.

"Look," Hendricks said, "this is a fascinating story, but I confess I'm still not clear on why we're sitting here together."

"Segreti's face was on every TV in the country. You think the people who tried to kill him seven years ago aren't going to see him and decide to finish the job?"

"Of course they're going to. Which means they'll be exposed. Considering the fact that you work for one of the most powerful law enforcement agencies on the planet, that should present you with more opportunities than problems. Scoop him up on the quiet. Lay a trap. Dangle him as bait. Roll up anybody who comes after him, and lock 'em somewhere deep and dark until they talk."

"You think I haven't thought of that? There's nothing I'd like more. The problem is, the Bureau brass won't hear of it—they're too focused on the attack. Trying to pick up Segreti is such a nonstarter, I can't even get my boss to run it up the flagpole."

"Isn't your boss Kathryn O'Brien? I thought you and she were…" He trailed off, unsure how to end the sentence.

Thompson's expression darkened. "We are," she said in a way that strongly suggested Hendricks drop that line of questioning. He couldn't blame her. Last time they'd met, he'd threatened O'Brien's life—and the life of Thompson's sister, Jess—in order to convince her to put Evie into witness protection. It was a bluff; Hendricks had no intention of hurting them. But, as he knew all too well, loved ones made good levers.

"So you responded by coming to *me?*"

"Protecting people with bounties on their heads is kind of your MO," she said. "And it's not like I had a lot of other options. Besides, in this one exceedingly unlikely instance, our interests are aligned."

"Yeah?" he asked. "How do you figure? Normally, I'm well paid for my services. I'm guessing neither you nor Segreti have enough socked away to cover my fee."

Thompson's mouth quirked into a tired smile. "Since I have you here, I'm curious: What *is* your fee? In all my interviews with Evie, numbers never came up."

They wouldn't have, Hendricks thought. When he was forced to confess to Evie that he'd spent the past several years working as a hired killer, he tried to play up the whole helping-people-marked-for-death angle, and he'd glossed over the charging-them-boatloads-of-money side of things.

"Ten times the bounty on their heads," he said.

"And if your would-be clients can't afford you?"

It was a loaded question, one Hendricks had asked himself a thousand times. "Then at least they have a heads-up so they can run."

"That's pretty fucking cold."

"That's life. Most of the people I protect aren't saints. And I never kill without good reason."

"Sounds to me like bullshit semantics, if money counts as 'good reason.'"

"Most of that money went to Evie," he said. "Not that she knew where it came from. She thought it was part of a wrongful-death settlement against a manufacturer of faulty body armor. The rest, once operational costs were taken care of, went to Lester."

"Oh, I suspect you've got a little set aside for a rainy day."

"I did," he said. "But this past year, it's been pouring."

"Why? Nobody in need of saving?"

"It's not that," he said. "My mission's changed, is all."

"Let me guess: From redemption to revenge?"

"I prefer to think of it as justice. I got sick of nipping at the monster's heels. Decided my time might be better spent aiming for its head."

"Yeah? How's that going?"

"Slowly," he admitted. "But then, I shouldn't have to tell you that. The FBI's been trying to stamp out organized crime since before it was the FBI."

"True enough," she said. "Which is why Segreti resurfacing is a stroke of luck for both of us."

"Yeah? How so?"

"When I first saw the video, I remembered what he'd

said when he walked in. That you couldn't even move a kilo without the Council's say-so. And then I asked myself, if the Council is for real, wouldn't they *have* to've been the ones to give the order to have Michael Hendricks whacked?"

Hendricks said nothing. His body remained still. His face showed no reaction except the subtle clenching of his jaw. But it was enough. Thompson saw it and knew that she was right.

"Do you understand what you're asking? You expect me—a wanted man—to wade into one of the largest investigations in U.S. history and attempt to locate a man who will doubtless do everything in his power not to be found. Then—if I'm very lucky and actually manage to find the guy—I'm supposed to protect him from the most powerful criminal organization in the world."

"Yes."

"You're out of your mind."

"Am I? Think of the damage you could do to the Council with Segreti's help!"

"Assuming his intel's still worth a damn," Hendricks replied. "Say, for the sake of argument, I find him. What makes you think I'd hand him over to you?"

"Honestly? I'm not sure you will. But at least with you on his side, he'll stay alive long enough for me to have another crack at him one day. And who knows? Maybe you *will* hand him over, if for no other reason than you're unlikely to bring the Council down all by your lonesome."

"You underestimate me."

"No. I don't. I just think you're smart enough to understand the value of a strategic alliance."

"Is that what this is?"

"For lack of a better term."

Hendricks fell silent. Steepled his fingers in front of his face, his elbows resting on the table. Pondered. Thompson watched him intently but said nothing. Finally, he put his palms down on the table, looked her in the eye, and said, "No."

"Excuse me?"

"I said no. This whole situation's lousy. Lots of opportunities for it to go sideways and damn few for it to go well. And that's if you're telling the truth. If you're lying, my odds of survival get even worse."

"Why would I lie? If I knew Evie had a way to draw you out, why go to the trouble of pointing you toward some random old man when I could just have this place surrounded and arrest you here?" She saw him tense up and added, "Relax. I'm just saying."

"Look, with Lester dead, all I've got left to rely on is my gut—and my gut says this is a bad idea."

"Segreti's going to die out there, you know. The Council is going to find him, and when they do, they're going to make him pay. They'll take him apart slowly, piece by piece, until his body finally fails. Is that what you want?" She was playing on his sympathies by reminding him what Engelmann had done to Lester. The ploy was as underhanded as it was obvious. Hendricks wasn't about to give her the satisfaction of rising to the bait.

Hendricks shrugged. "If he dies, he dies. That's on you for losing him in the first place. Besides, if everything you've said is true, the guy's as dirty as they come. My guess is, no one's gonna miss him when he's gone."

He finished his coffee. It was bitter. He winced as

it went down. Then he stood and reached for his back pocket. Thompson flinched, her right hand ducking beneath the table, toward the piece Hendricks knew she must have secreted somewhere. But when he removed his wallet from his pocket and tossed some bills onto the table, she relaxed.

"Coffee's on me. I don't want you thinking I owe you anything."

"Here," she said, fishing a business card and a pen from her purse, her movements slow, deliberate, unthreatening. She scrawled a number on the back and offered the card to him. "In case you change your mind and need to get in touch. The one in pen's my personal cell."

He took it. Looked it over. Then he crumpled it and dropped it into his empty mug. "I'm not going to change my mind," he said. "Don't contact me again."

17.

FRANK SEGRETI SAT with Lois Broussard on her living-room couch. Her house was lit only by the flickering glow of the television. It was after midnight. The curtains were drawn. Lois's dog, Ella, snored at Frank's feet. Sirens droned in the distance, sometimes rising, sometimes falling, but never passing too close by. The house was not on a major through street.

A smattering of empty glasses, plates, and takeout cartons covered the coffee table. Two empty bottles of white wine sat on the floor beside it. Thanks to Frank's encouragement, Lois had polished off most of the wine herself and—with an assist from whatever pharmaceuticals she'd taken before he arrived—wound up sloppy drunk. His plan had been to keep her drinking until she passed out so he'd have the run of her place until the heat died down.

As the evening wore on, Lois careened wildly between

manic oversharing—about her childhood in Gulfport, Mississippi; about her garden; about some old jazz record he *absolutely had to hear*—and long jags of tense silence during which Frank could feel the hitch of her quiet sobbing through the couch. When the second bottle ran dry, he told himself he should go grab another, but the truth was, he'd begun to worry about her. So instead, he raided her fridge and laid out an elaborate spread of all the leftovers he could find.

He'd figured if he could get some food into her, he could sober her up some. The fact that he hadn't eaten since first thing this morning didn't even occur to him. Adrenaline had suppressed his appetite. But when he caught a whiff of cold Hunan pork, he started salivating. They both dug in with gusto, wolfing down enough food to sustain twice their number, and Lois even perked up for a while.

Now she dozed fitfully—brow furrowed, whimpering occasionally—while, on her television screen, Jimmy Stewart fished a despondent Kim Novak from San Francisco Bay, two miles and sixty years from where Frank and Lois sat. The bridge towered over them, its supports blissfully undamaged. The choreography of the scene was quite formal by modern standards. Novak dropping flowers one by one into the water before she leaped took on a ritualistic air, and when Stewart emerged slowly from the water with Novak in his arms, it seemed less a rescue to Frank than a baptism.

A few hours ago, Frank had cleaned himself up in the downstairs powder room and—at Lois's insistence—changed into one of her husband Cal's sweat suits so she could throw his clothes in the wash. The house was too damn quiet with the television off and Lois wouldn't let him put on CNN, so Frank was idly flipping channels when he came across his all-time favorite movie—Alfred Hitchcock's *Vertigo*. If Frank were being honest with himself, it's why he settled in San Francisco. There was something haunting and romantic about the way Hitchcock shot the city; the first time he saw the movie, as a teenager, he fell in love.

Turned out, *Vertigo* was one of Cal's favorites too, so they left it on.

"He should have been home by now," Lois told him more than once, "but his flight was grounded...*because of what happened*." Always the same euphemistic phrase, always delivered at a stage whisper, as if she couldn't bring herself to fully acknowledge it.

Lois told Frank that Cal's construction firm was putting up a new hotel in Reno, and he'd been out there all week supervising their progress. It was obvious she was having trouble coping without him, and in her medicated, booze-soaked stupor, she found Frank an acceptable enough replacement. He worried about what she'd think of him being here when she finally sobered up—or what Cal would think if Frank was still around when he got home.

Lois shifted on the couch, her eyes active behind closed lids. Then, without waking, she leaned toward him and placed her head on his shoulder. Her cheek was warm against his neck. Her breath was honeyed by the wine. Her hair smelled faintly of apples. Frank's pulse quickened. His face grew hot. It had been a long time since he'd been this close to a woman.

Feeling suddenly uncomfortable, he cleared his throat, and Lois opened her eyes drowsily. She regarded him with an unfocused gaze that made him feel as if she were look-ing past him—or through him, as if he were a ghost. Her expression indicated neither recognition nor fear.

"C'mon," he said. "Let's put you to bed."

"Yes," she said, fighting through her mental cloudiness, the strain evident in her face. "That's probably a good idea."

Lois tried and failed to get off the couch. She could barely hold her head up, much less stand. She leaned heavily on Frank the whole way upstairs, Ella trailing close behind. Occasionally, Lois's knees would buckle and she would stumble, then brace herself on the banister while Frank struggled to set her right once more. By the time he got her into bed, he was sweating, and his bum knee was on the verge of giving out. He took her slippers off and tucked her in.

Lois's eyes focused briefly on Frank, lucidity sparking behind them, and then widened. "Wh-who are you? Where's Cal?"

"Cal's stuck in Reno, Lois," Frank said gently. "Be-cause of what happened, remember? I'm Max. You know me."

"Max," she echoed, eyes tearing up a little. "Of course. Will…will you stay the night?" Then she colored, her face a boozy caricature of embarrassment. "Not, uh, *here*…I didn't mean…it's just, the house is so quiet with my Calvin gone…"

"Don't worry. I'm not going anywhere. And it looks like Ella's more than happy to steal Cal's spot." The tiny dog hopped in place, trying in vain to get on the bed. "Do you mind if I help her up?"

But Lois's eyes drooped, her moment of clarity dissipating as her adrenaline waned. In seconds, she was unconscious. Frank shrugged and set Ella on the bed.

Just leave the lady be, Frank thought. *She's not your fucking problem.* But he couldn't shake the notion she was going to feel like hell tomorrow morning.

He sighed and picked up the empty glass on her nightstand. Then he ducked into her master bathroom to get her some water.

The bathroom was spacious and dramatic—white walls, ceiling, and vanity, with an original wood floor painted glossy black and a white shag rug. There was a freestanding shower in one corner, and a claw-foot tub tucked into an alcove at the far end of the room.

He started to cross the room to the vanity, then froze. A cell phone lay in the rug's deep pile, where the edge of the rug came closest to the tub. It was one of those oversize Galaxy phones they advertised during ball games, as much a tablet as a smartphone. Water beaded on its glossy surface. In fact, half the rug was soaked, and water pooled in the cracks between the floorboards.

Frank approached the tub. It was still half full, a sopping towel draped over its rim. He remembered Lois's hair was wet when she came to the door. Remembered that the cops had knocked for some time shortly before he tried to break in but had received no answer. She'd been up here in the tub, it seemed—and when she came down, she must have thought Frank was the one she'd heard knocking.

That's when he spotted the side table.

It was black lacquered like the floor and partially hidden from view by the tub. On it was a Bose Bluetooth speaker, a sandalwood pillar candle on a small wrought-iron tray, and a toppled prescription bottle, its lid beside it, pills spilling to the floor.

Frank picked up the bottle. It wasn't Xanax or Valium, as he'd initially suspected, but Flexeril. The label said to take it three times a day as needed for muscle spasms— and warned it didn't play well with alcohol.

He gathered up the scattered pills and put them back in the bottle. A few had rolled under the tub, so he reached under and dragged a palm across the floorboards, trying to blindly sweep them out. His fingertips brushed against something larger and heavier than he'd expected, something about the size of a roll of quarters, but made of wood. He strained to reach it. Managed to grab it between his first and second fingers and tweeze it out.

It was an old-fashioned folding pocketknife with a single blade and a burl handle. At present, it was open— which made Frank grateful it was the handle, and not the blade, his fingers had grazed. Carved into the handle was a set of initials: *CWB.* Calvin Broussard, he assumed, and idly wondered: *William? Walter? Wayne?*

Frank closed the knife and slipped it into his pocket. Then he walked around the tub and picked the phone up off the floor. He fumbled with the thing a moment, trying to figure out how to turn it on or wake it up or whatever. Frank was no good with gadgets. He didn't trust them, cell phones in particular. All that information floating around freaked him out. Seemed like it'd be way too easy to tap, track, or intercept.

Something he did worked. The phone lit up in his hand. He found himself looking at some kind of keypad without any numbers. *Okay,* he thought, *let's treat this like a break-in. Look for fingerprints. Guess the pattern.* He tilted the phone a little and saw a streaked zigzag fingerprint overlaying the keypad. Lois didn't seem the sneaky sort, so he tried the most obvious possible direction—top to bottom, left to right—first. The lock screen disappeared immediately, and Frank found himself in Lois's voice mail.

The message that was queued to play was twenty-seven seconds long. Lois must've listened to it multiple times, because there were several fingerprints on the play button, their lines and whorls intersecting. Frank added another and held the phone up to his ear to listen.

"Hey, babe, it's me. Where are you—out in the garden? If so, I hope you get this before I get home, so you have a chance to clean up. I know my flight's not until this evening, but hanging out in Reno alone on a Saturday seemed like a waste, so I rented a car and booked us some massages for this afternoon, followed by dinner at Aziza. Had to call in a favor to score a table, so don't you dare tell me you're in the mood for takeout. I'm on the bridge now, so I'll be home in a few. If you've got some handsome young thing keeping you company in my absence, you'd best tell hi—"

And then there was a roar of fire and static. An explosion of glass, oddly melodic. A sound like a lead weight tumbling in a clothes dryer as the car rolled, Cal screaming the whole time. A rapid series of snaps—the bridge's vertical support ropes, Frank guessed—followed by a moment's silence and then a splash. Cal's screams ceased. The call ended.

Cal Broussard wasn't stuck in Reno. Cal Broussard was dead.

And until the cops had come knocking, Frank realized, Lois had intended to join him.

18.

Jake Reston trudged from the hospital cafeteria back to his family carrying a green plastic tray loaded precariously with food and drink. It was early Sunday morning. The world outside the hospital's windows was bathed in cool predawn blue.

His head pounded, thanks to the tension in his neck and shoulders. His ears still rang from the explosion. His broken nose throbbed dully. A stink like burning plastic clung to his hair and clothes, although he'd gotten so used to it he barely noticed. He hadn't eaten since yesterday, and now that blind panic had given way to boredom and exhaustion, he was starving, the kind of gnawing hunger that bordered on queasy.

The tray held an egg-and-cheese croissant for Emily. Cereal with almond milk for Hannah, who'd been going through a vegan phase ever since she turned thirteen. A pile of corned-beef hash for Aidan, who enjoyed taunting Hannah by scarfing down all the meat he could. A bagel with cream cheese for himself. A plate of home fries to share. Coffee for the grown-ups. OJ for the kids. And as much bottled water as he could carry because they were all dehydrated and hoarse from smoke inhalation.

The night had been a trying one. Though Hannah had seemed fine at the scene, and she'd never once complained, it turned out she'd fractured her wrist when she fell. The ER physician splinted her arm and told her parents that she'd need to follow up with the orthopedic docs in a few days. The gash on Emily's forehead required twenty stitches. Hannah said they made her look like the bride of Frankenstein—mostly, Jake thought, to get a laugh out of poor Aidan. His leg was badly broken and required surgery. The hours he'd been under were the longest of Jake's life. But the surgeon said that it went well, and Aidan had been moved to a room shortly after. He'd slept on and off throughout the night but woke up hungry and in good spirits not long ago. The whole family was now camped out in Aidan's room, which the staff had mercifully allowed them to take over.

Sophia's brief bout of unconsciousness was still troubling to Jake and Emily, but the baby's head CT was negative, and the doctor who examined Sophia gave her a provisional thumbs-up, although she recommended they monitor her behavior for a couple days. The doc had insisted it was fine for Sophia to sleep, but Emily found herself unable to let her do so for more than ten minutes at a time. As a consequence, both of them were up all night.

Thankfully, Emily had finally nodded off two hours ago, and Sophia had followed suit.

Hannah spent half the night watching the hits climb on her cell-phone video—over two million views, last Jake heard—but eventually her phone died and she was forced to get some rest.

Jake, too wired to sleep, had just watched them until Aidan woke. Then he'd headed out to fetch some breakfast.

Jake rounded the corner toward Aidan's room and then stopped short. There was a man waiting just outside. He was lean and weathered—fiftyish, Jake guessed. He had on a navy canvas blazer, a white button-down, and well-worn jeans. Cowboy boots, as creased and tan as the man's face, graced his feet. His thick, wavy hair was dyed a shade too dark to be convincing, gray roots starting to show. A .357 Magnum jutted from a holster on his hip.

The man was scowling at his cell phone when Jake spotted him, but when he sensed Jake's presence, he tucked the phone into the front pocket of his jeans and broke into an easy grin, the corners of his eyes crinkling, smile lines bracketing his mouth. There was something vulpine about his face, Jake thought.

"Jacob Reston?" he said.

"That's right," Jake replied.

The man produced a wallet from the inside pocket of his blazer and flipped it open with one hand, a practiced motion. There was some kind of government ID inside, the man's face staring back at him. "Chet Yancey," he said. He put his wallet away and extended his hand. Jake raised the tray a tad to indicate his hands were busy. As Yancey

151

dropped his arm, Jake noted the turquoise pinkie ring the man wore.

"What can I do for you, Mr. Yancey?"

"I had some questions about what happened down at the bridge yesterday, and I thought maybe you could answer them."

"I already spoke to the police."

"Course you did. You're a good citizen. Eager to help. You understand that when an attack like this happens, you've gotta step up and do your part. That's why you're gonna talk to me too. It won't take but a minute."

Jake looked down at the tray in his hands. Thought about telling Yancey to wait a sec while he delivered breakfast to his family. But something held him back. He suspected Yancey would simply follow him, and that didn't sit right with Jake. So he said nothing and stood his ground.

"Sure," he said.

"Attaboy." Yancey clapped Jake on the shoulder. The food on Jake's tray jostled, but thankfully nothing fell. Yancey removed a small notepad and pen from his back pocket and clicked the latter open. "How's your family doing, by the way? I peeked in on them, but when I saw your wife and baby were asleep, I thought it best I wait out here for you. I didn't want to disturb them," he said brightly.

"Uh, they're fine. My littlest—"

"Sophia, right?" Yancey interjected, reading from his notepad.

"That's right," Jake said, slightly unnerved. "She took a good bump to the head when my wife, Emily, fell, and was unconscious for a few minutes, but the docs say she's doing okay now. They even let her stay down here with the rest of us, instead of up in Peds, but we're supposed to keep an eye on her behavior. Emily needed some stitches, but she's otherwise okay. My son—"

"Aidan," Yancey said.

"—broke his leg and needed surgery to set it. He's been groggy ever since he came to, but they cleared him for solid food a little while ago and told us he should heal up just fine. And Hannah—the toughest of us, I think—fractured her wrist, but she barely seemed to notice."

"Hannah's your oldest, right?" Jake nodded. "What a pretty, pretty girl. Takes after her mother, if you don't mind my saying."

"Actually," Jake said, bristling, "I kinda—"

"Anyway," Yancey continued, breezing past Jake's obvious discomfort, "I'm glad everybody's doing okay." His tone didn't match his words. It sounded hurried, perfunctory, as though Jake's family's well-being didn't matter to him one way or the other. "Now, as my daddy used to say, let's talk turkey. You live in Eugene, right?"

"That's right."

"Nice country up that way. Lots of green. A little chilly for my taste. What brought you and your lovely family to San Francisco today, Jake?"

"We were headed home from Disneyland," he said, "and thought we'd stop and see the sights." He had no wish to tell him the story about his parents' photo.

"Did you visit anyone while you were in town?"

The question puzzled Jake. "No. We just headed to the bridge to get a family picture."

"A video, you mean."

"Excuse me?" Jake was thrown by Yancey's correction.

He felt defensive, suddenly, as though he'd been caught in a lie, which was ridiculous—he had nothing to hide.

"You headed to the bridge to get a video. It's been all over the news."

"Yes. Right. Of course. Hannah posted it on Facebook when her friends started asking if she was okay—she'd mentioned we were stopping off in San Francisco. One of them put it up on YouTube. The video was supposed to be for my parents. A surprise for their anniv—"

"What can you tell me about the man who shot the video?"

"Come again?"

"The man who shot the video. Is he an uncle, maybe? A family friend? When I poked my head into your boy's room, I didn't see him."

"Uh, he wasn't with us. We just bumped into him on the path."

"Is that so."

Jake waited for Yancey to continue, but for a long while, he didn't—he just looked at Jake unblinkingly, a silent challenge. Jake withered beneath his gaze like a child called before the principal but said nothing.

"You stopped a stranger on the path and asked him to take a video for you?"

"Yes. It was my son's idea," he added lamely, wondering why that made his story—the truth, he reminded himself—sound more believable. He somehow felt like he'd just ratted out his own flesh and blood.

"Why this man in particular?"

Jake shrugged, the food on the tray shifting as he did. "I don't know. He was walking alone. Everybody else was in a group or busy."

"What happened to him? After the blast, where did he go?"

"I have no idea. When the bomb went off, I lost consciousness. By the time I came to, he was gone."

"Did you happen to get his name?"

"No. It was just a quick thing. A chance encounter. If it wasn't for the explosion and the fact that he caught himself on camera, I doubt I'd even remember what he looked like."

Jake saw a head poke out of Aidan's room and look his way. It was Hannah, her hair mussed, her face puffy from sleep, her expression one of puzzlement. "Dad? I thought I heard you out here. Who's this guy?"

Jake looked from his daughter to Yancey and back again. Yancey's attention lingered on Hannah, a wide grin spreading across his face. "The name's Chet Yancey, little lady—and I work for your dear old Uncle Sam," he said, winking.

Jake cleared his throat loudly and said, "Mr. Yancey's got some questions about what happened at the bridge, is all. We're almost done. Go back inside and wake up Mom. Tell her I'll be in with breakfast in a sec." Hannah ducked back into the room. Jake relaxed perceptibly once she was out of sight.

Yancey's…flirtation?…hadn't been sexual, exactly, but it still felt to Jake as if it were miles from appropriate. Jake couldn't shake the feeling that it had been intended to unnerve him—and it had worked.

Yancey flashed his pearly whites at Jake as if pleased by his discomfort. Then he reached over and plucked a home fry off Jake's tray. He dunked it into one of the paper condiment cups that Jake had filled with ketchup and stuffed it in his mouth. He chewed slowly, as if savoring the tasty morsel. After he swallowed, he licked the grease off his fingers one by one.

"What I'm hearing from you, Jake, is there's not much that you can tell me about the old man in the video. Is that a fair assessment?"

"Yes. I guess. I'm sorry I couldn't be of more assistance," Jake lied. In truth, all he wanted was to be rid of Yancey.

"You're not holding anything back, are you? Because I'd like to think our conversation's been a friendly one, but if I find out you've been lying to me—and believe me, if you are, I *will* find out—our next talk's gonna be a lot less pleasant. And if I'm forced to haul you in for questioning, who'll look after this beautiful family of yours?" His smile vanished. In its absence, Yancey's face was cold and hard.

"I've told you everything I know. I have no reason to do otherwise."

"Well, then," Yancey said, his smile lighting up once more, "thanks for your time!" He clicked his pen closed. Stuck it and his notepad back in his pocket. Produced a card and dropped it onto the tray full of food. It contained nothing but Yancey's name and a phone number—no address, no title, no mention of the organization he worked for. "But do me a favor and hold on to this in case you remember anything else you think I ought to know. And please give my regards to Aidan, Emily, Hannah, and Sophia. You're very lucky they all came through this okay."

Yancey started to put out his hand again, and then, remembering Jake couldn't shake, he made a pistol of his fingers and aimed it playfully at Jake. He mimed shooting, his thumb twitching as he dropped the hammer, and then he took off down the hall.

Without looking back, he called, "Don't you worry, Jake—if I need anything else from you, I know where to find you." Then he began whistling idly to himself.

As Yancey rounded the corner, his whistled song echoing down the hall, Jake realized Yancey had never asked him anything about the blast.

19.

THE CHARTER JET touched down in Palo Alto a little after
nine a.m., jarring Hendricks awake when the landing
gear connected with the tarmac.

Pale sunlight poured through the cabin's windows.
Hendricks yawned and stretched, plush leather creaking
beneath him. His limbs were stiff and sore but he was
happy for the rest. Cameron, who sat facing him in a beige
leather recliner of her own, looked as if she'd fared less
well. Her face was pale. Her eyes were bloodshot, the
flesh around them dark-smudged. She pecked idly at her
laptop—which was plugged into the outlet beside her and
tapped into the aircraft's Wi-Fi—as she'd been doing before Hendricks dozed off hours ago.

When Hendricks had returned to Cameron's car after
his meeting with Thompson, she'd cocked her head and
said, "You don't look happy."

"The person waiting for me wasn't who I was expecting."

"Yeah, I gathered that much from your tone when you walked in. Then the line cut out, and I got worried. I had half a mind to come in after you."

"It didn't cut out. I hung up on you."

"Why?"

Hendricks's mind conjured an image of Lester's mangled corpse cast aside like shreds of orange rind once Engelmann had extracted the information he'd desired. "We were discussing things I didn't want you overhearing. Things it isn't safe for you to know."

An awkward silence stretched between them. "So what happens now?" Cameron asked eventually. "I drop you somewhere, and we go our separate ways?"

He shook his head. "The situation's changed. You said you grew up in the Bay Area?"

"That's right."

"Do you know it well?"

"Are you kidding? My parents worked like a hundred hours a week, and I was a good kid, so they were more than willing to leave me to my own devices. I spent more time in the city than I did at home."

"Congratulations, then. You're officially my tour guide."

"Come again?"

"You heard me. We're going to San Francisco."

Hendricks had called in a favor and got them on a private jet out of Philly—a sleek, luxurious Citation X+ with room for twelve and twin Rolls-Royce Allison engines so powerful that its top speed bumped up against the sound barrier. Cessna claimed it was the fastest civilian aircraft in the world, and unlike most charter jets, it could travel

159

coast to coast without refueling. It cost just shy of twenty-three million dollars, not counting fuel and upkeep. A single cross-country flight ran twenty-five grand.

Hendricks knew all that because the guy who owned the plane—a former client named Morales—had made sure to tell him. It was clear Hendricks's request had put him out. Hendricks hated cashing in so big a chip, but time was of the essence, and the TSA was on high alert, which made traveling-while-criminal a bad idea. Plus, commercial flights to the Bay Area were grounded. The only reason the tiny Palo Alto Airport—which boasted a single runway, and warned pilots on approach to watch out for jackrabbits—was open to private travelers was its proximity to Silicon Valley. The tech lobby had pressured Congress to ensure their top executives could get in and out, and Congress had in turn pressured the FAA.

The flight from Philly had taken five hours—two with the time change. The Cessna had raced the breaking dawn across the country, flying toward darkness pricked with stars, the sky bloodred behind it the whole way. Hendricks had dozed off long before daylight overtook them. Cameron, apparently, hadn't.

"I thought I told you to get some sleep," he said.

"I tried. My brain wouldn't let me. I don't know how you do it."

"What, sleep?"

"Yeah. After everything that happened yesterday. Knowing what we're walking into."

"*We're* not walking into anything—*I* am. You're going to hang back and support me from afar, like we discussed."

"I've been keeping an eye on the coverage," she said. "It's getting ugly out there. Someone set fire to a mosque in Dearborn, Michigan. A Sikh cabbie in Los Angeles was dragged from his car and beaten. And the Feds raided some poor guy's apartment in Alameda an hour ago on what turned out to be a false lead called in by a pissed-off neighbor."

"Any follow-up attacks?"

"Not yet, and I've seen no further mention of the old guy from the video."

"How about the mess we left in Port Jefferson?"

"Nothing new, although the paper speculated it was a gangland killing."

Not too far off, Hendricks thought, and at least that line of questioning kept interest away from Cameron. "Anything else I ought to know?"

"I downloaded some apps to your phone because the preinstalled ones sucked. Maps, GPS, video chat—the BART app too, while I was at it."

"Bart?"

"Bay Area Rapid Transit."

"You think I'm gonna catch a lot of buses while I'm in town?"

Cameron reddened. "It's more than buses. The app keeps track of trains, cable cars, ferries…although I guess not so much that last one lately."

"Water traffic's still shut down, huh?"

"Yeah. Sounds like the search has been slow-going. They've been bringing food and water out to the smaller vessels to tide them over until they can be cleared. Anyway, I figured the app might come in handy for a guy who doesn't know the town. Chance favors the prepared mind, as my mom would say."

"Thanks," he said.

The aircraft taxied to a stop. Silence descended upon the cabin as the engines wound down. Then the cockpit door opened, and the pilot stepped out. "Welcome to sunny Palo Alto," he said, his tone teetering between bored and irritated. "Enjoy your stay."

The air was cool, the airport quiet. Small private aircraft were parked in rows, two- and four-seaters mostly, single-engine prop planes belonging to rich hobbyists. Most of the airport's outbuildings were shuttered and dark. Palo Alto was situated on the southwestern tip of San Francisco Bay, where the water peters off to wetlands. The airport was bordered by a salt marsh to the north and east, and a municipal golf course to the south and west. Through the morning haze, Hendricks could just make out the gentle rise of the mountains across the bay.

A man in an orange vest and coveralls pointed them toward a nondescript gate in the chain-link fence that surrounded the airport. From this side, at least, it was unlocked.

When they reached the parking lot, Hendricks frowned. It contained maybe a dozen cars.

"What's wrong?" Cameron asked.

"We need a ride."

"And?"

"This is a short-term lot. If any of these went missing, they'd be reported by day's end. Besides, without proper tools, boosting one could take a while, and we're liable to be seen."

"I'm guessing Uber's not an option."

Hendricks shook his head. "In my line of work, it doesn't pay to leave a trail."

Cameron poked at her phone a moment. Then her face brightened. "I have an idea."

She led him southwest on Embarcadero Road, four lanes bracketed by sidewalks and lined with trees. To their right, as they walked, was the golf course. To their left, an office park. The golf course was empty. Most of the businesses were closed.

After a quarter mile or so, they reached a shuttered auto-rental agency. Cameron circled it, glancing at her phone from time to time. Then she sat down in the shadow of a live oak and took her laptop from its bag.

Hendricks eyed the building with suspicion. Surveillance cameras monitored the parking lot. Sensors protected the windows and doors. "I don't know what you're thinking, kid, but I can tell you that it's not a good idea."

"Shh."

"Rental places track their inventory pretty closely—"

"I said be quiet."

"—and this place is wired for security, which means—"

"For Christ's sake," Cameron snapped, "would you shut up and let me work?"

Hendricks fell silent.

Three minutes later, the overhead door on the far side of the building rattled open.

"Cameron," he said warily, "what did you do?"

"You said we needed a ride no one would miss. This place is closed until Monday, and their after-hours return slot drops the keys into the garage. If we swipe a car before it's checked back in, they'll just assume it hasn't been returned yet."

"What about the security system?"

"Please. I shut it off before I triggered the door. If they were serious about security, they would have locked down their wireless network. They're practically begging to be hacked."

"And the cameras?"

"Currently experiencing technical difficulties. Why, I wouldn't be surprised if the whole day's feed was compromised."

"That's a damn shame," Hendricks said, smiling.

"Isn't it?" Cameron replied. "Now, how about we go pick out some wheels?"

20.

C HET YANCEY SLURPED terrible coffee from a Styrofoam cup and watched the rescue efforts from a scenic overlook while he waited for the new guy to arrive.

Though the fireboats had quelled the blazes in the wee hours of the night, the sky was still dulled by smoke. The road along the water's edge was crowded with rescue workers and equipment. The bay was choked with police boats and Coast Guard cutters. A pair of tugboats maneuvered a massive crane barge into place beside the Golden Gate Bridge, their engines laboring.

Most of the survivors had been successfully evacuated, but seventy-five or so were still up there, trapped or pinned down by rubble. Throughout the night, the bridge's vertical suspender ropes had snapped at random, steel cable nearly three inches thick breaking loose and slicing through cars and asphalt like razor wire through flesh. The remaining support ropes squealed under the added strain. Rescue workers hoped to use the crane to clear the roadway and support the bridge's weight until the remaining survivors could be reached.

The hills flanking the walking trail were dotted with yellow flags, indicating debris, and red flags, marking spots where biological evidence—a polite euphemism for bodies and body parts—had lain. The debris sat where it landed. The biologicals were moved once they were flagged and photographed, to avoid predation.

Upslope, at the Golden Gate Bridge Pavilion—which served as the command center for the rescue effort—FEMA and local fire-and-rescue crews argued with state and federal crime-scene investigators over priorities. SFPD and U.S. Park Police quibbled pointlessly over jurisdiction. Homeland Security and the FBI's National Security Branch butted heads and measured dicks. The bickering—and the lousy coffee he'd grabbed—gave Yancey flashbacks to his public-sector days.

Yancey'd spent two decades in the FBI's employ, even heading up the Albuquerque field office for a time, but he'd gotten out years ago. Now he worked for Bellum Industries as manager of West Coast operations, a title intended to obfuscate rather than describe.

Bellum was a private security contractor, a major player in the Middle East, with nearly sixty thousand private military contractors in the region. Bellum's duties included securing borders, bases, embassies—even entire cities—at the U.S. government's behest. Protecting the interests of well-heeled multinational corporations—their oil fields, shipping routes, employee housing—and any private citizens who could afford to pay. Supplying the CIA with manpower—called consultants, officially, although in reality they were off-the-books hit squads.

Bellum's domestic interests included training members of the U.S. military and law enforcement at their compound north of San Francisco, the translation and analysis of electronic intelligence at their headquarters in DC, and protecting foreign diplomats on U.S. soil. Bellum also, via its subsidiary companies, provided more prosaic security measures, such as CCTV monitoring and personnel, to everything from amusement parks to schools.

As Yancey stared out over the bay, his thoughts returned unbidden to the phone call he'd gotten yesterday.

"Hiya, Chet. It's been a while."

The number had been blocked, but he recognized the voice immediately. It was the Council's mouthpiece, Lombino.

"Why the fuck are you calling me? I paid my debt, and haven't so much as lost a nickel on a friendly game of cards in seven years."

"Good for you, pal, only here's the thing: your payment bounced."

"The hell it did," Yancey whispered. "I put Segreti in the ground, just like you asked."

"Yeah? Then how'd he just end up on my TV?"

"What do you mean, your TV?" Yancey hadn't seen a television in days. He'd been tied up dealing with a crisis at work—unsuccessfully, as it turned out.

Lombino filled him in. Yancey lit a cigarette with trembling fingers while he listened.

"Look, Chet," Lombino said, "I'm not an unreasonable man. I can tell this was an honest mistake. As far as I'm concerned, if you fix it, we're square. Of course, this time

167

we're gonna have to ask for video evidence. I'm sure you understand."

"What if I say no?"

"Seems to me our deal last time was, you take out Segreti and we forgive your debts, you don't and we kill your daughter. But that was seven years ago, which means there's interest to consider. Speaking of, I hear she just had twins."

"You don't understand. I'm in the middle of a work thing. I'm not sure I can—"

"Lemme stop you, Chet. That sounds more like a you-problem than a me-problem. See, I don't care *how* it gets done, but I care very much that it *does* get done. Understood?"

"Yeah. I hear you," Yancey had said, and Lombino's words had echoed in his mind ever since.

Footfalls behind Yancey brought him back to the here and now. He turned to find the new guy, Reyes, strolling down the path in a pale summer suit, a venti Starbucks in his hand.

"Morning, boss."

Yancey downed the rest of his own coffee and pitched the cup into the bushes. Then he tapped a cigarette from his pack and lit it. "Is it still?" he asked, exhaling smoke. "I've been waiting so goddamn long, I thought for sure it would be afternoon by now."

Bellum had hired Oscar Reyes three months ago, and Yancey was still breaking him in. There was no denying Reyes had talent, but Yancey found his swagger grating. He seemed to Yancey like a horse that wouldn't take a saddle. The ivy-educated son of Dominican immigrants, Reyes was recruited out of grad school by the CIA and had spent the past decade running solo ops throughout Central and South America. Consequently, he was accustomed to his independence, and—unlike the majority of men in Yancey's employ, who hailed from the military—punctuality was not his strongest suit.

"Yeah, sorry about that. I got tied up with this kid from the Park Police who wouldn't shut up. Then—"

Yancey cut him off. "Bellum doesn't pay you to make excuses, son, and they don't pay me to stand around. How about you skip 'em and just give me the fucking sitrep?"

"You got it, boss." Reyes took an infuriatingly long sip of his coffee before continuing. "First off, the subject's still alive, near as I can tell. I spent half the night looking at bodies. Saw some seriously gory shit—and probably won't be eating lasagna for a while—but none of them matched the stills you sent me from the video."

Fuck, Yancey thought. He'd been hoping to get lucky. "So if he isn't dead, where is he?"

"Good question," Reyes replied. "We found his hat in the bushes not far from here. He must've lost it when he fell. And that kid from Park Police I mentioned had a run-in with a guy matching our subject's description not long after the blast. Sounds like he was banged up. Disoriented."

"Where was this?"

"About a quarter mile uphill from here."

"I thought the local boys were tasked with bringing the injured to the medical tents for triage. Why'd Ranger Rick let him go?"

"He claims our guy told him that a family downslope needed his help—the people from the video, maybe—and promised to stay put until the cop returned. The kid combed the scrub beside the trail for half an hour but couldn't find any family, and when he came back, our guy was gone."

"So he's in the wind?"

"I don't think so. I've spoken to my contacts at Homeland Security, since they're the ones patrolling the park's perimeter. Far as they know, nobody meeting his description has left the grounds, which means he's likely still inside."

"They sure?"

"Sure as they can be, given that they've got over three miles of perimeter to cover. And they've got the Coast Guard monitoring the beaches, so we know he didn't leave by sea."

"Okay, say you're our guy. You get caught pants-down when shit meets fan, but you can't get out before the Feds drop the net. Where do you go?"

"That's the question, isn't it? Obviously, it'd help if I knew more about him. His background. His training. His identity. Without more intel, I feel like I'm conducting this investigation with one hand tied behind my back."

"Sorry, no dice. All I'm authorized to tell you is, he's a person of interest in the bridge attack," Yancey lied.

"That and a blurry picture's not a lot to go on."

"True enough," Yancey agreed, "but Lord knows, I've tracked down men with less. What's your next move?"

"I've dispatched a four-man team to his last known location. They're conducting a grid search as we speak. And I've got dogs en route. I figure if he's hurt, he may've left a blood trail, and if he's holed up nearby, they'll take us right to him. It's just a matter of time."

"Good. Keep me posted. Text me if you find anything."

"You're not sticking around?"

"I can't. I've got another matter to attend to."

"Which is?"

"Way above your pay grade, son."

21.

"Y OU SURE YOU wanna do this?" Cameron asked.

"Nope," Hendricks replied, "but I don't have any better ideas, so this one'll have to do. Are you clear on your part of the plan?"

Cameron smiled. "Are *you?*"

They were in San Francisco, parked on the northbound side of Lyon Street in the Nissan Altima they'd lifted from the rental agency. The Presidio was to the west behind them. Hendricks twisted in his seat, the stitches in his side pulling, so he could keep an eye on the two Home-land Security officers within sight of their position. One was stationed at the Presidio's Lombard Street gate. The other was nearer to where they sat, leaning against the low stone wall that encircled the old base. Though the day was warm and clear with an easterly wind holding the city's trademark fog offshore, they wore full tactical gear, all of it

172

black: helmets, fatigues, ballistic vests, utility belts, hard plastic elbow and kneepads. Both looked hot and tired, but watchful.

Homeland Security had the Presidio pretty well locked down. There was an agent stationed at the end of every dead-end road that jutted north from Lake Street, which ran east to west along the westernmost half of the park's southern border. East of Lake Street, the park's edge became more accessible, so agents were stationed line of sight from one another just outside. There were regular foot patrols along the Mountain Lake Trail and vehicular patrols along West Pacific Avenue, both of which ran just inside the southern edge of the park's stone fence. But to the east, no road or trail ran along the inside border, and closing Lyon Street—which ran parallel to it just outside—was impractical, so Homeland Security's presence was thinner there. Not *much* thinner, but still, it was a weakness Hendricks had every intention of exploiting.

"I'm serious," he said. "I need to know you're good to go."

"I am."

"All right, then," Hendricks said. "Let's do this."

The plan was Cameron's.

"So," she'd asked as they sped north from Palo Alto, "this Segreti guy you're looking for—how do you expect to find him?"

The highway had been eerily devoid of traffic. In the wake of the attack, it seemed Bay Area residents were staying home.

"I'm working on it."

"You mean you have no idea."

"I mean I'm working on it."

"Are you open to suggestions? Because I spent most of our flight thinking about it, and I have a thought. A couple, actually."

"Okay," he said. "Let's hear 'em."

"First off, it seems to me the most logical place to start would be the family from the video."

"Too risky," he replied. "Anybody looking for Segreti would be onto them, which makes approaching them dangerous."

"That's not an issue if you look into them online."

"Which I'm guessing you did."

"Yup. First, I combed through their social media—the parents are on Facebook, the mom's on Pinterest, the eldest child is on Instagram and Snapchat—but found no pics of Segreti or anyone who looks like him in their lists of friends. Then I hacked the parents' e-mail—"

"You did *what?*"

"—but none of the searches I ran turned up anything of interest. It looks to me like bumping into him was a chance encounter."

Hendricks thought back to the video, which he'd watched on Cameron's laptop a couple dozen times on the plane before dozing off. "Yeah, that seems to track."

"But I still think they're worth questioning. They might've seen which way he went or gotten something useful out of him before the camera rolled—"

"Much as I'd love to, we can't. If I were the Feds or the bad guys, I'd put someone on the family as a matter of course, which means they're off-limits to us."

"But what if I—"

"Seriously, drop it. It's not going to happen. What else

have you got?" Hendricks felt bad slapping her down, but after the mess at the Salty Dog, he couldn't afford another sloppy play, and approaching the Restons qualified.

"If you didn't like my last idea, you're going to *hate* this one."

"Why don't you let me be the judge of that?"

"You ever heard of COWs?"

"Sure. Big, dumb, tasty things, go moo."

"Not cows like dinner," she said. "COWs like cells on wheels."

"Can't say as I have."

"A COW is basically a cell-phone tower attached to a trailer that can be rolled into an area as needed. It's meant to support the existing system when there's an increase in demand, which could be due to anything from the Super Bowl to September Eleventh. Hell, during Obama's inauguration, they brought in twenty-six of them to accommodate the million-odd spectators, most of whom expected to be able to live-tweet and Facebook the event."

"Okay," he said. "Now I know what COWs are. The question is, why?"

She held up a picture on her phone for him to see. "That's why."

He took his eyes off the road just long enough to glance at it. The image was grainy but seemed to show precisely the sort of device she'd described. It was in the middle of a broad expanse of pavement, enough dotted lines visible on either side of it for six lanes of traffic at least. In the background, out of focus, Hendricks saw some kind of tent.

"I take it this is somewhere near the bridge?"

Cameron nodded. "That's a detail of a still I pulled from CNN. They've set up a command center for the rescue effort right outside the toll gates, and they brought in that tower to support their data needs."

"And?"

"And I think that we should hack it."

"Come again?"

"It's not as crazy as it sounds. I did some digging on the dark web about that model. Turns out, it's an old one and easily exploited. So I talked to a gamer buddy of mine—an off-the-grid crypto-anarchist type who siphons off of local cell systems when he wants to go online—and he sent some code to get me started. I tweaked it to suit our needs, and the end result's a program that'll gain us access to all the data passing through that tower—calls, texts, photos, you name it."

"I'm guessing you've never broken into one of these before. How do you know it'll work?"

"Code's code. It'll work. And it sure beats knocking on doors."

"Assuming we could get access, what would we do with it?"

"Anything we want!" she said. "See, unlike the Super Bowl or Obama's inauguration, there aren't a bunch of these towers, because there's not enough demand to warrant them. There are only eight hundred or so full-time residents in the Presidio. Most of the residents and all the businesses are clustered on the western edge, which is served by several towers atop buildings in the city proper. So almost all the traffic on that mobile tower is directly related to the bridge investigation, and almost every aspect of the bridge investigation is passing through that tower. Witnesses' cell-phone pics. Written statements. Surveillance feeds, probably. There's a good chance all we need to do to get a bead on Segreti is run the data through some keyword searches and facial recognition."

"Jesus," Hendricks said. "That's incredible."

"Right?" she replied, obviously pleased by his compliment. "But there's a catch. A big one."

"What's that?"

"The tower can't be hacked remotely. The program has to be physically inserted into a port on the control panel for this to work. And the tower's parked right next to, like, half the law enforcement agents in the state."

Hendricks fell silent for a mile or so, thinking.

"How hard is it to install?" he asked finally.

"Not very. Insert a thumb drive, maybe execute a few commands."

"So you're saying I could do it?"

"If I walked you through it, maybe. But if you fucked up, the techs responsible for keeping the tower operational would know immediately."

"Then I guess I'd better not fuck up."

As Hendricks rounded the corner onto Lombard Street heading east, away from the Presidio, it was all he could do not to look at the agent manning the gate. He'd left his sweatshirt in the car, and he carried the backpack Cameron had bought for him over one shoulder. A navy windbreaker, its nylon stiff and crinkly with newness, was tied around his waist and whispered to itself with every step. "Has the guy at the gate got eyes on me?" he muttered.

"Yeah," Cameron said, her voice tinny through the cheap Bluetooth earpiece. "But he doesn't look particularly interested."

"Be sure to tell me if that changes."

"Roger that," she said.

Hendricks strolled casually down Lombard, then took a right onto Baker Street, a wide, tree-lined drive where stylish, single-family row houses with oversize bay windows and roofs of Spanish tile sat shoulder to shoulder with funky midcentury multi-unit buildings. Peppered in between were local businesses: grocer, bistro, bar, dry cleaner. It was midafternoon. The sky was clear. The sun was warm and bright. Hendricks suspected this area, which exuded a friendly neighborhood vibe, would typically be bustling with activity and good cheer on so lovely a Sunday as this. Sidewalk brunches. Dog walkers. Newspapers read on narrow balconies. But today, the streets were empty of cars save for those parked at the curb. Businesses were shuttered, blinds drawn. People were afraid.

It broke Hendricks's heart. He'd seen this kind of fear too often overseas. Children cowering behind their parents' legs as drones passed overhead. Wide eyes peeking around parted curtains as war erupted in the streets. *We played our part in the name of freedom*, Hendricks thought, *but what good were our reasons to the innocents we killed or displaced? All our fighting ever seemed to do was feed the military-industrial beast, which profited mightily from every ratcheting of tension, every escalation of conflict, every convoy attacked, every hovel destroyed.*

When war became big business, shareholders were bound to demand more of it, regardless of how many young men and women it left abandoned, rudderless, adrift. Too many of them found solace in extremism, only to discover the life vest they'd been tossed was laced with explosives, and thus the beast was fed again. The fatter it got, the greedier it became, like a rat that learned to push a button or an addict who lived needlestick to needlestick.

Hendricks loathed the notion of perpetuating the cycle.

But today, he didn't have much choice.

With a glance up and down the block to see if anyone was looking, he trotted into the street. He walked calmly and quickly, his head down, his eyes fixed on the mottled pavement at his feet.

In the middle of the road, he shrugged off the backpack and set it down. Then he took off, running south toward Greenwich Street.

As he rounded the corner, his laden cargo pockets thudding heavily against his legs, he glanced over his shoulder toward the backpack, but it was no longer in his line of sight. And though he strained to hear, there was no indication anyone had seen him and followed.

He slowed to a walk and dabbed the sweat that had sprung up on his brow with his sleeve. "It's done," he said to Cameron through his Bluetooth earpiece once his heart had stopped racing. "You're on."

22.

SARAH KLINGENBERG POLISHED off a can of Red Bull—her third today—and chucked it into a trash bin as she trotted across the bustling pier. Yesterday, Pier 80 had been just a barren stretch of weed-cracked pavement in San Francisco's Central Waterfront jutting six hundred yards into San Francisco Bay. Now it was the base of operations for one of the biggest Bureau manhunts in history.

The Port of San Francisco was primarily designed for break-bulk cargo, the sorts of things that had to be unloaded individually, such as wooden barrels, steel girders, and industrial-size paper reels. The advent of containerization had sounded San Francisco's death knell as a shipping hub because the port's old-fashioned piers were ill suited for unloading container ships, and there was little real estate to expand them. As a consequence, the majority of cargo shipped to the Bay Area headed to Oakland instead, and many of San Francisco's piers sat vacant.

Today, though, Pier 80 was crowded with armored SWAT vehicles and police helicopters, cop cars and unmarked government sedans. Police boats came and went in a steady stream. Inside the command trailer, dispatchers studied maps and blueprints and coordinated with the tactical units in the field.

The Bureau had learned a lot about the True Islamic Caliphate in the last twenty-three hours. They were part of Sunni Islam's ultraconservative Salafi Jihadist sect, mostly operating out of Syria's lawless southeastern region, and their hatred of the West was second only to their violent opposition to the Assad regime. What the Bureau didn't yet know was why they'd suddenly decided to execute an attack on American soil, where they'd staged it from, or what they intended to strike next.

The Bureau had, however, identified three men associated with the group who'd entered the United States on student visas in the past six months. They'd soon apprehend them, Klingenberg thought, provided her boss—James to his wife and friends, Jimmy to the president, and Assistant Director Osterman to those who worked beneath him in the FBI's Counterterrorism Division—stopped saddling her with bullshit assignments when there was real work to do.

She reached the unmarked sedan the San Francisco office had provided her—a nondescript Ford something-or-other, its once-glossy black faded by years of sun and salt air—and ducked inside. When she closed the door, the relentless din of the command center receded. Then she opened Osterman's e-mail on her phone and clicked the number he'd provided.

Osterman had instructed her to call the CEO of Bellum Industries, Harrison Wentworth, and update him on the investigation. Why, she had no idea. Wentworth was a former three-star general who'd served as the head of the Defense Intelligence Agency under the prior administration, and his son, Trip, headed up the Senate's Appropriations Subcommittee on Homeland Security, so he had a lot of juice inside the Beltway. Lately, he'd been using that juice to lobby for more domestic contracts for his corporation, citing Bellum's successful peacekeeping efforts in New Jersey after Hurricane Sandy hit and in Baltimore during the recent racial tensions. But, to Klingenberg's relief, the widespread privatization of domestic security had proved a nonstarter on the Hill. As far as she was concerned, profit margins had no place in law enforcement, and even if they did, there were half a dozen other firms better suited for the gig; Bellum's reputation overseas was less than stellar.

Wentworth's receptionist answered—icy, competent. Klingenberg explained who she was and why she was calling. The woman put her on hold, no company but the hiss of the open line. Klingenberg had expected better from the private sector. They didn't even have the decency to pipe in music or tell her how much her call mattered.

She remained on hold for eleven minutes. Eleven minutes, as it turned out, was long enough for her to crash, for adrenaline and caffeine to abandon her. As she languished on hold, her thoughts wandered, and her eyes began to close.

"Wentworth here."

His authoritative baritone startled her awake. She

dropped her phone and had to scrabble to pick it up. "Hello, sir. This is Special Agent Sarah Klingenberg. My AD instructed me to update you on the status of the investigation."

"Yes. I gathered as much from my girl."

His girl, she thought. *Jesus*. "Okay, then. What specifically would you like to know?"

"Specifically," he said, "I'd like to know the status of the investigation."

"We're currently pursuing a number of leads in parallel."

"I'm certain you are," he said. "Perhaps you could indulge me by walking me through each of them."

Klingenberg sighed. "State's identified three known associates of the TIC who entered the country separately on student visas in the past six months. We believe they're responsible for executing the attack, although their whereabouts are currently unknown. We're attempting to reconstruct a timeline of their movements now, working forward from their points of entry."

"A sensible approach," he said. "I assume you're pursuing leads nearer to the attack as well?"

"Of course," Klingenberg replied, tetchiness creeping into her voice. "As I'm sure you're aware, all commercial and recreational boating in San Francisco Bay has been suspended. The Coast Guard is in the process of inspecting any vessels already on the water and clearing them to dock at designated locations. It's been an arduous, time-consuming operation, and by their own estimates, they're only halfway through."

"Have they found anything yet?"

"A party boat full of hookers and hedge-fund managers.

A pot shipment coming down the coast from Humboldt County. A few commercial vessels with expired paperwork. Some workers with lapsed visas."

"Are you searching the waterfront as well?"

"Yes. But there's over eight miles of urban waterfront in San Francisco alone, which adds up to a lot of boats and buildings. Washington's pitched in with dedicated satellite coverage and fast-tracked warrants, but boots on the ground are still a limiting factor, and we can't rule out the possibility that the tug might have originated from Oakland or Sausalito."

"Have you the manpower to search nearby municipalities?"

"We've enlisted local PDs, and we've got FBI SWAT on standby, should anybody find anything." She looked through the car's side window at the helicopters lined up at the far end of the pier, dark and sleek, and the armed men milling anxiously around them, all itching for the go order.

"That sounds like a no, which explains the debacle in Alameda."

"The neighbor's tip sounded credible at the time," she snapped.

"The dentist whose apartment you raided has adopted a less charitable view of the situation. He's been crying racial profiling to anybody with a microphone, and I understand he's enlisted the assistance of the ACLU."

"With all due respect, sir, we're doing the best we can with the resources we have."

"What about the threat of additional attacks? I heard something on the news about a gunman in San Mateo."

"False alarm," Klingenberg replied. "Some poor bastard with a BB gun attempting suicide by cop. Truth is, our sources have been quiet. But then, they didn't see the first attack coming either."

"No one did," he replied. "I assume you're in San Francisco now?"

"Yes, sir."

"If you don't mind my asking, how long's it been since you last slept?"

"I don't know. Since before the bomb went off, I guess."

"You must be exhausted."

"I'm fine."

"Of course you are. I didn't mean to suggest otherwise. Tell me, Klingenberg, do you have a room in town yet?"

"Uh, no?" In Klingenberg's confusion, it came out more a question than a statement.

"Then I'll have my girl book you one straightaway. I know some people swear by the Ritz-Carlton, but I've always been partial to the St. Regis. It's where I stay whenever I'm in San Francisco."

"That's very kind of you, sir, but I'm not sure it's entirely appropriate—and anyway, the gesture would be wasted; I'm too busy to have much use for a room."

"Not anymore," he said.

"Come again?"

"Didn't your director tell you? Oh, never mind—how could he have? You were on hold for me when last we spoke."

Klingenberg's stomach went all fluttery. It felt like something more than hunger, exhaustion, and Red Bull. It felt like that moment on a roller coaster where the bottom drops out. "Didn't tell me what?"

"Bellum will be taking command of the investigation from here on out."

There it was. The reason for the call. Klingenberg was being benched—by a goddamn private contractor, of all things. "I don't understand. Have I done something wrong?"

"Of course not. Under the circumstances, your performance has been exemplary. But, thanks to Bellum's efforts to secure Iraq's northwest border, we're well acquainted with this group and their methods, which affords us a tactical advantage you simply do not have."

"Then read me in," she said, her words hollow, reflexive, because she knew how he'd respond.

"Much as I'd like to, I'm afraid you don't have the clearance. It's nothing personal."

"But—"

"Listen," Wentworth said, "I understand how this must seem to you, but in the end you and I both want the same thing. Bellum just happens to be better suited to the task at hand. We're nimbler. More knowledgeable. Less encumbered by red tape. And we have equipment at our disposal that, frankly, the government can't afford. Obviously, your AD and the president agree—they're pushing the proper authorization through Congress as we speak. Don't worry; I'll make sure they both know you did outstanding work. If you ask me, you deserve a break. Take a bath. Get some rest. Order up some room service, if you like, courtesy of your friends at Bellum. I'm sure your AD won't mind; he and I are old friends."

Klingenberg's face burned with anger and shame, but she was too good an agent to let it show in her voice. "Thank you, Mr. Wentworth," she choked out around the lump forming in her throat.

"Think nothing of it," he said.

Wentworth hung up. Klingenberg sat in stunned silence for a long while. Then some sort of commotion at the pier's guard booth caught her attention. An argument, it sounded like. She opened the car door and stood so she could see what was going on, but by the time she did, the argument was over, and the gate arm had been raised.

Sarah Klingenberg looked on in disbelief as thirty Bellum Humvees rolled, one by one, onto the pier—and she wondered how the hell they'd gotten here so fast.

23.

CAMERON DREW A steeling breath, and released it slowly. It came out shaky. She told herself that was okay— helpful, even.

She took out her Bluetooth earpiece and plucked a second burner phone from the center console. Using its browser, she Googled the number she was looking for and clicked the link to dial.

The phone rang twice; the call connected. "San Francisco tip line." The syllables tumbled out with neither inflection nor the appropriate stresses, as though the woman who'd picked up had said them so often, they'd ceased to have any meaning.

Cameron couldn't blame her. This number had been broadcast on every station, local and national, and printed in every story about the blast since Homeland Security had set it up late yesterday. She'd probably been dealing with cranks nonstop since she'd come on shift.

"I—I'm calling to report a crime," Cameron said, her voice a sharp whisper.

"Ma'am, if you're the victim or a witness of a crime in progress, you need to hang up and call 911."

"You don't understand," Cameron hissed. "I'm on Baker Street in San Francisco between Greenwich and Lombard. A man outside just dropped a backpack in the street and ran away. He...he looked *Muslim*."

Ugh. Just saying those words made Cameron feel dirty. She was preying on prejudice and the looming fear of follow-up attacks. But there was no denying, they had the intended effect.

"Please stay on the line, ma'am," the operator said, urgency creeping into her tone. "I'd like to put you on the phone with my superior. But first, can you confirm your location for me?"

"Baker Street, San Francisco, between Greenwich and Lombard."

"And what did this man look like?"

"He, uh, had a long dark beard and was wearing some kind of flowy off-white shirt, I think. Wait—something's happening. He's come back. It's...it's like he's looking for something. *Oh God, I think he sees me, please hurry!*"

Cameron hung up the phone. Then she popped off its back cover and removed the battery. The SIM card too, which she snapped in half.

That done, she replaced her Bluetooth earpiece, raised her binoculars—one of the two pairs she'd purchased at Walmart yesterday—and watched the Homeland Security agents manning the perimeter of the old base. It was hard to make out fine details because her hands were so unsteady, shaking not from fear, but from adrenaline. Still, she saw enough to get the broad strokes.

Both were startled into action when their radios went off. They conferred a moment and then left their posts and sprinted toward Baker Street, one down Greenwich, the other down Lombard.

"You still there?" Cameron asked.

"Yeah," Hendricks replied in her earpiece.

"They're on the move."

"Both of them?"

"Yeah."

"You must've been convincing, then. Good job."

"Thanks. I'll admit, it was a hell of a rush," she replied, grateful he wasn't here to see her dopey grin or the flush in her cheeks.

"Don't get used to it," he admonished. "Okay, I'm going dark. Remember: get clear, and hole up somewhere quiet—"

"—with an open Wi-Fi network," she finished, because they'd been over the plan a thousand times. "Got it."

"Good. I'll call you when I need you." Hendricks disconnected.

Cameron smiled again and started the car.

As far as she was concerned, his next call couldn't come soon enough.

Halfway up Greenwich, Hendricks ducked into the recessed entryway of an apartment building and patted his pockets as if looking for his keys. There was no need for the charade, it turned out—the Homeland Security agent who sprinted by didn't so much as glance his way.

Hendricks poked his head out of the entrance alcove and watched the man round the corner onto Baker Street. Then he headed west on Greenwich once more.

When he reached Lyon, he looked both ways and then crossed it at a trot, slowing as he reached the far sidewalk. Rather than heading north toward the Presidio's Lombard Street gate, Hendricks went south. The gate was too visible for his taste, Lombard Street too well traveled. Plus, half the cops in San Francisco were, at present, within the Presidio's walls. If they'd bit hard on Cameron's diversion, Hendricks figured they'd most likely leave via that gate to check it out.

The keening wail of sirens behind him—quiet at first, but building quickly, like a migraine—confirmed Hendricks's assumption. He didn't turn around; he just kept walking and watched three SFPD cruisers rocket through the gate, lights flashing, in the distorted reflection of a parked delivery van's windshield. Then they were swallowed by the neighborhood, their sirens muffled slightly by the buildings.

The backpack he'd dropped contained a pair of road flares and a scissor jack he'd scavenged from the Altima's trunk and taped to a spare burner phone. It was utterly harmless, but when the Feds X-rayed it, it'd look scary enough to keep them busy for a while.

Hendricks passed behind the delivery van and stopped. It blocked him from view of the row houses to his right. To his left, beyond the low stone wall that marked the edge of the Presidio, was an overgrown rise, shrubs huddled beneath large trees. Hendricks glanced around to be sure there was no one else in sight and then he vaulted over the wall.

He crouched behind it for a second, listening for any indication he'd been spotted. He heard none, so he scrabbled upslope through the trees until the ground leveled.

When he reached the edge of the tree cover, he untied the windbreaker from around his waist, turned it right-side in, and slipped it on. Emblazoned on the back, both shoulders, and left breast were yellow block letters that read FBI.

On a campus crawling with law enforcement, blending in made more sense than slinking around. The problem was, official uniforms were hard to come by. It always looked so easy in the movies: knock a guy out, drag him into a supply closet, emerge seconds later in his clothes. In reality, it was damn near impossible to put a guy down with one blow, much less strip someone while he was unconscious. Which was what Hendricks had told Cameron when she'd suggested it.

She'd frowned then. Fell silent. Opened the browser on her phone. Then she turned the screen around to face him. On it was an image of an FBI raid jacket. "Is this really what they look like or is that only in the movies too?"

"That's really what they look like."

"Then why not just make one?"

Cameron bought a roll of yellow duct tape and an X-Acto knife at a craft store just off the highway. Then they'd hit a uniform-supply place to pick up the jacket. She carved the letters freehand and applied them in the parking lot of a tamale joint that was closed on Sundays, the jacket laid out on the hood of the car. Hendricks had been dubious, but once she was done, he was forced to admit the illusion was convincing. Sure, it fell apart if you put your face right up to it, but if anybody got that close to him, he had bigger problems than the texture of the duct tape showing.

Afterward, since Cameron didn't need it any longer, he pocketed the X-Acto knife. You never knew when a sharp blade would come in handy.

Hendricks watched from the trees awhile, taking in the scene. He was at the edge of a winding drive. A neighborhood of connected townhomes disappeared into the green off to his left. A pair of low-slung buildings stood to his right. Everything was off-white with red roofs, some of them actually clay tile, the others red shingles meant to convey the impression of clay.

A Park Police cruiser rolled by. Hendricks ducked into the shadows as it passed. Once it was no longer in sight, he stepped out of the woods. The command tent—and, therefore, the cell on wheels—was northwest of his position. He could either head west through the neighborhood or go north toward the commercialized end of the old base.

He chose north. Walked past a tennis court, a social club. A couple of uniformed cops loitered outside the latter, and they eyed Hendricks as he approached.

He nodded at them, heart thudding.

They nodded back, and he continued on his way.

24.

S WEET JESUS, DID Lois feel like shit.

Hangover seemed like such an insufficient word for what she had. It suggested a sense of mild discomfort that could be dispelled by aspirin, water, and a greasy breakfast. This wasn't that. No, what she had was an *affliction*. A full-on disability.

Lois had slept deeply through the night—no surprise, since she vaguely remembered washing down several back-pain pills with wine yesterday. While she slept, she'd dreamed of loss, of ache, of big events forgotten until too late and important things misplaced.

Daylight was an assault—a sharp stab between her eyes, a slithery uncoiling in her stomach. Every time her eyelids flitted open—from pain, anxiety, or her uneasy dreams expelling her from sleep—she immediately regretted it. Even the red-black static of the light through her closed eyelids was almost more than she could bear. For a time, she slung a forearm over them to block it out, but her own body heat began to make her queasy.

She wondered how she'd managed not to throw up yet. Then she ran her tongue across her lips, tasted bile, and wondered if she *had* thrown up but was simply too foggy to remember.

Lois's bedroom was airy and light. Blond wood, mismatched whitewashed furniture, and soft-hued fabrics combined to give the place a beachy feel. Oversize mirrors, one freestanding and another on her vanity, made the space seem even bigger than it was. Her husband, Cal, called it their island retreat. Today it seemed to amplify the afternoon light. Lois felt like she was at the center of a boardwalk busker's steel drum.

I swear, if I survive this I'm never going to drink again, she thought.

As her eyes adjusted to the sunlight, Lois realized someone was standing in the doorway. Male, and visible only in silhouette.

"Cal?" she asked hopefully, though some small aching part of her knew that it wasn't.

"Lois, I'm sorry," Frank said softly, "but Cal's not here."

The unfamiliar voice startled her. She jerked upright, her face twisting in agony as her head responded to the sudden movement. "Wh-who are you? What are you doing here? Where's Cal? Why are you wearing his things?"

"Easy," he said, stepping just inside the doorway but not approaching her. He was white. Older. Rail-thin. His eyes were the palest blue she'd ever seen. His hair was mussed, and he had on one of Cal's sweat suits, the sleeves of the sweatshirt pushed up to expose wiry, liver-spotted forearms. His elbows were at right angles, his hands in front of him. One was balled into a fist; the other held a glass of water. Ella, improbably, followed him into the room and stopped at his feet, her fluffy tail wagging. "My name's Max Rausch, remember? We met yesterday. You...had a little too much to drink last night, so I helped you up to bed."

Lois's face fell as the events of yesterday came rushing back. Her brow furrowed. Her lip trembled momentarily, and then stilled. As fear abandoned her, the tension drained from her muscles, and her shoulders sagged. "Max. Of course. Forgive me. Yesterday, I...I wasn't at my best."

"There's nothing to forgive," he said. "I brought you some aspirin and a glass of water. I figured you might need it."

She beckoned him closer. He dropped the pills into her hand. She popped them into her mouth and took the glass from him to wash them down.

"Easy," he said. "Sip, don't gulp. You probably don't remember, but the water you drank last night didn't stay down."

Lois flushed with embarrassment and looked around but saw no sign of any mess.

"It's fine. I took care of it. The empty glass fell off the nightstand when you tried to put it back, and I heard it shatter. When I came in to check on you, you said you needed a trashcan. I barely managed to get to the bathroom and back in time. Then I, uh, sat with you awhile to make sure you were okay."

"Thank you," she said. "You're very kind."

Frank startled her by laughing.

"Did I say something funny?" she asked.

"No," he said, smiling. "It's just...*very kind* is not something I'm called often."

"Really? That surprises me. It seems to me you've been nothing but kind since you arrived."

"Maybe so," he said, "but when I was younger, I was not the nicest guy."

"I doubt that's true."

"It is. I was a thug. A criminal. Sometimes I hurt people."

He wasn't sure why he'd told her that. He expected her to recoil. To ask him to leave. Instead, she said, "Are you familiar with Heraclitus of Ephesus, Max?"

He cocked his head, confused by the conversational hairpin. "Can't say as I am," he said. "Is it a person or a thing?"

"A person," she said, smiling. "A pre-Socratic Greek philosopher, in fact."

"Oh. I don't know a thing about philosophy. Never had much use for it."

"Mr. Rausch, you wound me. I spent thirty years teaching Classics before retiring."

"You were a teacher?"

"A professor, yes, first at UNC and eventually across the bay at UC Berkeley."

"Huh. Then you *extra* wouldn't have liked the younger me. He never met a teacher he didn't manage to piss off."

"Clearly the two of you have little in common, then—just as Heraclitus would have predicted."

"How's that?"

"He believed that change was the only constant in the universe. As he observed, 'No man can step into the same river twice, for it is not the same river—and he is not the same man.'"

"So you're saying I ain't that guy anymore."

"I'm saying everything, even what we think of as our essential self, is fluid."

"I dunno," he replied. "Seems to me, most people never change."

"I think you're wrong. We all do. Most of us simply never change *direction*."

"Maybe," he said. "Maybe not. But I don't see how it matters. Either way, I'm stuck carrying around the memories of what I've done."

"Those memories might be not a burden, but a gift. It's possible you carry them to remind yourself why you've chosen a different path."

"That's a nice thought," he said. "But if I could, I'd ditch 'em in a heartbeat."

Her face clouded. "I suppose we all have things we wish we could forget."

"Listen, Lois. About Cal—"

"Has he called?" she asked, sounding shrill and desperate but not disingenuous, as if she'd convinced herself that he was somehow still okay but knew the illusion wouldn't hold if examined closely. "Is he on his way?"

"No, Lois, he hasn't called," he said, his tone gentle but insistent. "That's what I wanted to talk to you about."

A brief glimmer of understanding flickered across her face and then vanished, replaced once more by that same odd incuriosity Frank witnessed yesterday and had attributed to the drugs. "Perhaps later," she said flatly, and then, the topic dismissed, she perked up some. "First, I think I'd like to try to eat some breakfast, since it seems these aspirin are staying down."

Last time Frank had taken notice of a clock, it was after three—a little late for breakfast, but he didn't bother to point that out to her. It was one of many things he didn't bother pointing out.

Lois threw back the covers and tried to get out of bed, but she was shaky, her body weak. Frank wondered how many of those muscle relaxants she'd taken yesterday before the Park Police interrupted her by knocking on her door. Not enough to kill her, it would seem—but if he had to guess, he'd say she hadn't been far off.

He watched uncomfortably for a minute while she struggled to get up, uncertain if she'd accept his assistance. But when it became clear she'd never make it downstairs on her own, he took her hand and helped her to her feet. She frowned but didn't object.

Once she got going, she did okay, although he linked arms with her on the way downstairs for safety. Frank's strength wasn't what it once was—there was a time when his slender frame had been coiled with muscle—but Lois was so slight, he had no trouble keeping her upright. They apparently moved too slowly for Ella, though, because she raced past them down the stairs.

"So," Frank said once they'd reached the kitchen and he'd deposited her on a stool beside the island, "what can I get you?"

"That's very kind of you, Max, but I can't have you cook me breakfast in my own home."

"Of course you can. In fact, I insist. So what'll it be? I make a mean omelet. You want one?"

He watched her expression cycle from disgust to curiosity to outright hunger as she tried the idea on for size. "I'll take that as a yes," he said. "How about coffee? I made some earlier—I hope you don't mind—but I finished it hours ago. I'd be happy to put on some more."

This time, she ran through the same cycle of expressions in reverse and wound up little green. "I think I'll stick to water for now, thanks," she said.

Frank got Lois some more water. Then he opened her fridge and dug around. Even after their feast last night, it was well stocked—eggs, milk, several kinds of meats and cheeses, and scads of local produce. He selected an herbed goat cheese, thin-sliced prosciutto, and some leftover asparagus, as well as a few sprigs of chive to chop for garnish. Then butter for the pan—an expensive, restaurant-grade nonstick made of anodized aluminum—and three eggs.

He set the pan on the Viking cooktop, put two pats of butter inside. The burner clicked three times when he cranked the dial and then lit with a whoosh, blue flames licking the underside of the pan. He cracked the eggs into a bowl. Seasoned them with salt and pepper. Beat them while the butter melted. Poured the mixture into the pan. Fed Ella a small scrap of prosciutto while the eggs set. All the while, Lois watched in bemused silence.

"What?" he asked when he noticed her expression.

"It's just…" She hesitated—maybe wondering if she was about to offend him—and then continued. "You must be the most thoughtful home invader on the planet, to make me breakfast."

The briefest frown touched his features, an expression he replaced immediately with a genial smile. "I didn't invade nothing—you let me in!"

"Did I?" she asked as he added filling to the omelet and folded it. "I confess, it's all a bit fuzzy. I remember I was in the tub and heard you knocking."

It was the Park Police she'd heard, not Frank. "You came downstairs," he said, rooting through the cupboards, "saw me outside"—he found a plate and set it on the island in front of her—"and let me in." He grabbed the pan and expertly slid the omelet onto the plate with a nudge from the spatula he'd taken from a ceramic crock beside the stove.

"To the left of the sink," she said, when he looked flummoxed trying to find the silverware drawer. "No, your other left."

Frank found the drawer, opened it, and handed her a fork. She cut a bite from the center of the omelet and put it in her mouth. At first, she chewed tentatively, as though worried it would be terrible or—more likely—that her body would rebel. But when she swallowed, she immediately took another. By her third bite, she was practically shoveling it in.

"This is delicious," she said around a mouthful of omelet. "Thank you."

"My pleasure," Frank replied. "It's been a long time since I got to cook in a kitchen this nice. You have a lovely home."

"Thanks. I think so too. Of course, it's not actually *ours*—we pay the Presidio Trust twelve grand a month for the privilege of staying here. Cal always tells me that it makes more sense to buy than rent, that our money would go farther elsewhere. But I like it here, and in the end, we're all just renting anyway, aren't we?"

On that point, Frank agreed.

He watched with a chef's satisfaction as she demolished the omelet. When she was finished, he took the plate and cleaned it, Lois objecting all the while.

"How're you feeling?" he asked finally as he dried the plate.

"Better," she replied. "More myself."

She *looked* better. Her eyes clearer. Her color returning. Her movements more assured. "Good, because we need to talk. About Calvin. About you."

"I don't know what you mean. Cal's stuck in Reno."

"No, Lois, he's not."

Her face was a mask of innocent surprise, brittle and unconvincing as a porcelain doll's. "Oh, are the flights back on schedule? If so, there's every chance he's in the air by now. In fact, he'll probably be here any minute—and he'll doubtless think me a fool for letting a stranger spend the night."

"You don't really believe that, do you?"

"Of course I do. Why shouldn't I?"

"Lois, I was in your master bath last night. I saw the pills, the knife. I heard Cal's message."

"I…I don't…"

Lois didn't finish her sentence. She couldn't. Because when her mask slipped, it shattered. What began as a slight tremor in her hands as she raised them to her face in shock and horror became a series of violent, choking sobs that racked her body. It was as if she'd just heard Calvin's final message for the first time, not simply replayed it in her mind.

Her breath came in ragged gasps, and she released it in keening wails, her mouth wide open, her eyes clenched shut, the cords of her neck straining from the effort. Tears and snot streaked her face. These were not dignified widow's tears; this was the ugly cry of a woman who'd had her heart ripped out. Frank recognized the difference because he'd put his share of husbands and fathers in the ground.

Unconsciously, Lois drew her knees upward, primal instinct reducing her to a wounded animal, curling into a fetal position for protection. Frank reacted without thinking and was glad of it. She would have fallen off her stool if he hadn't rushed around the island to catch her.

He wrapped his arms around her and held her close while she shuddered from grief. He said nothing, just squeezed with all he had and let her cry. There was no point in saying anything—she was beyond the comfort of words.

Eventually, her cries subsided. Her breathing slowed. Her body stilled. Frank released her and was pleased to see she stayed upright. She dabbed her eyes with her pajama sleeve and wiped it across her nose like a child. Her eyes were bloodshot and glistened with tears.

A hysterical laugh escaped her lips. It startled Frank, and worried him too. He hoped he hadn't pushed her to some kind of psychotic break. "What's so funny?"

"I just remembered an old joke my mama used to tell, is all."

"A joke." Not questioning, exactly, but skeptical.

"That's right. It was about a righteous man and a terrible storm. Town officials warned him the river that ran beside his house was going to overrun its banks and ordered him to evacuate, but he refused. 'I put my faith in God,' he said. 'If I'm in danger, He will protect me.'

"As the storm raged and the waters rose, his neighbors loaded up their car and said, 'We're headed to higher ground, and we've got room for you—come with us!' But the man declined. 'I'm in no danger. God will save me,' he said.

"The river breached its banks and lapped against his

porch. A man in a canoe paddled by. 'Hurry into my canoe! I'll take you to safety!' But the man said, 'No, thanks. God will save me.'

"As the floodwaters rose higher, the man retreated inside and was eventually forced onto his roof. A helicopter spotted him and lowered down a rescuer who shouted, 'Grab my hand so I can pull you up!' But still, the man refused. 'God will save me!' he said. Shortly after, he was swept away and drowned.

"When he reached heaven, the man said angrily to God, 'I put my faith in You—how could You just let me die?' And God said, 'My son, I sent you a car, a canoe, and a helicopter. What more were you looking for?'"

She laughed again, the sort of raw, guffawing laughter that strikes at funerals and is only encouraged by attempts to suppress it. Frank tried his best to smile politely, although he thought that as jokes went, this one was pretty weak. When Lois saw his pained half-smile, it only made her laugh harder.

"I know," she said, tears streaming down her cheeks. "Mama must've told that joke a thousand times, and I never found it funny either!"

"Then why are you laughing?"

"Because it occurred to me that you're my goddamn helicopter. And now I can't get my Mama's smug-ass voice saying 'What more were you looking for?' out of my head."

"You saying you believe all that 'God works in mysterious ways' bullshi—er, stuff?"

That elicited a fresh peal of laughter from Lois. "No!" she said. "That's the point! Mama dragged my ass to Sunday service every week until I went away to college, and it never meant a thing to me. But here you are, and thanks to you, here *I* am. Now, maybe I'm just grasping because"— and here her smile faltered, a deep reservoir of sadness peeking through—"because of Cal, but to me, it feels like fate. And if that's the case, when I finally do pass through the Pearly Gates, that old biddy's never going to let me hear the end of it."

"I hope you're right about all that," Frank said, and he meant it. Not because he much believed—he'd seen so many senseless acts of violence in his life, he figured the universe was either random or outright cruel—but because he liked the notion that in his useless, fucked-up life, he might've done one good thing, if only by accident.

"I do too. But either way, thank you."

"Anytime," he said.

The moment was interrupted by an unexpected sound: the melodic tinkle of glass breaking. It happened so quickly and with no evident cause that at first Frank thought he had imagined it. But then Ella growled, her hackles rising, and a matte-black cylinder skittered down the hallway from the living room into the kitchen.

"Get down!" Frank yelled. He threw himself at Lois, knocking her off her stool. She shrieked as they fell and was silenced when the landing knocked the wind from her lungs.

A half a second later, the room was filled with blinding light, followed by a firework pop so loud that Frank's ears ran warm with blood. He collapsed, disoriented, atop Lois, who struggled to get free.

Then, as one, the front and back doors imploded with a brittle snap of wood—not that Frank or Lois could hear or see—and armed men in riot gear stormed the house.

25.

As Hendricks scaled the Lincoln Boulevard on-ramp toward the Golden Gate Bridge tollbooths, the Homeland Security agent stationed at its top looked him up and down. The man's expression was inscrutable, thanks to a pair of sport sunglasses, and his gloved palms rested on the butt of his MP5 assault rifle, which hung from a tactical sling across his chest.

Hendricks was flushed and short of breath. Because of the hike across the Presidio, he told himself, although he worried it was more than that. Sweat beaded on his brow. His skin crawled. His wound itched like crazy. He worried he'd look like he was going for a weapon if he scratched at it. He worried he'd look shifty if he didn't.

The stolen .45 rested heavily in the pocket of his cargo pants. After a brief internal debate, he'd elected not to move it to his waistband once he made it onto Presidio grounds. Now he regretted that decision. He had no intention of using it against law enforcement, but damn if having it within easy reach wouldn't offer him some comfort now.

The route to the bridge had taken him down Pilots' Row, a neighborhood of Colonial Revivals originally built for army aviators. He caught glimpses of the bridge through the trees to his left as he walked, but he couldn't see it in any detail. When he climbed the on-ramp, the trees dropped away. The view that greeted him was heartbreaking and confounding. Even as tense as he was, marching into the densest concentration of law enforcement agents this side of the Hoover Building, he couldn't help but stare.

The bridge's roadway was chunked and gapped as it drew near the southern tower. Cars were piled atop one another on either side. Charred bodies lay just outside open doors and protruded from shattered windshields. There were survivors up there too, some trapped inside their ruined cars, others wandering nervously while they waited for rescue. There'd been reports that a few of them had plunged to their deaths during the night. Whether they'd jumped or fell, no one was sure, but the result was the same either way. Two hundred and seventy feet is a long way to fall—four full seconds from bridge to bay. When they hit the water, they were moving so fast that they might as well have landed on a city street.

The tower itself was blackened but stood true, although a few of the steel support ropes that ran parallel to the tower dangled freely, frayed at the ends and curled like broken guitar strings. Smoke still drifted on occasion from below as leftover accelerant caught fire, only to be quickly doused. The undamaged northern tower seemed impossibly small from where Hendricks stood, which made sense, given that it was almost two miles distant.

The bay was littered with government boats: police, Coast Guard, fire-and-rescue. Most were small, ugly, and utilitarian—scuffed hulls and faded paint, pilothouses crowded with antennas and equipment—but a few were quite large. Several hundred yards to the west of the bridge was a fog bank as pale and solid as the cliffs of Dover, and a Coast Guard cutter hovered like a ghost ship at its edge. A massive crane barge with a ruined pickup truck in its grasp sat to the bridge's immediate right, the twisted wreck swinging like a pendulum as the crane pivoted to deposit it on a flattop barge beside it.

As Hendricks approached the top of the on-ramp, he forced himself to give the Homeland Security agent guarding it a friendly nod. It felt awkward, insincere, and in that instant, Hendricks was painfully aware that this plan hinged on a disguise made out of duct tape.

The man eyed him a long moment. Shifted his weight and adjusted his hand on his gunstock. Hendricks tensed. He was too far away to engage hand to hand but not nearly far enough for the man to miss him if he opened fire.

Then the man said, "Fucking awful, isn't it?"

"You ain't kidding," Hendricks replied. "It makes me hope there's such a thing as hell—death's too easy for anybody who could do a thing like this."

"I hear you," the man said, and then a quadcopter camera drone zipping toward the bridge from the command tent drew his gaze. Hendricks slipped past him without another word, into the teeming nerve center of the rescue effort.

From Hendricks's perspective, the place was an operational nightmare. There were cop cars, fire trucks, and military vehicles everywhere. At least half of them were occupied, their doors open, radios crackling. People seemed to dart around at random. SFPD and Park Police uniforms abounded, but FBI and ATF agents were sprinkled here and there as well, their nylon raid jackets fluttering in the breeze. Men and women in military fatigues trotted back and forth between the command tent to the south of the tollbooths and the sawhorses that marked the point at which the roadway was deemed structurally unsound. Homeland Security agents in riot gear stood guard at all the access points.

It looked to Hendricks like it had been a while since a survivor was extracted from the wreckage. Ambulances lined the FasTrak lane that bypassed the tollbooths, their drivers antsy and wide-eyed. Two Life Flight helicopters sat in the bridge pavilion's parking lot, their crews milling just outside. Some paced. Others smoked. All of them looked tired, strung out, on edge.

Hendricks took in most of this through the screen of his smartphone. He walked with it in front of him, scowling and occasionally tapping at it with his thumbs as if he were texting. Smartphones made for excellent camouflage. People were less likely to question your presence if you seemed like you belonged, and these days, belonging meant wandering obliviously around with your eyes glued to your phone's screen.

But the phone was no mere prop for Hendricks; it was also a useful piece of tech. He kept the camera app open as he walked, and, pretending that he was looking for a decent signal or trying to see the screen in full sunlight, he alternated between live shots of whatever was in front of him and glimpses over his shoulder, via the forward-facing camera, to see if he was being followed.

The cell on wheels was set apart a ways from all the chaos, which made approaching it tricky. It was a good fifty yards south of the command tent, to which it was connected by a cord the width of Hendricks's wrist, and twenty yards from the nearest cluster of vehicles. No one was guarding it, which was good, but no one passed near it either, which would make any attempt to do so painfully obvious.

He snapped a pic. Sent it off to Cameron via text. "You still with me?" he asked.

"Sure am," she replied in his Bluetooth earpiece. Hendricks could hear the clink of dishes and quiet conversation all around her. A coffee shop, she'd said. Then she'd hit him with some mumbo-jumbo about how she planned to use its unencrypted Wi-Fi network to gain access to the other computers on it, which would decrease the processing time for all the data they were about to steal. He'd barely understood a word.

"Good. I sent you something. Any updates on our bomb scare?"

"CNN and local news are on the scene. The bomb squad's cordoned off the area. They're waiting for a robot to arrive as we speak so they can safely detonate it."

Her tone was sharp. Brittle. "You sound annoyed," he said.

"More like disgusted. Two more witnesses came forward claiming they saw, and I quote, 'an Arab-looking guy' drop the bag and flee the scene. One of 'em swore up and down this nonexistent perp was wearing some kind of explosive vest."

"People are scared. Nervous. Bracing for the next attack. They see what they expect to see. That's why eyewitnesses are so untrustworthy. You'd be surprised how easy it is to plant the seeds of false memory. They probably don't even realize they're lying."

"Somehow," she said, "that doesn't make me feel any better."

"Did the pic come through yet?"

"Yeah. Pulling it up now."

"Is that what I'm looking for?"

"Yup. That's our Bessie, all right."

Hendricks smiled despite himself. "You really want to make that happen, don't you?" She'd called the damn thing Bessie the whole drive north while they were hashing out their plan.

"What else are you supposed to name a COW?" she asked. "Have you reached it yet?"

"I'm headed toward it now," he said, head down, snaking through the crowd. "What next?"

"There should be some kind of control panel."

Up close, the cell on wheels looked to be part cargo trailer, part TV-news van, and part moon lander. It was a wheeled box of road-grimy white maybe four feet high with a ladder at one end and a trailer hitch at the other. From its center, a telescoping antenna pointed twenty feet into the air, and a triangular brace extended from each of its four corners, like landing gear, to hold it steady.

"The whole thing's panels," he said.

"The one we want would be waist height or higher. We're looking for electronics, not anything mechanical, and no designer in her right mind would put an access terminal at ground height."

Hendricks raised his phone into the air toward the tower as if he had just lost the signal and started to circle it slowly, taking pics and texting them to her. In the distance, an equipment tech in his midtwenties eyed Hendricks with confusion and then began walking toward him.

"There!" Cameron said. "Stop. Go back. Not the last pic you sent, the one before. Top left."

The panel Cameron directed him to looked like the door of a breaker box, except that it was white, not gray. There was a keyhole beside the recessed handle. Hendricks tried the handle anyway, hoping for a bit of luck. It was locked, because of course it was.

"Hey," the man headed toward him called, not angry yet, but agitated. He was taller than Hendricks by a few inches and well muscled beneath a layer of baby fat. He wore a tool belt low around his waist and soon was close enough—thirty yards or so—that Hendricks could make out its contents. Screwdrivers. Wire cutters. Voltmeter. Electrical tape. An assortment of pliers. They clanked and rattled as he walked.

Hendricks set his phone down atop the cell on wheels, reached into the right thigh pocket of his cargo pants, and took out Cameron's electric toothbrush. He'd come across it when they were taking inventory of their belongings on the plane and couldn't help but laugh. "What's so funny?" Cameron had asked, reddening.

"Most outlaws aren't so diligent about their oral hygiene," he'd replied.

Hendricks had removed its brush head and filed down the metal spindle on the curb while Cameron doctored up his windbreaker. Now he carefully inserted it into the lock.

The man was twenty yards away, the cell on wheels between them, so Hendricks was partially obscured from his view. "Hey!" he shouted. This time, several people glanced up at them.

Hendricks thought, *Please work*, over and over, a silent mantra.

Hendricks was not a seasoned lock picker. Give him a set of rakes and torsion wrenches, and he'd get through a door eventually, but not with any speed or grace. Lock-bumping—in which a specially made key is inserted partway into a lock and then rapped with a mallet so that the vibration causes the pin stacks inside the lock to line up momentarily—was far more reliable for an amateur like him. But each make of lock required its own bump key, and the process was far from stealthy.

Thanks to recreational lock picking's rise in popularity, Hendricks was able to learn a trick or two online. For instance, he'd found out that you could insert the spindle of an electric toothbrush into a lock and use its high-speed vibration like a computer hacker uses a brute-force attack. Instead of one rap of the mallet, one chance to turn the lock, the constant shaking knocks the pin stacks around until they line up just right.

At least, that was the theory. Until today, Hendricks had seen it only on YouTube. The guy who'd posted the video warned that the average electric toothbrush spindle was too short to work on a door lock and too thick to fit inside most keyholes. He'd also warned that if you filed the spindle down too far, it'd snap off and the lock would *never* open. But done right, he said, anyone could pick a lock this way, and to demonstrate, he'd popped open half a dozen padlocks, lockboxes, and storage lockers in seconds flat.

At the time, it had seemed impressive to Hendricks. Now he hoped he didn't wind up getting caught because he'd been dumb enough to believe something he saw on the Internet.

The tech was fifteen yards away and agitated enough that he'd attracted the attention of some nearby personnel. Hendricks pressed the button on the handle of the toothbrush and winced as the motor hummed to life. The spindle rattled in the lock like pennies in a cup holder.

He held his breath.

Twisted the handle.

To his surprise, the lock opened.

Inside the panel was a keyboard. A bunch of lights, toggles, buttons, and ports. A small display screen, green writing on black background, lines of data scrolling by.

"I'm in," he said quietly. He glanced up. Ten yards and closing fast.

"You see a USB port?"

"No," he said. Her tense silence spoke volumes. "Wait—yes. What now?"

"Pop in the thumb drive that I gave you."

"Done. Now what?"

"Is the screen giving you a prompt of any kind?"

"Uh…"

Cameron sighed. "Just show me."

"How?"

"Jesus, you're hopeless. Hang on."

Hendricks's burner began to vibrate atop the cell on wheels, spinning a minute or two clockwise with every pulse. He picked it up and clicked the notice. One of the apps Cameron had installed on it launched, and her face popped up on his screen. "Hold me up so I can see it," she said. He complied. "Okay, listen carefully."

She told him what to type. He set the phone back down and punched the characters into the keyboard, hunt-and-peck-style, with his index fingers. "Uh, the screen just went blank. Nothing but a blinking cursor in the top left corner."

"That's expected," she said.

"What do I do now?"

"Nothing," she said. "Once the exploit's done uploading, remove the thumb drive, close the door, and get the eff outta Dodge."

"How will I know the exploit's done uploading?"

"Just watch the screen."

"For what?"

"You'll know it when you see it."

"Uh, buddy?" The tech had reached the other side of the cell on wheels. "You want to tell me what the hell you think you're doing?"

Hendricks eyed the screen. Then the tech. Then the screen again. Nothing on it had changed that he could see. "I don't know what you mean."

"I *mean*, why are you fucking around with my machine?" He began to circle around to Hendricks.

"Oh, that," Hendricks said nonchalantly. "My signal keeps cutting out. I thought it'd get better the closer I got to the tower, but no such luck. So then I figured there's gotta be some kind of knob on this thing somewhere that'll turn it up. But the goddamn thing is locked."

The corner braces forced the tech to swing a little wide. Otherwise, he would've seen the open panel door and called to the guards—who were already a little too interested in this exchange for Hendricks's liking.

Hendricks glanced down. Saw the screen flicker. The code vanished, replaced by a message in block letters made of zeros:

HELLO MY NAME IS BESSIE

Then the message disappeared, and code began to scroll by once more.

Hendricks removed the thumb drive. Pocketed it, along with the electric toothbrush. Eased the panel door closed as the man rounded the corner. It locked automatically with a click.

The man had an ID badge on a lanyard around his neck declaring him to be Aaron Stanton of the NCSC—Homeland Security's National Cybersecurity Center. "This thing's locked for a reason."

"Which is?"

"So morons who can't stop the clock on their microwave from blinking twelve don't fuck with it and knock out our whole damn communications network," he said.

"Listen, asshole," Hendricks said, affecting umbrage, "I'm not some dipshit off the street—I'm a special agent with the FBI." He was always amazed at how well a little bit of swagger sold a flimsy grift.

"Oh. Sorry," Stanton said, his words dripping sarcasm. "I didn't realize you were a Feeb. I'll try to talk slower."

Hendricks leaned in close and grabbed Stanton's ID badge. He made a show of scrutinizing it closely. "Hey!" Stanton exclaimed, snatching at it. "What the hell?"

"I want to make sure I spell your name right when I report you," Hendricks replied.

"For what? Doing my job? You're lucky *I* don't report *you*. If you'd so much as pressed a button on this baby, I would've. So how about you get the fuck away from her before I change my mind?"

"Fine. Have it your way. I don't have time for this bullshit." Hendricks turned and walked off. Once it became clear the argument was over, the attention of the crowd began to wander. Stanton, though, was still suspicious. He looked the cell on wheels over carefully, even opening the panel door and checking inside.

When Hendricks was twenty paces away, Stanton shouted, "Hey, dipshit—not so fast."

Hendricks tensed. Reddened. Turned. Those near enough to hear Stanton turned too, their gazes focused on Hendricks once more. A few placed their hands on their guns. Hendricks broke out in a nervous sweat.

"What now?" he asked, as casually as possible.

Stanton smiled like a grand master declaring checkmate and waved something at Hendricks. "You forgot your phone."

Hendricks didn't have to feign embarrassment; his rattled nerves made his performance as convincing as it was effortless. He jogged over to Stanton and took his phone. Once he had it, he set off walking west—toward the nearest off-ramp, toward anywhere but here.

26.

YANCEY SET HIS items on the counter beside the register and flashed the teenage girl behind it a smile. She was young, pretty, and Somali. Her skin was light brown. Her hair was hidden beneath a vibrant head scarf of orange and pink. Her clothes were otherwise indiscernible from any reasonably modest Western teen's. She was chewing gum and texting someone as he approached, thumbs flying across her cell phone's screen. But when she turned her attention to him, her face went immediately expressionless. "That it?" she said, eyeing the items he'd set down, her tone bored, her accent Californian.

"Actually, little lady, I'd also love a book of matches, if you please." He cranked up the wattage on his smile and threw in a wink for good measure.

The girl snapped her gum, rolled her eyes, and rang him up. Then she grabbed some matchbooks from beneath the counter and tossed them in the general direction of his bag, her eyes glued once more to her cell phone's screen. A couple of the matchbooks landed inside. The others missed. One bounced off Yancey and landed at his feet.

The smile died on Yancey's face. He snatched the cell phone from her hand and launched it across the room. It ricocheted off a magazine rack and shattered when it hit the floor.

"Hey!" the girl exclaimed. "What the—"

Yancey flipped aside his sport coat to reveal the wooden grip of his revolver. The girl's eyes widened and she shrank a little behind the counter. Her chin quivered as tears threatened.

"T-t-take whatever you want, just please don't hurt me."

"I ain't gonna hurt you, honey—I'm one of the good guys. I keep this country safe so people like your folks can pour across our borders and take advantage of our social services. But I draw the line at letting 'em raise their kids to be spoiled brats. If you're gonna live here, you better learn to show some goddamn respect."

He fished his wallet from his pocket and tossed a twenty on the counter. "Ditch the scarf and use the change to buy a baseball cap," he said. "This is America, for Christ's sake." Then he snatched up his bag and headed for the door.

The air outside the convenience store smelled of exhaust. Yancey lit a cigarette on his way across the parking lot and then waited at the curb for the traffic to clear. Once it did, he jogged across the street to the mosque.

The place didn't look like any mosque he'd ever seen.

There were no domes. No minarets. No ornamentation of any kind besides the banner hanging off the roof with lettering in Arabic. It was just a squat, ugly commercial building that used to be a second-run movie theater—though the letters had been removed, the words DAYMARK CINEMA were still faintly visible in negative on the building's dingy facade—in a commercial stretch of Daly City, ten miles south of San Francisco.

Today, the mosque was closed. Its expansive lot—sun-bleached and in need of repaving, tufts of crabgrass sprouting through the cracks—was nearly empty. The only vehicles were his rental, a plum-colored Cadillac ATS; two unmarked Bellum Industries Humvees, identifiable as Bellum's only by their license plates, BI23 and BI27; and a green late-1980s Chrysler LeBaron with a Bondo'd front-right fender that likely belonged to the imam. Two Bellum men, both thickset and clad in sleek black body armor, flanked the front entrance.

Yancey headed toward the door. One of the men opened it for him before he arrived. He stepped inside, exhaling smoke, and looked around.

They hadn't done much with the place since its movie-theater days. Same carpets, same walls, same lights. The concession stand was dark, its glass case empty. There was a set of shelves beside the door for shoes, a couple pairs left on it, even though the imam was the only one here. Yancey wondered how the fuck somebody managed to walk out without his shoes. These people were a mystery to him.

He kept his on.

The lone theater had been converted into a prayer hall, its seats removed, its floor recarpeted but not leveled so it still sloped gently toward the curtained screen. Its entrance was to the left of the concession stand. Yancey headed right, to the imam's office—originally the theater manager's—and went in without knocking.

The imam was inside, zip-tied to a folding chair.

His desk—metal, institutional, painted antacid green decades before and left to flake—was shoved against the wall, as was the thrift-store office chair that normally sat behind it. Office chairs were lousy for interrogations. Always rolling away or slowly spinning around. They blunted the force of a good punch, and made it hard to intimidate the subject by walking in and out of his field of view.

The imam was in his early forties, tall and thin, with long limbs and delicate hands. He had a well-trimmed beard, black flecked with white, and wore a loose-fitting white button-down with no collar, a white skullcap, and gray trousers. His wire-rimmed glasses rested on his desk blotter. An oozing cut split his right eyebrow. His face showed anger. His feet were bare.

Yancey schlepped his grocery bag across the room and set it on the floor where the imam could see it. "He give you any more trouble since we last spoke?" he asked the black-clad man who leaned against the desk cleaning his fingernails with a carbon-steel tactical knife. Another Bellum man stood, silent, in the corner of the office behind the imam.

"No, sir. He hasn't said a word."

"Good." Then, to the imam: "I hear you gave my boys quite a fight."

The imam said something in reply but too quietly for Yancey to hear.

"What was that?"

"I said you cannot smoke in here. It is a place of worship." His voice was calm. Quiet. Full of rage and hurt, well mastered.

Yancey took a good, long drag. Let the smoke flow freely from his mouth. Inhaled it through his nose. Held it, savoring. Then blew it out again, smiling. "Seems to me, I can smoke in here just fine. And anyway, from where I'm standing, this place looks more like a porno theater than a place of worship. Now, you wanna tell me why you went all Taliban on my boys when they came knocking?"

"I did no such thing. I merely attempted to flee. When one is Muslim in America, one learns to be distrustful of masked men with guns. Given the proximity of their arrival to yesterday's tragedy, I surmised—correctly, it appears—that they were here in a misguided attempt to lay blame for this horrible attack at my feet."

"Seems to me that distrust cuts both ways," Yancey said. "We wouldn't come knocking if you people would stop attacking us on our own soil."

"The soil is as much mine as yours," the imam replied. "And I resent the implication that I am anything like the men who did this. Those men are zealots, savages, lost souls corrupted by leaders whose teachings are an affront to the true message of the Koran. I am not like them. I am a man of faith. A pacifist. Neither I nor Allah condone what happened yesterday."

"A damn shame those savages look so much like you, then."

"On that," the imam replied, "I do not disagree. Although I hasten to point out that I am not the one to resort to violence today. These restraints are unnecessary. Perhaps you'd consider removing them and having your men wait outside so that we two may continue this discussion in a civilized manner."

"Civilized," Yancey said. "Right. Listen, Muhammad—"

"Rafiq," the imam corrected.

"—as much as I'm enjoying our little chat, I don't have time to dance with you all day. Here's how this is going to work. The restraints stay on. My men stay where they are. I'm gonna ask you some questions. You're going to answer them. My satisfaction with regard to those answers will dictate how the rest of your day goes."

"I would like a lawyer," Rafiq said.

"Would you, now."

"Yes. If you wish to question me, it is my right."

"Well, would you look at that," Yancey said to his men, "Rafiq here knows his rights! Only here's the thing, Rafiq. I'm private sector. Your so-called rights don't mean shit to me. So, as I was saying, I'm going to ask you some questions, and you're going to answer them."

Rafiq set his jaw. "And if I do not?"

"Then you're going to find out what's in that bag."

"I see. Then by all means, please begin," Rafiq said, his quiet confidence in the face of Yancey's attempts to intimidate a subtle act of rebellion.

Yancey pulled up an image on his phone. It was a black-and-white ID photo of a thin young man with dark hair and deep-set eyes, his face clean-shaven, his expression neutral. He showed it to the imam. "Do you recognize this man?"

Rafiq said nothing.

"I asked you a fucking question. Do you recognize this man?"

Still nothing.

Yancey thumbed to the next image. A different photo. A different young man. "What about this one? Or this one?" he said, swiping again.

Rafiq looked Yancey in the eye. And remained silent.

"These men are terrorists," Yancey said. "Known members of the organization that claimed credit for the bombing. And these photos were taken from the visas they used to enter the country. Why, I wonder, would you elect to help them by refusing to answer my questions?"

"Perhaps it has something to do with the manner in which those questions are being asked. I am curious: What, besides my religion and the color of my skin, makes you think I know anything of these men?"

"Cry profiling all you want—it ain't gonna fly. We have a witness that puts them in this mosque." It wasn't technically a lie. But it also wasn't the whole truth.

"This is a place of worship," Rafiq said. "Many people come and go."

"Even terrorists?"

"If in fact these men were here, as you claim, they were not yet terrorists."

"So you *do* remember them."

"I did not say that. I simply inferred it, based on the fact that they were issued visas. It is my understanding that the U.S. government is not in the business of abetting the travel plans of known extremists."

"That's a funny argument to make, Rafiq. Kinda makes it sound like they were radicalized here."

"Impossible. As I have said, I neither preach nor condone violence. And if you must know, I truly have no memory of these men, which means if they passed through here, it was but briefly."

Yancey got down on his haunches so that he and Rafiq were eye to eye, and smiled. "Okay," he said. "Now we're getting somewhere. And you know what? I believe you. So let me make things easy on you. You want out of those restraints? You want me and my boys to leave you be? All you need to do is give me a list of congregants or whatever the fuck you people call 'em who might be sympathetic to these men's cause. The sorts of people who might, say, give them a boat or someplace to hole up when the cops come looking."

Rafiq shook his head. "As I said, I do not know these men. If I did—if I knew *anything* that could prevent further bloodshed—I would be happy to tell the proper authorities." The stress he put on *the proper authorities* made it clear he didn't think Yancey qualified. "I have no loyalty to this so-called True Islamic Caliphate. Their beliefs insult those who, like me, truly wish to follow the teachings of the prophet Muhammad. But while I would gladly aid in their apprehension, what I will *not* do is assist you in conducting a...*witch-hunt* is, I believe, the term, against the law-abiding men and women who worship here."

Yancey stood. Shook his head. Walked over to the convenience-store bag. "You know much about waterboarding, Rafiq?"

Rafiq's face tightened with worry. He shook his head.

"Well, I do," Yancey said. "See, the way it works is, you strap a guy down at a slight incline—ten, fifteen degrees will do—so that his lungs are higher than his head. Most folks picture a special table with straps and shit, but the fact is, you can use whatever you have on hand. That chair back you're fastened to would work just fine. Then you put a rag over his face, so his mouth and nose are covered."

Yancey reached down and removed from the bag a five-pack of small white terry towels, the type used to buff cars. "These'd do the trick," he said. "Once the rag's in place, you pour water over it real slow so that it fills his nasal passages, his sinuses, his throat. The idea is, the guy—or gal, there's no need to discriminate—won't drown, because his lungs are uphill from where the water pools, but honestly, most folks aspirate it anyway, or puke and fill their lungs with vomit. I've seen both, and it ain't pleasant. And of course, even though the manuals *say* water, really, any liquid will do. I like using something carbonated because the bubbles burn like a motherfucker and have a way of loosening the tongue."

Yancey reached into the bag again, and removed two forties of Colt 45. Rafiq began to struggle atop his chair, though the zip-ties held him in place.

"Oh, right," Yancey said. "You people are forbidden to consume alcohol, aren't you? Well, then, you'd better start working on that list I asked for, or hope your God ain't watching." He nodded to his men, who moved silently to either side of Rafiq, grabbed the chair, and tilted it backward, Rafiq screaming, until he lay with his head on the ground and his bare feet up in the air.

Yancey's phone chimed—a text. He read it. Smiled. Typed a brief reply.

"Sorry, Rafiq," he said. "It looks like I'm not going to get to stay for the festivities. I've got other business to attend to. But don't you worry—I'm sure my boys will take good care of you."

27.

W HAT'S THE word, kid?"

"The word is *ninja*," Cameron replied, excitement raising the pitch of her voice. "As in, I am one."

"Come again?"

"We got a hit."

Adrenaline surged through Hendricks's system like a drug, spreading warm and tingly through his limbs. He felt lighter, suddenly, more present, his aches, pains, and exhaustion chemically erased. "Your, uh, programs decoded a call or whatever?"

"Aw. It's cute when you pretend you have the faintest idea what you're talking about. But yeah, they found something, and it's way better than a phone call, it's a text. Well, two, to be exact."

"How's that better?"

"Because the first one included a pic. I'm sending you the details now."

His phone vibrated. He clicked the notification, and his text app opened. No names, just phone numbers. The first message read: *POI acquired. Awaiting instructions.* The attached photo was of the old man from the video, bound and bloodied on a couch. There was a woman beside him, bound as well. Men in body armor stood guard on either side of them, their heads cropped from the shot. The second message said: *On my way.* Time stamps indicated the second message had been sent less than two minutes ago.

"You get 'em?" Cameron asked.

"Yeah, kid. I got 'em. You did good—this is amazing work."

"Thanks," she said. She tried to toss it off all casual-like, but Hendricks could practically hear her blushing. "What's a POI?"

"Person of interest," he said. "Hey, what can you tell me about these guys besides their phone numbers?"

"Nothing," she said, "and not for lack of trying. Those phones are encrypted six ways from Sunday."

"Can you find out the point of origin for the text?"

"No—at least, not digitally. Since the phone's encryption prevents me from accessing its GPS, the best that I could tell you is the cell tower it went through, and we already *know* which tower it went through, or we never would've intercepted it."

"I sense a *but*. We don't have time for dramatic pauses, kid. If you've got something, just say so."

"I'm not trying to be dramatic. I'm multitasking."

"Meaning what?"

"Take a good look at that picture. Tell me what you see. Besides the guys, I mean."

"I dunno. A couch?"

"Sure, a couch. Also a fireplace, hardwood floors, distinctive molding, and what looks like a covered farmer's porch outside the window."

"Okay—but what good does that do us?"

"None of the houses on the Presidio are privately owned. They're all rented from the Presidio Trust. I'm on their website now. They've got pics of all their housing broken down by style and neighborhood."

"Good thought," he said, "but the Presidio is an old army base. There must be dozens of houses that match that description. I walked through neighborhood after neighborhood of identical homes on my way here."

"You'd think, but as it turns out, your boy Segreti has refined taste. Because I'm pretty sure I just found the place where they caught up with him, and there's only four like it on the whole base."

"You got any idea which one he's in?"

"No, but it looks like they're all clumped together, two on either side of Presidio Boulevard where it intersects with Funston."

Hendricks opened Google Maps. "That's almost a mile from my position. I need to get moving. And we're gonna have to disconnect, so you'll be on your own a little while."

"Why?"

"Because these guys don't look like mob goons; they look like law enforcement. And I need to make a phone call to see if I can find out who sent them."

"Law enforcement? That, uh, jibes with something I heard earlier," Cameron said.

"Which is?"

"The girl from the video—Hannah Reston—told me a Fed came by her brother's room super-early this morning and talked to her dad. Said the guy was gross. Winked at her and everything. Anyway, he asked a bunch of questions about our guy and leaned on her dad hard for answers. Sounds to me like the dad was pretty rattled by the whole experience. I had Hannah push a little, see what else she could find out, but her dad got pissed and snapped at her, told her to leave it be. She said it's not like him to yell."

"Wait—you talked to the Restons? What the hell were you thinking? I told you not to go anywhere near them!"

"Relax. I talked to Hannah in the hospital's restroom, girl to girl. Made up some story about the guy being my granddad. Said my family's trying to find him but we need to keep it on the down-low because he's technically an illegal. Met my grandma when he came over from Italy for college and stayed but never filed the proper paperwork. She bought it, hook, line, and sinker. Thinks she's digging in the name of love. Her parents don't even know I'm here."

"Wait, what do you mean, they don't even know? You're not still in the building, are you?"

"Yeah, why? I don't see the big deal. The hospital cafeteria's got everything I need. Great Wi-Fi signal. Loads of computers on the network for me to hijack. Tons of people hanging out and killing time, so I've got plenty of cover, and everyone from the docs to the patients' loved ones are so distracted, no one's even given me a second glance."

"You said you were in a coffee shop," he said, his voice an angry, gravelly monotone.

"Yeah, well, I lied."

"Listen to me. You're not safe there. You need to get

out of the building immediately, preferably through a staff exit."

"Why a staff exit?"

"Because if someone's watching the place, they'll be monitoring the doors civilians come and go through. But—and this is important—you need to stay within sight of two people and two routes of egress at all times. Don't allow yourself to be alone with anyone. Don't let yourself get cornered."

"You're scaring me."

"Good. You should be scared. Listen to your fear. It'll keep you safe. One more thing: Did Hannah tell you what this Fed looked like?"

"Uh...older guy. Really tan. Like, from the sun, not spray. Said he was wearing cowboy boots and a turquoise pinkie ring. That help?"

"Too soon to tell," he said. "Now go. Run. Don't stop until you're sure no one is following. I'll call back as soon as I can."

"But what if—"

Hendricks disconnected the call. Felt a pang of guilt for leaving her in the cold. Prayed his paranoia was unnecessary.

Then he pulled up his burner's keypad and punched in a number from memory.

28.

THE HOOVER BUILDING was a nest disturbed. Stuffed beyond capacity. Brimming with activity. Every phone, printer, and photocopier clamoring at once. The HVAC system couldn't keep up. The whole building smelled like overloaded electronics and unwashed bodies. With the threat of future attacks looming, none of them were willing to abandon their posts for long enough to shower or change their clothes, much less get some sleep.

O'Brien had moved her best agents from their offices to a conference room, the table buried beneath a foot-high layer of paper. "This represents every ounce of intel we have on Khalid Waheeb, Ahmed Muhammad Bakr, and Fazul Abdullah al-Nasr," she'd said. "Most of it is out of date. Some of it is doubtless inaccurate. But we're going to sift through every page anyway, because that's what NSB's asked us to do. So grab a stack and get to work."

They all knew it was a shit detail, that if there were anything worth finding in these documents, NSB would be combing through them instead of handing them off. But they buckled down and dug in anyway. Like it or not, that was the job.

They'd been at it for hours when Thompson's phone rang. It took a moment for her to locate her cell in the mess. It was wedged between a pile of phone records and some credit card receipts that in turn were hidden from view by the open lid of a pizza box.

Caller ID was no help. It was an unfamiliar number, no name attached.

"Thompson here."

"Tell me you sent them."

"Who is this?" she asked sharply enough that O'Brien cocked an eyebrow at Thompson over her laptop.

"You know damn well who this is."

Jesus. It was Hendricks. She got up from the table. Turned her back to O'Brien. Dropped her voice to just above a whisper. Ducked out of the conference room and headed down the hall. "How the hell did you get this number?"

"What are you talking about? You gave it to me."

"And you refused to take it."

"No. I took your number. All I left behind was the card you wrote it on." He sounded out of breath, Thompson realized, like he was on the move. "Now—did you send them?"

"I don't know what you're talking about."

"Five minutes ago, a team of men in body armor stormed a house in the Presidio and captured Frank Segreti. I need to know if they're law."

Thompson opened the door to the stairwell. It banged shut behind her once she stepped through. "Someone captured Frank Segreti?" She winced at how loud her voice sounded, amplified by the stairway's bare concrete.

"I'll take that as a no, then."

"No," she whispered. "I didn't send anyone. I wish to hell I had the clout to. The fact is, you were my last hope, and, as I recall, you turned me down. What changed your mind?"

"Nothing changed my mind," he said. "I gave you deniability, and gave myself some room to breathe. But now that someone's got Segreti, I can't afford to keep you out of the loop."

"What else can you tell me about these guys?"

"Not much," Hendricks said. "Although it's possible they're taking orders from a man claiming to be law enforcement."

"This guy got a name?"

"Probably."

"How about a description?"

"I haven't seen him personally, but I'm told he's older. Deeply tanned. Fondness for cowboy boots and turquoise jewelry."

"My God. That sounds like Chet Yancey."

"Who's Chet Yancey?"

"The good ol' boy I worked under when I graduated from Quantico."

"Wait. You're saying he was—"

"—special agent in charge of the Albuquerque field office when Segreti walked in."

"Motherfucker," Hendricks said. "I think we just found your mole."

"Sounds like. He left the Bureau shortly after the safe house was compromised. I hear he's some kind of bigwig at Bellum Industries now."

"That explains the men in body armor. He's got a goddamn private army at his disposal."

"Is Yancey with Segreti?"

"Not yet, but he's on his way. Which means Segreti's running out of time."

"Listen, Michael, I'm really glad you—"

But Thompson didn't bother finishing her thought because Hendricks had already disconnected.

When she left the stairwell to head back to the conference room, O'Brien was waiting for her in the hallway. "What the hell was that about?"

"What do you mean?"

"When your phone rang, you leaped out of your seat like you'd been zapped with a cattle prod. You onto something?"

"No, I..." Thompson began, color rising in her cheeks. "It was Jess."

"I thought Jess was backpacking through Costa Rica with her new boyfriend."

"She was. She is. But she got sick of camping, so they shacked up someplace with a TV for the night. When she saw the news, she called."

O'Brien was skeptical. "That warranted your leaving the room?"

"Oh, you know Jess. High drama. High volume. I figured I'd spare everybody the distraction."

O'Brien fell silent for a moment, her face set in a frown. "Charlie, this is me you're talking to. I know you. There's something you're not telling me."

Thompson took O'Brien's hands in hers. Looked her in the eye. "There's not."

"Promise?"

"Promise."

O'Brien seemed mollified. "Listen, I just got word from the director. Apparently, Bellum Industries is taking over the investigation. We've been instructed to coordinate with them from here on out."

"You're kidding me."

"I wish I were. Anyway, I'm told Chet Yancey's their top guy on the ground. We're tracking down his number now. You mind sitting in on the call?"

"Me? Why?"

"You know the guy. I don't. But if it's a problem—"

"No. Of course not. Count me in."

29.

CAMERON'S FOOTFALLS ECHOED like a snare drum down
the empty hall, mirroring the pounding of her pulse.
Just keep moving, she told herself, and don't look back.

She looked back. Locked eyes with her pursuer
through the hall door's inset pane, narrow and cross-
hatched with wire.

When Hendricks had told her to get out of the hospital,
she was scared—as anybody would have been—but she
was also half convinced that he was overreacting. She'd
been so careful. So clever. Sure, she'd walked past the Reston boy's room a few times. It had been easy enough to
find once she'd gained access to the hospital's electronic
chart system. She'd peeked through the open door as she
walked by, but she'd never slowed, never stopped, never
engaged. Instead, she'd set up in the waiting area beside
the nurses' station, which was just a widening of the hall-

237

way, really, with a few banks of chairs and a side table full of magazines, where she could keep an eye on them from a distance. When she saw Hannah head for the restroom, she followed.

She was sure no one had been shadowing her then. The only people in the waiting area were obviously camped out while their loved ones were being treated. They all had the greasy, stretched-thin look of folks who'd been awake too long and forced to consider the worst.

The restroom had been empty save for Cameron and Hannah. And once they'd spoken, Cameron relocated to the cafeteria.

So how had this guy gotten onto her?

She'd spotted him as soon as she'd finished talking to Hendricks, closed her laptop, and headed for the cafeteria exit. Not the main exit, the one that cut through the hospital's small courtyard. She figured the courtyard was less traveled, that someone following her would be more obvious if she went that way—and she was right.

It was no wonder she'd missed him before. He looked to be of average height and weight, and he was dressed to blend in—T-shirt, jeans, and canvas jacket. But his hair was cut high and tight like former military, and it was a little warm inside the hospital for a jacket. He wore it to conceal the shoulder holster beneath it, which was briefly visible when he moved just so.

She thought she'd shaken him when she exited the courtyard. She'd sprinted around the nearest corner, her laptop cradled to her chest like a football, and didn't slow until she'd taken two more turns. But then, as she headed toward the outpatient surgery entrance, he'd materialized as if from nowhere fifty feet ahead of her, between her and the door.

She turned and ran, slammed into a medication cart, and nearly wound up on her ass. "Watch it!" the nurse pushing it barked, although the damn thing was so heavy, it was in no danger of tipping over. Cameron spun and kept on going, her pursuer close behind.

She thought she'd lost him a second time when she ducked into the elevator as the doors were sliding shut. She got off at its first stop and darted through an automated door labeled AUTHORIZED PERSONNEL ONLY as it swung closed behind a pair of nurses wheeling an unconscious patient. But then, somehow, there he was again—scowling at her through the glass. She felt like she was wearing a goddamn tracking device.

He approached the door. Cameron's heart rate trebled, and she took off running. She ducked around corners at random—a left, a right, another left—and then ran smack into a security guard.

He was a husky kid in his twenties with dirty-blond hair and watery eyes. The kind of guy who looked like he ended up a security guard because he'd washed out of the police academy. But he had a badge, a radio, a gun. To Cameron, his chintzy brown-on-brown uniform seemed like a gleaming suit of armor.

"Are you lost, ma'am? This is a restricted area."

"I'm not lost—I'm being chased."

"Chased?"

"Yeah. You have to help me. Some creep's been following me all over the hospital. I think he has a gun. I only ducked in here because I was hoping I could lose him."

"Sure," he said, "No problem. How about we head back to the security office and sort this out? If there's a strange man chasing women through the hospital, I'm sure my boss will want to hear about it."

"Actually, I'm in a bit of a hurry, so if you wouldn't mind just escorting me to the nearest exit—" Cameron said, but the guard cut her off.

"Relax," he said, "this won't take long."

He put his hand around her upper arm—squeezing a little tighter than Cameron thought appropriate—and guided her down the hall the way she'd come. "Hey, easy!" she said and tried to yank her arm loose. But he held fast—and gave the surveillance camera in the corner a subtle nod.

Too late, Cameron realized why she'd been unable to lose her pursuer.

"Look," she said. "Clearly, there's been some kind of misunderstanding."

"I don't think there has."

"Excuse me?"

"We got word from HQ a few hours ago about a potential threat to the Restons, so we've been monitoring their son's room. The third time you walked by, we sent them your picture—and do you know what they found?" Cameron stared blankly at him. "A sheet as long as my arm. Identity theft. Bank fraud. Unlawful possession of prescription narcotics. You name it. What kind of sicko preys on people in a hospital?"

Theft? Fraud? Drugs? What the hell was he talking about? *You have to get out of this*, she thought. *Convince him to let you go. Beg, if need be.*

"Listen," she began, searching his chest for a name tag. But he wasn't wearing one. The only marking on his uniform shirt was an embroidered corporate logo made to look like a badge: a shield emblazoned with a crenellated tower. And stitched beneath it, in small block type, were the words CITADEL SECURITY: A BELLUM INDUSTRIES COMPANY. "You've got this all wrong. I never—"

"Save your breath. You're caught. Besides, my boss'll be here soon."

Cameron heard footfalls approaching, and her heart fluttered in her chest. She tried to squirm free of the security guard's grip. He shoved her backward into the wall and pinned her there, his forearm to her neck. She couldn't breathe. An involuntary squeak escaped her throat. He eased off just a hair. She sucked wind and sobbed. Tears and snot poured down her face.

"Please," she managed. "Please."

He was so close that she could see the pockmarks on his forehead. His fetid breath was hot against her cheek. "Beg all you want," he said. "It's not gonna do you any good."

Cameron swallowed hard, her eyes wide as silver dollars.

Then she kneed him in the balls with everything she had.

He released her and doubled over, red-faced and sweating. Cameron gripped her laptop with both hands and swung it at his face. A crack of plastic shattering as it connected with his chin, and he went down. Lettered keys scattered across the floor.

Cameron ran. Her pursuer rounded the corner, cursing when he spotted the fallen security guard. He leaped over the kid with ease and raced after Cameron, quickly closing the gap between them. She felt the fingers of his right hand graze her shoulder.

No. Not graze. Take hold of.

He grabbed a fistful of her shirt and yanked, but as he did, he slipped on a loose keyboard letter, and they toppled to the floor.

The man wound up flat on his back with Cameron on top of him. He tried to wrap his arms around her, but she threw fists and elbows wildly, and felt a surge of savage delight when one connected with his nose. It gouted blood, and when he reached instinctively toward it, she clambered free.

He grabbed her by the ankle. Cameron kicked him in the face, and he released her. She launched herself down the hall like a sprinter from the starting blocks, a feral smile parting her lips as she looked back at the bloody mess she'd made of her assailant.

Then the security guard tackled her and drove her to the floor.

She landed facedown, the wind knocked out of her. The linoleum was gritty from foot traffic and smelled of vomit, of bleach. The security guard climbed atop her and drove his knee into her back. Then he yanked her right arm upward in a hammerlock. Cameron's wristbones ground together in his grasp. The tendons in her shoulder burned white-hot as they overextended.

"You like that, you fucking bitch?"

He tried to cuff her, but she resisted, bucking beneath him with all she had, so he grabbed her by the hair and slammed her face into the floor.

Cameron stopped fighting.

Her world went dark and silent as consciousness abandoned her.

30.

HENDRICKS SPRINTED ACROSS the Presidio's grounds, vaulting fences, cutting through backyards, pushing through dense stands of trees. His lungs burned. His muscles ached. His stitches tugged uncomfortably. Blood oozed from his wound whenever his midsection flexed.

At least the fog provided cover. It began to blow in, cold and clammy, shortly after he fled the bridge pavilion. Gray-white tendrils reached inland, smelling of low tide and swallowing everything they touched. Shadows vanished as the fog blocked out the setting sun.

The temperature—low seventies when the sky was cloudless—plummeted. Hendricks's world shrank as the fog narrowed the margins all around. Distant landmarks became ghosts, fading into the swirling mist. Man-made objects dissolved into the scenery as edges dulled and angles softened. Sounds reverberated oddly, sometimes muffled, sometimes accentuated. His own footfalls sounded dull to his ears, like the idle tapping of an eraser against a desk, but more than once he heard a conversation or an engine's roar so loud that he assumed he was right on top of it, only to discover it was blocks away or more.

He crossed a street and plunged into a forest, branches lashing. A footpath ran parallel to his route, eastward, ever eastward, and he zigged toward it, picking up speed once he left the underbrush behind. Then, at once, the forest fell away and he was running through a rolling field of grass, the blades slickened by the moisture-laden air, the footing treacherous. A cemetery, he realized. Headstones, low and regular, dotted the field, and threatened to take his legs out from under him. Larger monuments loomed in the mist. A soldier. A cross. An angel. Each a blur as Hendricks ran past. Then the cemetery vanished as the woods enveloped him once more.

This time when he emerged, he found himself on a paved road at the edge of the Main Post. In the dim half-light, the place could be confused for a particularly quaint small town—the streets winding, the sidewalks broad, the houses tidy and attractive, the lawns well tended. Residential and commercial buildings mixed, the former Spanish single-family dwellings, the latter everything from clapboard to red brick. The streetlights flickered to life one by one and cast halos in the fog. Since there was no civilian traffic on the streets, the glow of headlights warned him of approaching Park Police patrols and afforded him a chance to hide, to duck behind a building or a parked car or merely linger in an entryway, face averted, pretending he belonged.

At one such stop, outside the old officers' club, he

checked his phone. According to the map, his destination was just around the corner.

He tried not to think too much about what he was walking into or what might happen to Cameron in his absence. The U.S. government had trained Hendricks and his unit to operate autonomously behind enemy lines, and it had trained them well. What he needed now was to trust in his abilities, his instincts, his muscle memory. Overthinking led to distraction, doubt, and failure.

His muscles twitched from the sudden stillness. His breath plumed with every ragged exhalation. Blood roared in his ears. He willed his heart to slow. Felt the wound in his side throb in time. He moved the gun to his right jacket pocket. Thumbed the safety off and kept his hand around the grip.

And then rounded the corner, headed toward Segreti.

31.

REYES GLANCED AT his watch and frowned when he realized the hands had scarcely moved since the last time he'd looked.

"If you've got somewhere else to be," Segreti said, too loud due to the aftereffects of the flash-bang grenade, "don't let us keep you."

Reyes eyed the man—whose name Yancey had never divulged to him—with disdain. He looked so thin and frail as he sat zip-tied on the couch, but the fact was, he'd put up one hell of a fight when they'd stormed the place. He'd played possum until the lead team got within striking distance, then attacked, slicing Liman's forearm open with a folding knife and kicking out McTiernan's legs. He'd nearly gotten hold of McTiernan's gun before Stahelski put him down with a rifle butt to the face.

Lois sat beside Segreti on the couch, frightened, trembling, with Ella on her lap. Lois's bound hands were buried in the dog's coat, and she muttered an endless string of soothing nonsense in her ear. It was unclear to Reyes whether she was comforting the dog or vice versa. Either way, it was getting on his nerves.

"I'm not going anywhere," Reyes said. "Just counting down the seconds until I'm rid of you."

"You wanna get rid of me? All you've gotta do is let me go. I swear you'll never see me again."

"Sorry, pal, but I'm not the guy to talk to. You want to plead your case, you're going to have to take it up with my boss when he gets here."

"Uh-huh. That'll go well. Anybody who'd order a raid on an innocent lady's house is bound to be real reasonable."

"I'm sure he had his reasons."

"Yeah? What are they?"

"Above my pay grade," Reyes replied.

"Oh, I see. You're just a goon. A lackey. You've got no idea what's going on here. Tell me, this boss of yours—he got a name?"

"Do you?"

Segreti ignored his question. "Whoever he is, I can tell you he's crooked as fuck. I don't know what sort of line he's fed you, but I can promise you he means to kill me."

Reyes said nothing.

"Maybe that's fine with you," Segreti continued. "Ain't like I know you from Adam. But if you people are gonna kill me, I say let's get it over with—don't make me wait around all day. But please, I'm begging you, let Lois go. She's not involved in any of this. Only thing she did wrong was let me in when I came knocking."

"For fuck's sake, nobody's killing anybody," Reyes snapped. Then, to his men: "Gag him, would you? In fact, gag them both."

The truth was, Reyes didn't know what to believe. Nothing about this assignment felt right to him. The guy was more dangerous than he let on, sure, but he didn't strike Reyes as a zealot—and if he really was involved in the bridge attack like Yancey said, why the hell had he been here playing house when they'd busted in?

Still, orders were orders—and Yancey had been hand-picked by Bellum's CEO to head up West Coast operations, which carried weight among the rank and file—so Reyes kept his questions to himself.

While McTiernan and Stahelski gagged the captives, Reyes parted the curtains and looked outside. Night had fallen and a fog bank had blown in. Visibility was terrible, but near as he could tell, the street was empty except for the Humvee he'd arrived in, which was parked along the curb. Civilian vehicles were temporarily banned from all Presidio roads—he'd had to send a man in the other Humvee to meet Yancey at the Veterans Boulevard barricades. Across the street, he could just make out the vague suggestion of two homes identical to the one in which he stood. The fog reduced the nearby streetlights to nothing more than faintly glowing orbs that seemed to hover in the milky white.

Eventually the second Humvee emerged from the mist and parked behind the first. Yancey climbed out, his cell phone to his ear. When he walked through the front door, Segreti's eyes went wide and he struggled against his bonds, grunting unintelligibly through the gag in his mouth. The Bellum operative standing guard to his right stilled him with a jab to the ribs.

"Listen, Yancey—" Reyes began, but Yancey held up a finger to say *Just a minute.*

"No shit? Charlie Thompson's on the line too?" Yancey said into the phone. "Tell me, is she still an insubordinate pain in the ass?" He chuckled. "Easy, Thompson, I'm just busting your balls. You never did know how to take a joke." A pause. "That's very kind of you, Assistant Director, but I think we can take it from here. How about you send us what you've got so far, and stand down—we'll let you know if there's anything else we need. In the meantime, I'm kinda busy here, so..."

Yancey rolled his eyes at Reyes and made a sock-puppet gesture that suggested the person on the other end of the line was blabbing on. "No, not at all. I'm glad you called. It's always nice to have a chance to catch up with an old friend," he said, his gaze settling on Segreti.

When Yancey hung up the phone, Reyes asked, "Who was that?"

"Feds," Yancey replied. "Offering assistance, they said. Pissing on their territory, more like." Then, to Segreti: "I've gotta hand it to you, Frank. You are one slippery motherfucker. I never thought I'd see your ugly mug again."

Reyes eyed Yancey with suspicion. "Wait—you know this guy?"

"Our paths crossed a thousand years ago when I was with the Bureau. Seems like folks are coming out of the woodwork left and right today. I know he doesn't look like much, but believe me, he's a grade-A shitheel. We liked him for dozens—if not hundreds—of deaths back in the day, but we could never make them stick. Once he got wind that we were onto him, he up and vanished."

Segreti snorted.

"That tracks," Reyes said, his doubts allayed somewhat. "He didn't go down easy. Had a folding knife hidden in the front pocket of his sweatshirt and wound up cutting Liman pretty good. Poor bastard's off getting stitched up as we speak."

"That true, Frank? You get a little feisty with my men?"

Segreti just glared.

Yancey turned his attention to the woman beside Segreti. "Who's the skirt?"

"Lois Broussard," Reyes replied.

"This her place?"

"Looks like. It's leased from the Presidio Trust under the name Calvin Broussard. I'm guessing he's the gentleman in all the pictures."

Yancey picked up a framed photo from the side table, glanced at it, and tossed it aside. "And where is ol' Calvin?"

"Credit card records put him in Reno. Business trip, looks like."

"Was our guy holding Mrs. Broussard against her will?"

"Not as far as we could tell—which is why we elected to restrain her."

"What's your connection to this lady, Frank? You keeping Calvin's side of the bed warm while he's gone?"

A single tear slid down Lois's cheek. Segreti made noises of protest through his gag.

"Sorry, buddy, I didn't quite get that. But don't worry, we'll have plenty of time to catch up when I transport you to our facility up north for questioning."

Segreti's eyes, wide and pleading, darted from Yancey to Reyes.

"If this guy's tied to the attack in some way, shouldn't we turn him over to the authorities?" Reyes asked.

"Sure," Yancey replied. "And I'll be happy to—just as soon as I'm done with him."

Segreti thrashed against his restraints. The dog on Lois's lap growled as Yancey stepped in close and hit Frank twice. Segreti doubled over and sucked wind through his gag. Yancey grabbed him by the hair and yanked him upright.

That's when the dog lunged.

Yancey yelped as Ella's teeth sank into his forearm. He released Segreti and flailed wildly until he shook the dog free.

Ella sailed past Lois and slammed into a side table. The lamp atop it rocked and fell, shattering when it hit the floor.

"You okay, boss?" Reyes asked.

Yancey cradled his injured arm to his chest. Blood seeped into his sleeve. "I'm fine."

"Weddle," Reyes said, "shut that thing in a bedroom, would you?"

"No," Yancey replied. "Leave it be."

Ella hunkered low and snarled.

"You sure that's a good idea?" Reyes asked.

Yancey drew his .357 and aimed it at the dog. "You're goddamn right I'm sure."

Lois shrieked through her gag. Segreti strained against his zip-ties.

"Whoa," Reyes said. "I think maybe we should all just take a breath."

Yancey ignored him and instead addressed Ella directly. "Christ, look at you. You're more throw pillow than dog—proof positive that man makes for a capricious god. It took only a couple thousand years for us to turn wolves into accessories for rich bitches."

"Seriously, boss. I get that you're pissed, but there's no need for this. Let me stash her somewhere out of sight, okay?"

"But it's all just window dressing, ain't it?" Yancey continued. "Deep down, you're still half wild; all you wanna do is fight and fuck. It's not your fault, really—it's ours for thinking we could change your nature. But if you wanna play Big Bad Wolf with me, I'll show you how we deal with wolves where I come from."

"For fuck's sake, Yancey, put the gun down!"

"You know, son," Yancey said without taking his eyes off the dog, "it seems to me this little shit ain't the only one around here who needs to learn who's in charge."

Yancey pulled the trigger.

His gun thundered.

But not before Lois threw herself off the couch.

With her arms and legs bound, she went down hard. Yancey's shot ran parallel to the couch and angled downward to the spot where Ella stood. As Lois fell, it caught her in the sternum. Segreti screamed into his gag. Reyes rushed to Lois's side—but there was no saving her. The bullet had passed clean through and left an exit wound the size of his fist. She was dead before she hit the floor.

"Jesus Christ," Reyes said. "What did you do?"

Yancey stared at Lois's corpse in wide-eyed disbelief.

"It wasn't..." he said. "I didn't..."

And then the lights went out.

32.

"WHAT THE FUCK is going on?"

The house's background whir ceased as appliances shut down. Yancey's voice echoed, shrill and desperate, in the sudden quiet. His hands were sweaty. His mouth was dry. He became painfully aware of his own breathing and the roar of his pulse in his ears.

A rustling to his left. A squeak of couch springs. A struggle. A thud. A grunt.

Then, one by one, flashlights came on around the room.

Reyes still crouched beside the fallen woman, blood pooling black beneath her; lifeless eyes reflecting the flashlights' beams, but now his gun was drawn and his head was cocked to one side, listening.

Segreti was sprawled beside him, straddled by two Bellum men. It seemed he'd tried to make a move despite his bonds. Yancey wished he'd died in the attempt. It would have saved Yancey the trouble of killing him.

Speaking of, that little shit of a dog was nowhere to be seen.

Yancey knew he was in danger of losing control of the situation. He tamped down his rising panic and forced some steel into his voice. "I want a goddamn sitrep *now!*"

"Could be an outage," one of his men replied. "FEMA sent around a memo about the rescue effort taxing the power grid. Warned the lights could flicker."

"It's not an outage," Reyes said. He nodded toward the curtains. Light shone through the narrow gap where they met. "The streetlights are still on. Which means we've got company."

"Get him up," Yancey said. The men who'd tackled Segreti hauled him to his feet and held him upright by his elbows. "Remove his gag."

Once they had, Segreti spat in Yancey's face. "You son of a bitch," he said. "I swear you'll pay for what you did to Lois."

"Don't you *dare* blame me for this! Her death is on *your* conscience, not mine. You're the one who put her in harm's way."

Segreti turned his head and locked eyes with Reyes. "That how *you* see it? His actions seem justified to you? Because I promise, Lois ain't the first innocen—"

Yancey pistol-whipped Segreti. Segreti's head rocked sideways, blood spraying from his mouth. He sagged, his weight supported by the men on either side of him, and his eyes showed only whites.

Yancey cocked back his hand to hit him again. Reyes grabbed his wrist to halt the blow.

"Yancey! He's had enough!"

Yancey yanked his hand free and wheeled on Reyes. They stood nose to nose in the darkness, grips tightening on their weapons. "Are you questioning my authority, son?"

The moment hung between them—fraught, electric. The armed men around them tensed. Yancey felt as if his future hinged on the outcome of this confrontation. Reyes's challenge painted him as fallible and weak. He couldn't afford to let it stand.

Reyes glanced around the room, and realized that he was on his own.

He relaxed his posture and backed down.

"No," he said.

Yancey smiled, wide and predatory. "I'm sorry—I must've misheard. No *what?*"

"No, *sir*," Reyes replied through gritted teeth.

"Attaboy," Yancey said, his confidence returning. He looked at Segreti, who was once again conscious, although his eyes swam woozily in their sockets. "So, Frank—who's your friend out there?"

Segreti frowned. Spat blood on the floor. "Fuck if I know. I didn't think I had any left."

"Don't worry," Yancey said, "you won't for long. Reyes, McTiernan, Bigelow, Stahelski, go check the perimeter. Weddle, Swinson, Lutz, you stay in here with me."

The men, save Reyes, muttered their assent and geared up.

Yancey gave Reyes a hard look.

Reyes returned it.

"There a problem?" Yancey asked.

"Not so long as the prisoner is still alive when we get back."

* * *

The streetlights looked like paper lanterns in the fog and bathed the neighborhood in gauzy white. In the long shadows of the Broussard house's backyard, though, their illumination dwindled to the false twilight of a horror-movie poster.

The back door creaked slowly open. For a long moment, nothing happened. Then two mercenaries slipped into the night, nearly invisible in their matte-black body armor. They moved with silent precision, one advancing while the other covered him.

Hendricks studied them from the shadows, assessing strengths and weaknesses.

He'd watched the house for ten minutes, trying to formulate a plan of attack, but when Yancey arrived, he knew he had to make his move. Hendricks had been creeping toward the house when he heard the gunshot. For a moment, he'd worried he was too late. Then Segreti screamed—which meant he might be injured but was still alive.

In every scenario he considered, Hendricks was outnumbered and outgunned. The mercs carried MP5 assault rifles, fully automatic, thirty rounds to a magazine, and spare mags in their vests. And if they'd sent two men out the back, it was safe to assume there were at least two more around front. All Hendricks had was Pappas's .45, which wouldn't penetrate their body armor.

Their armor, however, afforded Hendricks some advantages. It slowed reaction times. Limited mobility. Dulled hearing. Narrowed visual fields. And the night-vision goggles they wore beneath their helmets were next to useless in the roiling fog.

One of the men took up a position behind the Jaguar in the driveway and provided cover for the other while he jogged toward the tree line. Hendricks smiled. He'd figured that's where they'd begin their search, which was why he wasn't hiding in the tree line.

Training is good. Training is valuable. But the wrong training leads to regimented thinking, which can be turned against you on the battlefield.

Thanks to the fog, Hendricks couldn't see the one searching the tree line, so he closed his eyes and listened. Heard the muffled crunch of dropped pine needles beneath boots, the dry rustle of underbrush disturbed. When the man completed his search, he shouted, "Clear! You see anything on your end?"

"Nada," the one behind the car replied. "I've got eyes on the house's electric meter, though, and it looks like it's been fucked with. Come cover me, and I'll see if I can get the lights back on."

"Copy that."

The meter box was located on a small, single-story addition nestled in the back left crook of the house's original cross gable, where shadows ran thick. A flower bed encircled the addition. Shrubberies partially hid the meter box. A garden hose hung just beside.

On the roof of the addition, a gently slanting plane some fifteen feet off the ground, Hendricks lay in wait.

"Look at this—someone yanked the fucking dial off."

His partner glanced over his shoulder without lowering his weapon, which was aimed vaguely toward the tree line "That enough to kill the power?"

"Beats me."

In fact, it was. Electric companies aren't wild about supplying power free of charge, so juice will flow only if the meter is plugged into the meter box. Removing it is a simple—if illegal—matter of snapping off the wire security seal and yanking the piece containing the display dial from its housing.

"They take it with 'em?"

"Dunno. Maybe." He clipped his weapon to his vest and rooted around the flower bed for a second. "Wait—got it."

"Is it busted?"

The merc wiped soil off the meter and turned it over in his hands. On the back were four prongs, which corresponded to four exposed slots in the box. "Doesn't seem to be."

"Put it back, then. See what happens."

"On it. Watch my six."

He lined the prongs up with the slots and plugged the meter in.

A white-hot burst of sparks lit up the night. The air crackled with electricity. The smell of ozone and scorched hair invaded Hendricks's nostrils as 220 volts blew the man backward into the yard.

Hendricks had used the hose to drench the meter and the box before he'd scaled the trellis, and he'd counted on the darkness and the man's tactical gloves to hide that fact until it was too late. If he were being honest with himself, he wasn't sure if it'd work.

The electrocuted merc landed, limbs rigid, on the grass. His hair and clothes were smoking. An involuntary groan escaped his lips. The man covering him cried out and dropped his weapon when the sparks erupted from the meter box, his night-vision goggles amplifying the light and blinding him. He stripped them off and tossed them aside, staggering. Then he rubbed uselessly at his eyes and called to his fallen friend.

"Bigs? Bigs, are you okay? Talk to me—I can't see you!"

And that's when Hendricks leaped.

Reyes was inspecting the underbrush to the right of the front porch when the streetlights dimmed. On the far side of the house, a brilliant flash of white, accompanied by a firecracker pop, turned night to day. Stahelski shouted something and was quickly silenced.

Reyes took off running toward the backyard.

The fog was thick; the grass was damp. Reyes wished he were wearing a bulletproof vest beneath his suit jacket and cursed his treadless dress shoes with every slip. McTiernan—who'd been nearer to the backyard when the light show started—was well ahead of him and more surefooted in his combat boots. It wasn't long before he vanished into the mist.

Visibility was shit. Still, near as Reyes could tell, the backyard was empty. No Bigelow, no McTiernan, no Stahelski. They weren't far, though. He could hear them engaged in battle somewhere to his right: The dull thwack of blows exchanged. The wet, popping sound of tendons snapping. A crunch of bone. A strangled cry. And then silence. Reyes hoped the sudden hush meant his men had neutralized the threat.

When he turned the corner to the side yard, his foot caught on something, tripping him. It was Bigelow. He lay flat on his back in the grass and stank like a perm gone wrong. Portions of his uniform had either melted or blown off, and his exposed skin was badly burned. Reyes checked him for a pulse and felt one, slow and weak.

Stahelski was slumped against the house not far away, his tongue lolling, eyes bulging. His helmet had been yanked backward off his head and twisted until its chin-strap cut off blood flow to his brain. Beside him was Mc-Tiernan, his right leg bent at an unnatural angle, his face misshapen by what looked to be a broken jaw.

Their guns, Reyes noted, were missing.

Reyes scrabbled over to check on the men. They were alive, but barely. Somehow, Bigelow, McTiernan, and Sta-helski had all been incapacitated without anybody—friend or foe—firing a single shot.

Luckily for Reyes, McTiernan *had* managed to injure his assailant. His combat knife lay beside him on the grass, and a trail of blood led from it into the fog.

Reyes followed it, pulse racing, his finger on the trigger of his SIG Sauer. Fog obliterated the world around him. After thirty yards or so, the blood trail stopped. Then a cold circle of gunmetal touched the base of Reyes's neck, and he realized he'd been had.

"Slick move, leaving a decoy blood trail," he said. "What, did you slice open your own goddamn arm?"

"Shut up," the man behind him whispered. "Put your hands behind your head. And take your finger off the trigger or the last thing you'll ever see is your teeth leaving your face."

Reyes complied. The man behind him took his weapon. Nylon rustled as he stashed it in a jacket pocket. "Now get on your knees."

Reyes started to do so. Then he spun and looped his arm around the man's wrist, pinning the gun against his side and wrenching it sideways.

The gun fell. Reyes dove and grabbed it. The man tackled him, and the gun slipped from Reyes's hand and skidded across the lawn.

Reyes was on his stomach in the grass. His assailant drove a knee in his back and grasped for his forearm, trying to maneuver him into an armlock.

Reyes elbowed him in the temple and received three quick jabs to the kidneys for his trouble. Pain spread, wet and loose, in Reyes's guts. He curled up instinctively to protect himself. The man rose and kicked him twice. Reyes swept the man's legs out from under him, and he went down hard.

Reyes was on him in an instant, straddling his chest and raining punches. His opponent was well trained; he anticipated, blocked, deflected. As Reyes's speed waned, the man caught his swinging fist and responded with an open palm to Reyes's face, trying to break Reyes's nose. Reyes dodged it but overbalanced and toppled.

They rolled, grappling, for a moment, each struggling for an edge. Reyes's hands slipped free. He took hold of his assailant's neck and squeezed, only to release his grip when he felt the gun that he'd surrendered digging into the tender flesh beneath his chin.

The man rose but kept the SIG Sauer trained on Reyes's face. He collected his firearm from where it lay a few feet away and aimed that at Reyes too.

"There are more men inside the house," Reyes rasped between breaths. "If you shoot me, they'll come running."

"Not fast enough to do you any good."

Now that the man used his full voice, Reyes thought there was something familiar about it. He squinted up at him in the dim half-light, eyes widening as recognition dawned.

"Hendricks?"

33.

REYES?" HENDRICKS SAID. "What the hell are *you* doing here?"

The two of them had worked together years ago, when Hendricks's Special Forces unit was brought in on a mission to rescue eleven U.S. NGO workers—three of whom were actually CIA assets—who'd been kidnapped by narco-guerrillas in Colombia. Reyes had been the Company's top field agent in the area at the time, working out of the U.S. embassy in Bogotá, officially as a cultural attaché.

"That's a funny question coming from a guy I heard was dead."

"Those reports were greatly exaggerated."

Reyes looked him up and down. "Maybe not *greatly*. You look like shit."

Hendricks believed him. His cheeks felt flushed. His

throat was parched. The stitched-up knife wound in his side was burning up and seeping blood.

"Really? I've never felt better. When did you go private? Last time we crossed paths, you were with the CIA."

"Yeah, well, last time we crossed paths, *you* were one of the good guys."

"Funny. I was gonna say the same of you, but I don't know if you're crooked now or just a patsy."

"Fuck you, Mike. After what you did to my men—"

"Relax. Given proper medical attention, they'll recover. I don't kill without good reason. As far as I'm concerned, you guys aren't my enemies—you're just soldiers following orders."

"And what are *you?*"

"I'm the guy who's gonna leave with Frank Segreti. What'd Yancey tell you about him?"

"Just that he's a person of interest in the bridge attack. Until now, I didn't even know his last name."

"Segreti had nothing to do with what happened at the bridge."

"You sure about that?"

"Pretty sure."

"Then how about you put the guns down and we can sort this whole thing out?"

"I wish I could, but I don't know if I can trust you. Get on your knees. Put your hands behind your head."

"C'mon, Hendricks—don't do this."

Hendricks circled him, and put Pappas's .45 to Reyes's head.

"Don't make me ask again."

Finally, with obvious reluctance, Reyes did as Hendricks asked.

"For what it's worth," Hendricks said, "I'm sorry our reunion has to end this way."

"Forgive me if I don't find that terribly comforting," Reyes replied. Then he closed his eyes and waited for the gunshot that would end his life.

Hendricks wrapped his left arm around Reyes's neck and locked his right elbow around his left wrist. Reyes struggled as Hendricks tightened his chokehold, then slackened.

Hendricks lowered Reyes's unconscious form to the ground and searched his pockets. When he found what he was looking for, he smiled.

"Bigelow? Stahelski? Goddamn it, *somebody* report!"

The only reply Yancey received was static. Seven minutes had passed since they'd lost contact with the team outside. In the house, he and his men grew more anxious by the second. Even Segreti seemed to feel the strain because he was uncharacteristically quiet, his mouth a grim straight line. Then again, he might've been grieving. While Yancey's men glanced nervously from curtained window to curtained window, Segreti's gaze never left the body on the floor.

"You want us to go check out the situation?" Swinson offered.

"No," Yancey replied. "The prisoner's our first priority. Call for backup. We'll sit tight until they arrive."

He did as Yancey ordered. Yancey crossed the living room, parted the curtains slightly, and peeked outside.

"You got eyes on 'em, boss?" This from Lutz.

"Nope. I can't see shit through all this fog." But as he said it, he realized that wasn't quite true. Something big and dark was moving out there, too far away for him to make out the details.

Then its headlights lit up and its engine roared, and he realized what he was looking at.

It was one of the Humvees they'd left parked out front—and it was coming right at him.

"Look out!" Yancey shouted.

He staggered backward, releasing the curtain. The room darkened as it swung closed. Yancey's calves connected with the coffee table and he toppled over, the table splintering beneath his weight. Lutz and Weddle moved to help him, but he waved them off and rolled frantically to his left.

Then the front wall imploded as five thousand pounds of diesel-powered steel crashed into the house.

The rat-a-tat of automatic fire pierced the night as the Bellum men unloaded on the Humvee. As strategies went, it wasn't the smartest. For one thing, the vehicle was bulletproof. For another, Hendricks wasn't in it.

After he'd popped the hatchback and maneuvered it into position, Hendricks wedged one of the assault rifles he'd confiscated between the gas pedal and driver's seat. The engine screamed, but the Humvee, still in neutral, stayed put. When he reached through the open driver's-side door and dropped it into gear, the vehicle leaped forward like an animal released, damn near taking off his arm in the process.

It roared up the Broussards' walkway, snapped the porch supports like matchsticks, and buried itself to its rear tires inside the house before it stalled. Hendricks sprinted after it. Once the Bellum men stopped shooting, he climbed through the open hatchback and entered the living room via the Humvee's back left door.

The Humvee'd made a wreck of the beautiful old house. A portion of the ceiling had collapsed, half burying the vehicle in rubble and pinning its right passenger-side doors closed. One Bellum man was pinned between the Humvee and an interior wall. He was alive but screaming, and it looked as if his pelvis was crushed. Hendricks swore. He'd hoped the headlights would serve as fair warning.

Another had taken a ricochet to the knee when he'd opened fire on the Humvee. He was on the floor at Hendricks's feet, one hand pressed tight to the pulsing wound, the other trying to free his sidearm from its holster. Hendricks kicked him in the face and his eyes rolled up in his head.

A click behind Hendricks alerted him to the fact that someone outside his line of sight had just reloaded. He dove further into the ruined living room as the floor behind him was pocked with bullet holes, rolling as he landed and then putting three rounds into his would-be killer's chest. The man went down writhing in pain and pawing at the edges of his tactical vest.

The vest had kept him alive, as Hendricks knew it would, dispersing the energy of the bullets before they could punch through. Still, the force of impact was enough to squeeze the air out of his lungs and break his ribs. It'd be fifteen, twenty seconds before his body remembered how to breathe, and even then it'd be an agony.

Hendricks looked around. Saw the woman from the photo Cameron had intercepted lying dead on the floor, a gunshot wound in her chest. Then, on the other side of the Humvee, a handgun boomed, and the couch beside Hendricks coughed batting.

The shot had come from Yancey's gun. He was cut off from the living room by the vehicle, so he'd pushed aside enough of the rubble atop it to take aim.

Hendricks returned fire. He didn't expect to hit Yancey, but he wanted to make him think twice before he took another shot. Then he crawled behind the couch for cover and came face to face with Frank Segreti.

Segreti lay flat on his back, bound. His face was bruised and swollen. Fresh blood oozed from his nose. The man was a born survivor; it looked to Hendricks like he'd launched himself over the couch when the shooting started.

Hendricks fished the X-Acto knife from his cargo pocket, uncapped it with his teeth, and used it to cut Segreti's bonds. "C'mon," he said. "We're getting out of here."

"Who the fuck *are* you?" Segreti asked.

"Does it matter?"

The couch shuddered as Yancey fired again.

"No," Segreti said. "I guess it doesn't."

Hendricks shot off a few more rounds in Yancey's direction. Then he and Segreti cut through the kitchen to the back door, Yancey cursing loudly behind them.

When Hendricks yanked the door open, he heard sirens in the distance. But as he stepped into the night, Segreti grabbed him by the shirt.

"What?" Hendricks said. "We're kind of in a hurry here!"

Segreti snatched something off the countertop and slapped it into Hendricks's hand. Hendricks looked at it and broke into a grin.

It was a key fob for the Jaguar in the driveway.

They sprinted toward the car, a sleek two-seat coupe with the exterior of a 1960s race car and the interior of a fighter cockpit. It unlocked automatically as they approached. Somewhere behind them, glass tinkled. Hendricks climbed into the car, but Segreti struggled to figure out the recessed door handle. A bullet thunked into the pavement at his feet.

Yancey, unable to follow them, had headed upstairs and was shooting at them from a window on the second floor.

Hendricks leaned across the passenger seat and opened Segreti's door from the inside. Then he pressed the Jaguar's start button and the engine roared to life, 550 horses strong.

A bullet shattered the rear window. Another punched through the roof and buried itself in the dash, passing an inch from Segreti's head along the way.

The car lurched forward, tires squealing. Four Bellum Humvees pulled up in front of the house. One rocked to a halt at the end of the driveway, cutting off Hendricks and Segreti. Hendricks jerked the wheel and stomped on the gas. The Jaguar fishtailed when its tires hit the lawn. Then it took off like a rocket through the fog.

Hendricks killed the headlights and drove blind, instinct guiding him. They roared through gardens, down footpaths, and over curbs, no destination but away. Two of the Humvees gave chase, but they were too wide to slip through narrow gaps and no match for the Jaguar's speed.

Eventually, Hendricks and Segreti were alone save for the engine's roar and the endless wail of sirens in the distance.

34.

"So, Charlie, you want to explain to me just what the hell is going on?"

They were in O'Brien's office. The door was closed. O'Brien had dragged Thompson there by the arm as soon as the picture found its way into her hands.

A few minutes ago, CNN had interrupted their interview with that asshole senator Trip Wentworth—the one who'd raked Thompson over the coals after the Pendleton's Casino disaster—with breaking news of further violence in San Francisco. At first, the other agents in the conference room barely glanced at the television. CNN had already reported many spurious claims of follow-up attacks today: A federal building in LA evacuated for what turned out to be a gas leak. An active-shooter threat at a Seattle high school called in by a student unprepared for a test. A backpack in San Francisco detonated by the

270

bomb squad that turned out to contain nothing more than roadside-emergency supplies.

But Thompson knew in her gut this one was different. She'd been waiting for an update from Hendricks ever since that torturous conference call with Yancey. Hell, she'd half expected Hendricks to strike while she and O'Brien were still on the line, and the longer Thompson went without hearing a word, the more she began to worry he hadn't gotten to Segreti in time.

Her fellow agents started to take note when CNN spoke via phone to several Presidio residents who reported shots fired near the Main Post. One claimed to've seen an explosion light up the night sky. Another swore vehicles in a high-speed chase had cut through her backyard. Details were scant, though. Thanks to the fog, news helicopters were grounded, and officials on the scene weren't talking to the press.

Then Bellum Industries issued an urgent memo to the FBI and Homeland Security. It claimed they'd been pursuing a lead when their operatives were ambushed. Seven men were injured in the attack, two critically, and a civilian woman was dead. The memo included a still image of the perpetrator, isolated from body-cam footage.

When O'Brien saw it, she recognized Michael Hendricks instantly.

"I don't know what you're talking about," Thompson lied. Her tone was indignant, unequivocal, but her head was spinning, and her insides roiled.

"You mean to tell me it's a coincidence that Michael Hendricks just waltzed smack into the middle of our investigation?"

"Must be," Thompson said.

"Must be?" O'Brien parroted snidely. "You're kidding, right? You're lucky there aren't a lot of people in this world who know his face. But the director does, and you'd best believe I'm going to get a phone call the second he sees that photo. I'm wondering how much I can protect you without lying."

"What do you want me to say, Kate?"

"I want you to tell me you haven't been in contact with a criminal. That you didn't hire him to protect a man you believe to be a long-dead federal witness. That you're not complicit in a fucking shootout that resulted in the death of an innocent civilian and the hospitalization of half a dozen government contractors. And I want it to be the truth."

"I did not hire Michael Hendricks," Thompson replied.

"That's a strangely specific denial."

"It's true. You can testify to that fact if need be, and so can I."

"That's not fucking good enough, Charlie! This is me you're talking to, not some random higher-up. We share a bed, for God's sake. We share a *life*. I want you to tell me exactly what is going on."

"No, you don't. Your career—"

"If you gave a shit about my career—or yours—we wouldn't be having this conversation. You want to convince me otherwise, you're going to need to tell me every-thing—*now*."

"Fine. You want the truth? Here it is. I put Hendricks onto Segreti. I had to. The Council was going to kill him if I didn't."

O'Brien's face showed disgust. She shook her head in

disbelief. When she spoke, it was barely audible, every syllable sagging under the weight of her hurt and disappointment. "How long have the two of you been in touch?"

"We haven't been! Not until last night."

"But you knew *how* to get in touch with him, and you withheld that information, despite the fact that it's your fucking job to catch him."

"I *didn't* know how to get in touch with him—not specifically. But I had a hunch that Evelyn Walker might have a way to reach him, and I was right."

"You could have laid a trap. Brought him in. A win like that would have made your career."

"That's funny," Thompson spat, "I was told by my superior that now wasn't the time for side projects. That our efforts were required elsewhere."

"Don't you dare put this on me. You're the one who fucked up here."

"You know as well as I do that Evelyn Walker would never have given me his contact information if I'd had any intention of using it against him, so bringing him in wasn't an option. And besides, none of this matters, because when I met with him and explained the situation, he turned me down."

"It sure as hell doesn't look like he turned you down."

"What do you want me to say? He told me he didn't want to get involved. Until he—" Thompson stopped herself abruptly.

"Until he what?" O'Brien asked. Then her expression shifted. "The phone call you ducked out to take. It wasn't Jess, was it? It was Hendricks. You *knew* he planned to make some kind of move."

"I had no idea what he intended to do."

"Oh, I think you could've guessed. He's a hired gun, for Christ's sake!"

"Look, I didn't think—"

"You're goddamn right you didn't think. They'll have your badge for this, you know. You'll be lucky if you don't wind up in prison."

"If they find out," Thompson said carefully.

"Oh, so you're asking me to cover for you now? To lie to the Bureau and risk a career it's taken me a lifetime to build? How could you do this to me, Charlie? How could you do this to *us?*"

"How could *I?* How could *you* refuse to even broach the topic of picking up Segreti when you were on the phone with the director? How could you deny my request to go track him down myself when you knew how much this case meant to me? I'm talking about nothing less than shattering the largest criminal organization in U.S. history, one so far-reaching and shadowy, most people don't even realize it exists. So don't go lecturing me about shirking my responsibilities, not when you're the one who turned a blind eye to the opportunity Segreti presented us just so you could avoid making a few waves."

"Oh, I see. First you stab me in the back, and now you call me a coward?"

"If I stabbed you in the back, it was with the same knife you buried in mine."

O'Brien's jaw clenched. She shook with rage. "Get out of my sight. As of now, you're relieved."

"Now? You can't be serious."

"Yes, now. I don't trust you anymore, which means you're of no use to me."

"So, what—you want me to just go home and sit on my hands in the middle of an investigation?"

"No," O'Brien replied, tears brimming. "I want you to go home and pack."

"You're kicking me out?"

"I...I don't know. But what I do know is, I need some space, because right now, I can't even look at you."

"Kate, c'mon. You know me. You know I didn't mean for this to happen—or for any of it to blow back on you."

"I thought I did," O'Brien said. "It turns out, I don't know you at all."

35.

WHEN A BLEATING horn pierced the quiet, Hendricks went, by instinct, for his gun. Then he realized the sound was coming from his burner phone. Cameron—ever the technological smartass—must have set his ringer to the James Bond theme when she was mucking with it on the plane. He hadn't heard it before because the phone had been silenced. Now the brassy music echoed shrilly through the cavernous space. He couldn't help but think that Lester would've approved.

He and Segreti were holed up in a warehouse at the water's edge. It was used to clean and store boats. The interior reeked of mildew and toluene. Water lapped against the nearby pilings. Amber light spilled through the filthy windows from the streetlights outside.

All around them were yachts of various sizes, shrink-wrapped in white plastic and propped up with rusted stands that looked like camera tripods. The warehouse doors—front, back, and enormous overhead garage-style—were sealed with police tape (which parted easily when sliced with an X-Acto knife and cut so cleanly that when the door was closed, it still appeared unbroken from a distance), and an official notice stuck to each declared the building cleared. The cops had searched it and moved on, which made it the perfect place to hide.

They never would've made it out of the Presidio if it hadn't been for the fog, which only grew denser as the night wore on. Though the neighborhood surrounding the Broussard house was soon crawling with patrols, and the park's perimeter was on high alert, no one could see more than ten feet in any direction. The toughest challenge in eluding them was not wrapping the Jaguar around a tree.

They ditched the car soon after, in a parking lot beside the Palace of Fine Arts. Then they hoofed it downslope to the marina. A lone uniformed cop walked its grounds. Slipping by him had been a breeze.

One of the larger yachts had an inflatable dinghy strapped to its stern. Hendricks and Segreti wrestled it into the water, and Hendricks rowed it into the bay, taking them as far as his arms could manage. Once they were a ways from shore, he let the motor do the work, wincing as it rumbled noisily to life.

Hendricks had been trying to contact Cameron ever since. Phone. Text. The e-mail account they'd set up for her in case she was forced to ditch her phone. But the calls went unanswered, the texts and e-mails unread. His failed attempts hung like ellipses, like a circuit waiting to be completed.

He answered the phone "Cameron?"

"Who the hell is Cameron?" was the reply.

Shit. Thompson.

"No one. Don't worry about it. Why the hell are you calling me?"

"Are you fucking kidding me? Your handiwork at the Presidio is all over CNN."

"I have no idea what you're talking about," he lied—immediate, automatic.

"Cut the bullshit. I've seen pictures. You were there."

Pictures? How? And then it clicked. "Son of a bitch," Hendricks muttered, as much to himself as Thompson. "The Bellum operatives were wearing body cameras, weren't they?"

"Yeah. Which means you can add the death of Lois Broussard, conspiracy to commit an act of terror, and a handful of federal assault charges to your résumé. The Bellum men are expected to pull through, in case you're wondering."

"I wasn't. If I'd wanted to kill them, they'd be dead."

"Like the Broussard woman?"

"I didn't kill Lois—Yancey did."

"That's a fucking relief. Oh, wait—no, it's not, because now my boss, my..." Thompson's voice hitched with emotion. She gathered herself and tried again. "Now O'Brien knows we've been in touch. Knows I sent you. My career is ruined. I might wind up in jail."

"You're not going to wind up in jail. In fact, they'll probably throw you a goddamn parade once you bring Segreti in from the cold and he clears this whole mess up."

There was a long pause, and when Thompson next spoke, her tone was tinged with hope. "You're telling me you have him, and he's willing to testify?"

"He's got some demands, but yeah."

"What kind of demands?"

"For one, he'll talk only to you—and he wants you to personally oversee the details of his protection."

"Me? Why?"

"He remembers you a bit. Thought you seemed like a straight shooter."

"I doubt it. When we met, I was just a green kid in over my head."

"Yeah, well, I also might've vouched for you. Said you were trustworthy. That you'd keep him safe."

"Okay," she said, "what else?"

Hendricks hesitated. "Wherever you stash him, it has to be near a hospital with a decent oncology department."

"You mean..."

"He's sick."

"How sick?"

"Hard to say. Last time he saw a doc was seven years ago. She told him he was in remission but that it could return at any time. He's pretty sure it's returned."

"Fuck. Fuck, fuck, fuck. You know how hard it is to make a case on the videotaped testimony of a criminal?"

"No. My methods are a little more direct."

"Your methods are illegal."

"So's jaywalking. That doesn't mean it's not the fastest route. Consider his illness motivation to make your case in a timely fashion."

"Anything else?"

"Yeah." Hendricks filled her in on the rest of Segreti's demands. "So what do you say? Can you make that happen?"

"I—I think so."

279

"You think so?"

"Well, I'm not exactly in the Bureau's good graces right this second, but I'll try."

"Okay," Hendricks said.

"Okay as in he'll do it?"

"Okay as in I'll talk to him and see what he has to say."

"Thanks," she said. "Stay safe out there. And try not to shoot anyone else."

"I'll do my best," he said.

He hung up. Segreti, beside him, asked, "So how'd it go?"

"About as well as could be expected."

"You okay? You ain't looking too good."

"I'll be fine," Hendricks said—although in truth, he was pretty sure his wound was infected. He felt achy and feverish. His skin was slick with sweat and radiated heat. He crossed his arms to quell his shivering. "Right now, I'm more worried about keeping you alive long enough to deliver you to Thompson."

"Thanks, but I'll tell you, I'd trade places with Lois in a heartbeat if I could."

"Were, uh, you two..."

Segreti looked aghast. "No! Nothing like that. Not that I *wouldn't* have...it's just...when I found her, she was in a bad way. Her husband was on the bridge when the tugboat hit."

"Jesus."

"Yeah. We met by accident. I thought I was busting into an empty house. Turns out, I interrupted her while she was trying to off herself. She thought maybe I was meant to, that God had sent me to save her life. I don't usually go in for that kind of thinking, but I really wanted to believe her. She was a nice lady. A good person. The world was better with her in it, and I figured that if I'd played a part in keeping her here, maybe my life wasn't so worthless after all."

"Is that why you walked in seven years ago? You were trying to square your accounts?"

"Yeah. No. I don't know. I mean, my doc first diagnosed me eight years ago. Put me through surgery, chemo, radiation. It was hell, but when I came out the other side, I thought I'd beat this thing. So it's not like I thought I had to prepare my soul for the great beyond or anything. It was more that I felt like I'd been given a second chance. Like the cancer was a shot across the bow. After, I was changed. And the business changed too. I found I didn't have the stomach for it anymore."

Hendricks nodded. He could relate. The moment that had changed him was a brush with mortality as well. Not his own, but a young soldier's whose throat he'd slit, a man scarcely more than a boy who'd died, terrified, in his arms, his blood flowing between Hendricks's fingers.

He shuddered. Pushed the memory away. Blamed the goose bumps on his fever. "What do you mean, the business changed?"

"Look, I'm not one to make excuses for what I've done. I was a criminal. A murderer. And I enjoyed it. Not the killing, you understand. That was just the cost of doing business. Every made guy on the planet knows going in they're playing for keeps. Knows if they're not sharp enough, careful enough, good enough, they'll get got. But the lifestyle...the lifestyle's fucking glorious. And we did enough good, I could get to sleep at night."

Hendricks was incredulous. "You did good?"

"Damn *right* we did. The fact is, much as the white hats wanna pretend like organized crime is a scourge on society, we serve a fucking purpose. Some places, the family—or gang, or whatever—is all a community's got. We clean up neighborhoods the police won't touch. Make it safe to walk the streets."

"Yeah, you're fucking saints."

"I ain't claiming we are. We took our piece. We got rich. We lived the life. But the family I came up through had rules: No dope, no girls, and no tolerance for anyone who moved 'em on our territory. Did we charge local businesses protection? You're goddamn right we did. But you wanna know something? We fucking *earned* that money. In twenty years, there was maybe five holdups in my neighborhood. Probably twice as many rapes and muggings. Know how many the cops solved? Not a goddamn one. But thanks to me and mine, every one a them fuckers paid."

"So what happened? How'd you get from there to talking to the FBI?"

"Used to be, our business was about community. We provided what the cops and straight businesses wouldn't, or couldn't. But then we got greedy. We formed ourselves a council. Stopped thinking like a bunch of family businesses and started thinking like a global fucking corporation. Stopped taking care of our own. We'd deal in anything that paid. It began in the seventies, with dope. Smack, coke, and crack. Then came guns—to gangbangers, militants, whack-job cult leaders, whoever had the cash. Ain't like we asked 'em their intentions. Then came girls. Most of 'em unwilling. Brought into the country and kept like fucking pets, only we don't force-feed our pets junk to keep 'em docile. Next thing you know, our communities are rotting from the inside, but we don't care, because we've never been richer. And then the Council decided to aim higher."

"Meaning what?"

"Meaning some Council members realized we could lower our overhead if we took the operation international. Next thing I knew, we were buying off lawmakers and bureaucrats in Sarajevo, Amsterdam, Johannesburg. Making deals with fucking warlords to trade girls for guns. Watching the evening news and seeing the weapons we'd sold turned on the poor and helpless. I couldn't stomach it. Then I got sick—which was a blessing, in a way, because it removed me from the day-to-day. But the young punk who covered for me while I was undergoing treatment had designs to make his new position permanent, and he had some shady partner he said could take us legit and make us rich beyond our wildest dreams—if we made the partner chairman, that is."

"Who?"

"Hell if I know. But he must've had enough clout that the Council thought he could deliver, because next thing I know, I'm on a one-way ticket to the desert. I barely escaped with my life, and when I did, I went straight to the fucking Feds. You know how that turned out."

"Yeah. What I *don't* know is how you survived the blast at the safe house."

"Somebody with a cleaner conscience than mine might say it was divine providence. I think it was dumb fucking luck. I was in the basement when the bomb went off—doing laundry, if you can believe it. Half the house came down around me, but somehow, I walked away."

"But I understand they found your DNA."

"When the Feds heard I'd been sick, they brought in a doctor on the quiet to check me out. He drew some samples and packed 'em up to send 'em to the lab. They were sitting on the counter when the bomb went off. Seemed like a goddamn gift to me when I found out. I thought about hunting down the bastards who tried to kill me. I thought about making them pay. Then I figured, fuck it— maybe being dead's the best thing that ever happened to me. Maybe it means I can start fresh. Live out whatever days I've got left in peace. I'd always said that when I retired, I was gonna move to San Francisco—so that's exactly what I did."

Hendricks was envious of Segreti's fresh start. He wished he could have allowed himself to walk away. But then, Segreti hadn't gotten as far away as he'd thought. "What was your role with the Council, exactly?"

"There ain't really a name for what I did, but I used to say I was the Devil's Red Right Hand. I made sure the Council's word became deed."

"So if, for example, the Council were to hire a hitter to take care of a problem…"

"I'd be the guy to hire him, yeah."

"The guy who pushed you out—what was his name?" Hendricks asked casually, but Segreti was too smart to fall for it.

"I'll tell you what. First you deliver me safely to this Agent Thompson. Then I'll give you his name."

"Deal," Hendricks said. "Just do me a favor and don't go dying in the meantime."

36.

CAMERON CAME TO in a dingy room no more than four feet across. A bare lightbulb was screwed into the fixture above her. The floor on which she sat sloped toward a drain at its center. The wall they'd left her propped against was water-stained and smelled of cleaning products. A utility sink jutted from the wall.

A janitor's closet, she realized.

Apart from Cameron, it was empty. No mops, no tools, no cleaning products—nothing she could use as a weapon. Not that she was in any shape to fight. Her head pounded. Her limbs ached. Her thoughts were slippery, and she had difficulty holding on to them.

She rattled the door. Locked. She banged on it awhile and shouted herself hoarse, but no one came.

An hour or so later, the door opened. The hallway's fluorescent light was an assault. A wild-eyed man in filthy clothes and cowboy boots stood just outside, conferring with the head of hospital security. The latter's nose was packed with cotton, and when he looked at her, his features warped with rage.

"She's all yours, Mr. Yancey—but be warned, she's scrappier than she looks. "

They yanked her to her feet and zip-tied her hands behind her back. Then Yancey dragged her out a service entrance, identifying himself as law enforcement to everyone they passed so they'd ignore her cries for help.

As they crossed the lot to Yancey's rental car, the fog enveloped them. Cameron managed to writhe free of his grasp when he took a hand off her to open the back door, but Yancey grabbed her by the collar and punched her in the face. His ring split her cheek open like an overripe tomato. She crumpled, dazed, to the concrete. He kicked her until she blacked out, and possibly a while longer.

When she came to, she was lying across the backseat with what seemed to be a pair of dress socks in her mouth, her feet now zip-tied too. Her arms burned from lack of blood flow. Her ribs ached with every breath. Her face was so swollen that she could barely open her left eye, and it was sticky from drying blood.

The cabin of the rented Cadillac was thick with cigarette smoke. Pavement clattered by beneath. Yancey was on the phone.

"…about fucking time we caught a break. Hold position until I arrive—I want to be there when you go in." A pause. "No, I'll call the boss myself and let him know."

They jounced over a set of train tracks and Cameron was momentarily airborne. Her cheek slammed into the armrest on her way down. The pain was excruciating. Her eyes watered. Her vision went spotty. She cried out involuntarily, but it was stifled by the gag in her mouth.

Sometime later—five minutes? an hour?—the Caddy rocked to a halt. Yancey put a hand on the passenger-seat headrest, turned around, and favored her with a manic smile. His cheeks were flushed. His eyes were wide. "Sit tight, darlin'. Daddy's got some work to do. But don't you worry, he'll be back soon enough. And then you and me are gonna make your buddy pay."

He engaged the backseat child locks and climbed out of the car.

As soon as she was reasonably sure he was out of sight, Cameron began to move.

"What's the sitrep?" Yancey asked, out of breath from having trotted across the parking lot. He'd left his rental car around the corner of a nearby building because he couldn't risk the girl making noise and compromising the mission—or seeing something that she shouldn't.

"Heat signatures indicate two people inside," the man who'd called him—Osborne—said, "which is consistent with our intel."

"Armed?"

"Hard to say. It looks to me like they're asleep. Near as we can tell, they have no idea we're here."

The imam, it turned out, had been telling the truth; he'd had nothing to do with the bombing or the men who perpetrated it. But then, Yancey'd already known that, just as he'd known the men in question *did*, in fact, attend that mosque while they were in town. Eventually, though, with enough cajoling, that imam coughed up a list of names—almost literally, in fact, along with a pint or so of malt liquor and the contents of his stomach—of congregants who might be sympathetic to those espousing extremist views. Bellum dispatched a team to each, and they repeated the process. Eventually, one interview bore fruit. Yielded an address. The man who gave it to them had—along with his family—been taken into Bellum custody until Yancey's people could determine whether his information was legitimate.

The address was of a shuttered body shop in South San Francisco. Bellum's source said it was where the remaining members of the True Islamic Caliphate were hiding out and planning their next attack.

It's no wonder the business didn't last, Yancey thought now—the place sat in a desolate stretch of self-storage facilities, warehouses, and old factories, train tracks slicing up the parcels of land at odd angles.

That was good.

It meant fewer witnesses.

"Are your men in position?" Yancey asked.

"Yes, sir. We've got teams stationed at all three entrances, and snipers on the adjacent roofs. All we're waiting on is your go-ahead."

"You've got it," Yancey replied.

Osborne gave the order. His men breached all three entrances at once. For a moment all was chaos. Shouting. Screaming. Frenzied action. Yancey hung back and braced for gunfire—but there wasn't any. It was over in seconds, the men inside subdued without a shot.

"Clear?" Yancey called from just outside the door.

"Clear!"

He dropped his cigarette. Ground it out beneath his boot. Picked up the butt and slipped it into his pocket before he entered.

Two Arab men were hog-tied on their stomachs in the middle of the floor, their backs arched, ankles in the air. Gags stretched across their mouths. Both were young, skinny, and hollow-eyed. One was quiet, still. The other sobbed. Surrounded by armed men in riot gear, they looked more frightened than frightening. That was always the way, Yancey thought. In the end, every monster he'd ever met was just a man, full of hopes and fears and weaknesses of mind and flesh. But that didn't mean they weren't also monsters.

Flashlights swept across the darkened space as Yancey's men searched the building. It smelled of sweat and motor oil. Three sleeping bags lay beside the bound men, two open and mussed, one rolled neatly, its nylon straps clipped and yanked so tight that its ends flared out. A camp stove and a couple pots sat nearby. Empty cans were scattered all around—SpaghettiOs, fruit cock-tail, Coca-Cola. Funny to think of terrorists eating like four-year-olds. Yancey wondered if any of the food quali-fied as halal. Maybe their God didn't care. Maybe bomb-ing the bridge earned them their virgins no matter what they ate.

"Sir!" one of the men called. Who, Yancey didn't know. Bellum's matte-black ballistic masks rendered them indis-tinguishable from one another.

"What is it, son?"

"Come look at this."

The man panned his flashlight across a digital cam-corder on a tripod and the filthy sheet that it was pointed at, which hung from the wall, a makeshift backdrop. Be-side the sheet was a workbench. Yancey wandered over and inspected it. On it were two combat knives. Three handguns. A Kalashnikov. A MAC-10. Assorted maps, blueprints, and bomb schematics. A cling-wrapped brick of plastic explosive the dusky orange of Wisconsin cheddar. And two partially assembled suicide vests festooned with braids of multicolored wire and studded with ball bearings.

Yancey poked at the vests. Examined the schematics in detail. Hefted the MAC-10, testing its weight. He ejected the magazine, peeked inside, and reinserted it with a click. Then he trotted over to where the terrorists lay and crouched beside them so he could see their faces.

"Evenin', gentlemen," he said. "Long time, no see."

One of the men stared at Yancey, hatred glimmering in his eyes. The other's eyes were shut tight. Tears streamed down his cheeks.

"Jesus, Waheeb. I never pegged you for being such a whiny little bitch. You should take a lesson from al-Nasr here and man up. You're embarrassing yourself."

Al-Nasr attempted to reply, but the gag prevented it. Yancey watched him with amusement for a moment, and then removed it.

"Do not speak to Waheeb this way," he said, his English heavily accented. "He is ten times the man you will ever be."

"If you say so," Yancey said. "Since you two are still alive, I'm guessing Bakr must've been the one piloting the boat. Does that mean he drew the short straw or the long? I can never tell if you people are serious about dying for your God or if you're all just beating your chests and secretly hoping one of your buddies will volunteer."

"Bakr was a hero," al-Nasr said. "He died with honor. We should all be so fortunate."

"You think? Because I think he was a fucking coward who killed a bunch of innocent people for no reason. A worthless piece of human trash too dumb to realize he'd been misled for his whole miserable life. I bet he died with shit-stained trousers."

"I would not expect you to understand his sacrifice."

"Let me tell you what I understand. I understand that Bellum brought you here to train you to better fight Assad, and in return you promised us intel and freedom to operate within your territory. I understand you disappeared from the safe house we set up for you right around the time a massive cache of Semtex went missing from our training facility. I understand a member of the local mosque we recommended told you that this place was vacant and suggested you could hole up here without attracting attention. What I *don't* understand is why you decided to dick us over or where you got the boat and bomb schematics, because they sure as shit didn't come from us."

"Suffice to say, we have some very generous friends."

"And here I thought *we* were your friends—but apparently you'd rather bite the hand that feeds you than free your homeland from oppression."

"You think we owe you loyalty?" Al-Nasr's face showed disdain. "We owe you *nothing*. Allah will reward us for what we've done."

"Yeah? Be sure to say hello to Him for me." Yancey raised the MAC-10 and loosed a flurry of bullets into al-Nasr and Waheeb. He didn't ease off the trigger until the gun clicked empty and the two men were scarcely more than meat and gristle.

Bellum men came running but lowered their weapons

when they realized there was no threat. Yancey's ears rang. The room stank of voided bowels and spent ammo.

Osborne, red-faced with fury, grabbed Yancey by the lapels. He had three inches and forty pounds of muscle on Yancey, easy. "What the fuck was that?" he asked.

Yancey dropped the MAC-10 and placed his hand on the wooden grip of his revolver. "Get your goddamn hands off me. Our orders were clear."

"But if we'd had the chance to question these assholes, we might've discovered who helped them carry out the attack!"

"Sure, unless the Feds caught wind of the fact that we had suspects in custody and took them from us before they cracked. What do you think would happen if the world found out that Bellum brought these fucking towelheads into the country under false pretenses and gave them access to explosives? I'm guessing that scenario ends in prison sentences, and I'm not eager to play bitch for the same lowlifes I spent twenty years putting away."

"When we brought them here, we had no way of knowing that they planned to double-cross us."

"Listen to yourself. Do you really think that matters? The longer these two remained breathing, the greater the chance that Bellum's role in the attack, however inadvertent, would be exposed. If you'd just put them down when you came in, we wouldn't be having this conversation."

"My men and I aren't trained to shoot people who don't pose a threat."

"Well, then, I guess you should be thanking me for saving you the trouble."

"You think I ought to *thank* you? I—"

Yancey held up a finger to silence him. His phone was

humming in his pocket. He took it out and answered it. "Hello, Mr. Wentworth. Yes, it's done. Thank you, sir, but our tac team deserves most of the credit—they did good work." He covered the mouthpiece of the phone and said to Osborne, "Anything you'd like to add, or are we good?"

Osborne fumed but said nothing.

Yancey terminated the call. Then he knelt, fished a handkerchief from his pocket, and used it to wipe his prints off the MAC-10.

"Comb this place from top to bottom," he said. "Take the Semtex and anything else that could lead back to Bellum. Then send teams through the surrounding buildings to look for witnesses and cameras."

"That could take all night."

"Then it takes all night. We're on the one-yard line, son. Let's not fumble now because we forgot to dot our *i*'s or cross our *t*'s."

"Yes, sir," Osborne replied through gritted teeth.

"Good man." Yancey clapped him on the shoulder condescendingly and headed for door, lighting a fresh cigarette as he stepped once more into the fog.

Cameron sat in the rancid muck that had leaked out of a rusty dumpster and tried to use the hole's jagged edge to saw through her zip-tie handcuffs. She couldn't see what she was doing because her hands were behind her back, but her wrists burned with every downstroke, and blood dripped freely from her fingers.

I'll be pissed if I survive this only to die of tetanus, she thought.

Earlier, as soon as Yancey's footfalls had been swallowed by the fog and Cameron knew she was alone in the backseat of the Caddy, she had curled into a fetal position and tried to bring her hands around front by sliding them past her butt and pulling her legs through. But she was bound too tightly, the V made by her arms too narrow.

The exertion winded her. Yancey had stuffed a pair of balled-up dress socks in her mouth, and she could barely breathe through her nose because it was crusted with dried blood. *If I want to get out of here*, she thought, *I'm going to have to get rid of these goddamn socks.*

She'd opened her jaw as far as she could and pushed at the socks with her tongue. It seemed to take forever, but eventually, she succeeded in getting them out. She licked her lips and spat lint onto the backseat.

Yancey had engaged the rear child locks. With her hands and feet bound, she had no hope of climbing into the front seat and unlocking the door. That left one option... and it was going to be noisy.

Cameron scooted into position. Drew her knees up to her chest. Kicked the Caddy's back right window as hard as she could.

The car shook. Her legs ached. But the window didn't break.

She tried again. Still nothing.

Automatic gunfire echoed through the night. Cameron shuddered with terror and willed herself not to cry. Then she doubled her efforts.

On the seventh kick, the window shattered. She threw herself out of the aperture and landed face-first on the pavement, her hands useless behind her. For a moment, agony blotted out the world. It took every ounce of will she possessed not to scream.

With some assistance from the car, she'd managed to

stand. She tried to hop away but soon toppled and was forced to inch along on her stomach. The fog enveloped her. Eventually, she wriggled around a corner, out of sight of anyone near the car.

She'd found herself in an alley between buildings. It was shrouded in long shadows, its only illumination the distant streetlights through the fog. Her first thought when she'd crawled behind the dumpster was to hide, but then she saw the hole and thought the edge might be sharp enough to sever her bonds.

Now, Cameron wondered about the gunfire. Hoped that Yancey had been killed. But she kept sawing because, deep down, she knew he hadn't.

She heard sounds coming from around the corner, a muffled curse and a fist pounding the Caddy's roof in frustration, and she realized he'd returned. She froze and tried to breathe as quietly as she could.

Seconds passed that way, or maybe hours, or maybe years. Then she caught a whiff of cigarette smoke, and a voice nearby said: "There you are, you little bitch. Didn't I tell you that I'd be right back?"

Cameron cowered. Tried to kick him with her bound feet as he approached. He slapped them aside, hoisted her up by her hair, and punched her twice in the gut.

The air whooshed out of her like a bellows. She doubled over in agony. Yancey used her momentum to throw her over his shoulder. Then he carried her back to the car.

As he stuffed her in the trunk, she begged, "Please don't kill me."

"Don't worry, kid. I'm not gonna kill you—not until you help me get Segreti back, that is."

37.

W E NEED TO TALK."

The voice was male and had a smoker's rasp. The number was Cameron's.

"Where did you find this phone?" Hendricks asked.

"That's what we need to talk about. See, I've got your girl."

Hendricks's stomach dropped. "What girl?"

"C'mon, jackass. You know what girl. Cute little thing. Fresh-faced, resourceful. Well, a little less fresh-faced than she was before I got my hands on her, to own the truth. Anyway, she's got your number in her contacts and no one else's."

"That chick doesn't mean a thing to me," Hendricks bluffed. "She's a groupie. A dilettante. A spoiled little rich kid looking for a thrill. I've been trying to shake her all week."

"Is that right."

"Yeah."

"Then why are there twelve missed calls from you on her phone?"

Hendricks took a deep breath and let it out slowly. "Why don't we skip to the part where you tell me what you want?"

"It's simple, really. I've got someone you're interested in. You've got someone I'm interested in. Seems to me we ought to make a swap."

"What makes you think I'll give up Segreti that easily?"

"If you don't, this little bitch'll die slow."

"So you say. For all I know, she's dead already."

There was a rustling on the other end of the line. Then, away from the phone's mike: "Say hello to your buddy, darlin'."

"M-M-Michael?" Hendricks's heart ached when he heard the tremor in Cameron's voice.

"Hey, kid. You okay?"

"Whatever Yancey tells you, don't believe hi—"

Cameron's words came out in a rush, and just as quickly, Yancey yanked the phone away. "I think that's enough for now," he said. "So, where and when you wanna make the swap?"

"I haven't said I'll do it, yet."

"Oh, you'll do it, but if I were you, I wouldn't take too long to come to that conclusion. If I don't hear from you soon, I'm liable to get bored."

"Keep this phone on," Hendricks said. "I'll be in touch."

He hung up before Yancey had a chance to reply. When

he tried to slide the phone back into his pocket, he realized he was trembling. The air around him suddenly felt
too close, too stale, too musty. He leaned heavily on the
boat beside him for a second. Then he decided he needed
to get the hell out of the warehouse. Without a moment's
concern over who might see him, he pushed out into the
darkness, gulping air as he walked down the pier.

The night was cool, silent. The fog was even thicker
than before. Hendricks could feel it part around him. It
smelled of ocean—salt, sulfur, and rot—and blunted the
lights along the waterfront, reducing Hendricks's world to
ten square feet of murky gray. He felt trapped, floating in
the void between day and night, life and death, between
his desire to avenge Lester and his wish that no one else
be sacrificed for his cause.

Close behind him, a throat cleared.

Hendricks wheeled and drew his gun. He was unaccustomed to being snuck up on. Fever had rendered him
weak. Distracted. Off his game.

It was Segreti. Hands in pockets. A sympathetic frown
on his face. He didn't flinch when the .45 came to a stop
an inch from the bridge of his nose. He just stared calmly
down the barrel until Hendricks lowered it.

"You okay?" Segreti asked.

"Honestly? Not really."

"Lemme guess: Yancey's got your friend."

"She's not my friend," Hendricks replied. "The truth
is, I hardly know her."

"Clearly, Yancey sees things differently, and whatever
else he is, he ain't stupid."

"Yancey can go fuck himself."

"No argument here, but that don't help the girl none."

"Hey, she sought me out, not the other way around. I never asked for her to get involved. I came here to find out what you know about the Council so I can take them down. The smart play would be for you and me to walk away and not look back."

"Guys like us ain't always cut out for the smart play. Besides, I'm not sure taking on the Council qualifies as one. What's your beef with them anyway?"

"Last year, they hired a hitter to come after me. He killed my partner."

"I'm sorry to hear it. Listen, not for nothing, but I know a thing or two about the Council, and betrayal, and revenge. The path you're on...no good ever comes of it."

"So what do you suggest I do instead?"

"Big picture? No fucking clue. But there's a girl out there who could really use your help. That seems as good a place to start as any."

"You know he wants me to trade you for her, right?"

"Yeah, I figured. Just like you probably figured he plans to screw you over and kill all three of us."

"The thought had crossed my mind."

"Then I guess the question is, what're we gonna do about it?"

"Actually," Hendricks said, "I have an idea—but it's not a good one. You'd be nuts to go along with it."

"Will it save the kid?"

"I think so, yeah."

"Do I get to live?"

"If you're very, very lucky."

Segreti laughed. Genuine and unself-conscious, it echoed loudly through the night, blunted only slightly by

299

the fog. "Easy, pal," Segreti said eventually. "Try not to oversell it."

"I don't want to bullshit you. I want you going in eyes open."

"Fair enough," Segreti said. "Let's hear it."

38.

THE TRUNK HATCH opened, and cool, clean air rushed in. Cameron's eyes fluttered. She whimpered as she stirred, the sound muffled by the socks once again in her mouth.

"Up and at 'em," Yancey said. Then he slapped her awake and dragged her out of the Cadillac by her hair.

Tears welled in her eyes. Her face and scalp burned. She tried to get her feet beneath her, but after a night spent zip-tied in the trunk, her limbs were clumsy, leaden, unresponsive. She wound up lying on the concrete, its chill leeching through her clothes.

They were in a parking garage, empty on this level except for the Cadillac. Dawn threatened but had yet to break. The world outside was bathed in blue, its details blurred by fog.

"I'm gonna remove your gag and cut you free, but if

you scream or try to run, I swear to Christ I'll shoot you. Understand?"

Cameron nodded.

He sliced through her zip-ties with a utility knife and pulled the socks from her mouth. Cameron coughed so hard she thought she might throw up. He'd stuffed them in way farther than last time, and his extracting them had triggered her gag reflex.

"Here," he said, uncapping a bottle of water and handing it to her. "Drink this."

She took a cautious sip. Swished it around her mouth. Swallowed, wincing. Then she gave the bottle back to him, her hands shaking so badly, it spilled.

"That's all you want?"

She colored. "I...I have to pee."

Yancey made her squat behind the Cadillac while he watched. The moment seemed to stretch on for hours. As she was zipping up, she caught a glimpse of her reflection in the window. He'd beaten her so badly, she didn't recognize herself.

"These are for you." He placed a floppy hat and oversize sunglasses on her head. "Now gimme your hands."

She did as he asked. He zip-tied them again—in front of her this time—and draped a cheap plastic tourist poncho over them.

"I don't understand," she said. "What's happening?"

"That's up to your buddy. He called a few minutes ago. Said be ready to move come sunrise. Guess you must mean something to him after all."

"You won't beat him, you know. He's too good."

"Funny. That's exactly why I think I will."

* * *

Yancey drove them to a parking lot in Laurel Heights. It was teeming with Bellum operatives when they arrived. He backed the Cadillac into an empty spot and pocketed the keys.

"Here's how this is gonna go," he said. "You don't do as I say, I fucking kill you. You speak out of turn—to my men, your buddy, anyone—I fucking kill you. You so much as look at me funny, I fucking kill you. Are we clear?"

"W-we're clear," Cameron replied.

"Good. Now stay put, and don't touch anything."

As he climbed out of the car, Yancey's phone chimed, indicating a text. It appeared to have originated from an anonymous e-mail account rather than another phone. The sender's name was Tick Tock. The content of the message was a photo of his daughter and her young twins, taken through the window of their nursery.

A shiver crawled up Yancey's spine. He cursed Lombino under his breath and shot off a quick reply: *Stand down. Target acquired.* Then he stuffed his phone into his pocket as Reyes spotted him and trotted over.

Reyes's suit was rumpled and grass-stained at knees and elbow. His neck was mottled with bruises. He looked as if he hadn't slept or showered. When he spotted Cameron through the Caddy's windshield, he stopped short.

"Jesus, boss, that girl's a mess. You didn't—"

"Of course not," Yancey snapped, irritation masking his fear. "She was like that when I picked her up. Near as I could tell, it was justified—she did a number on the men who apprehended her."

"If you say so," Reyes replied doubtfully. "Who is she? What's her connection to our POI?"

"Sorry. All I'm authorized to say is, she means enough to the guy who snatched our prisoner from us that he's agreed to make a trade, so if we're lucky, all three of them will be in custody by day's end." Yancey had no intention of allowing any of them to be taken alive, but he needed Bellum's resources to get him close enough to put them down. If that meant feeding Reyes a heaping helping of bullshit, then so be it. "Did you do as I requested?"

"Yeah. Local law enforcement's on the lookout for the man who attacked us at the Broussard house. They've got strict instructions to inform us if he's spotted but to keep their distance. I leaked his picture to the press too and warned he might be planning follow-up attacks; there are stories posted online already, and his photo will be on TV within the hour. The Feds assure me they're going to funnel anything credible that comes in via the tip line straight to us. And I've stationed Bellum teams throughout the city, so we can move on him wherever he pops up. Not as many as I'd like, since some of our guys are busy doing God knows what—"

Yancey raised a hand to stop him. "Look. You're frustrated. I get it. Being out of the loop sucks. You gotta understand, though, you're still new to the organization, and you've yet to prove your worth. This op could be your chance to do just that, but first, I need to know that I can count on you. So whaddya say, Reyes: Are you in, or are you out?"

Reyes eyed the girl inside the Cadillac and frowned. "I'm not going to lie to you. None of this makes any sense to me—and when it's over, I expect some goddamn answers. But Bigelow's in the ICU right now, and Weddle's been in surgery all night. The bastard responsible should be made to pay for what he's done. If, as you say, this girl's our chance to make that happen—"

"She *is*."

"—then I'm in."

39.

H OW YOU HOLDING up, kid?"

Hendricks was clearly trying to keep his tone light, his demeanor confident. But Cameron could tell, even through the tinny speaker of the cell phone, that he was worried, and it terrified her.

She looked at Yancey. He nodded. "I—I'm okay," she said.

"I assume Yancey's listening in."

"Yeah. You're on speaker."

"How many men did he bring with him?"

"Don't answer that," Yancey snarled, and then, to Hendricks: "You never said to come alone."

"No," Hendricks replied mildly, "I didn't. Listen, kid, do you know where you are right now? Can you see any street signs or anything?"

Again Cameron deferred to Yancey, who said, "What the hell's that matter?"

This time, Hendricks wasn't so mild. "Yancey, if you ever want to see Segreti again, you'll shut the fuck up and let her answer."

Yancey frowned but didn't object.

"We're in the parking lot of some old UCSF building in Laurel Heights," she said.

"Okay," Hendricks said, and he fell silent for a moment. "I want you and Yancey to walk to the bus stop on the corner of California and Laurel. An eastbound bus will be there in three minutes. Be on it, both of you. Leave the goons behind."

"Then what, smart guy?" Yancey asked.

"I'll call you back shortly. I expect to talk to Cameron when I do."

Hendricks disconnected.

Yancey turned to a man holding a tablet computer with rubberized edges, built for field use. The guy'd perked up when Hendricks called, but he was scowling now. "Anything?" Yancey asked him.

"Not yet." He opened the rear door of a nearby Humvee with an oversize antenna on top and fiddled with an electronic device inside. It was a StingRay, Cameron realized, her stomach acid surging as panic gripped her. StingRays were cell-phone surveillance devices. They worked by sending out a pilot signal that outcompeted the nearest cell tower's and convinced cell phones in the immediate area to connect to the StingRay instead. Once a phone connected to the StingRay, it could be tracked by its GPS coordinates. "I'm picking up the conversation clear as day via the girl's phone, but wherever he's calling from, he's too far away to track. I'll need to get closer to lock onto his position,"

"All right, then. We'll play his game for now. Me and the girl are getting on the bus. You follow with the StingRay. I want additional units no more than two blocks away to our north, south, east, and west. The second we have a bead on him, the nearest team moves in. Remember, this asshole's ruthless and well trained, and he's proven he won't hesitate to act. If you get a shot, you take it. That's an order."

His men muttered their assent and started piling into Humvees.

"Reyes," Yancey continued. "Take the Caddy and cover my six. Make sure you're not spotted. You're my insurance policy in case shit goes sideways."

"You got it."

"But he said we were supposed to go alone," Cameron protested.

Yancey grabbed her by her shirt and raised his hand as if he meant to slap her. "You insolent little shit. I thought I warned you about speaking out of turn."

Cameron flinched and stammered unintelligibly.

"Easy, boss," Reyes said. "She won't do it again—will you?"

She shook her head emphatically. Yancey released her with a shove. "He told us to get on the *bus* alone—he didn't say fuck-all about anybody following. Now, Your Highness, can we go, or do you wanna talk this out some more?"

Cameron swallowed hard and said, "We can go."

"Good," Yancey said. He stuck a Bluetooth earpiece in his ear and said, "Let's move out."

It was early Monday morning. Sunrise had failed to burn off all the fog. The air was cool and clammy, the sky above, a hazy white. By the time they reached the bus stop, the driver had already closed the doors and seemed disinclined to reopen them. Yancey banged until he acquiesced then spent a minute digging through his pockets to find exact change for their fare. The driver glared at him with thinly veiled irritation.

The bus was half full of morning commuters, blue-collar types, mostly. Their eyes were wide and furtive. Their features were taut with stress. Cameron, bruised and bloodied beneath her hat and sunglasses, felt the weight of their attention as Yancey nudged her toward the nearest open seats, which turned out to be behind an older Asian woman in multicolored scrubs who watched them closely as they passed.

When Cameron sat down, the woman twisted in her seat and opened her mouth to speak, a look of concern on her face, but Yancey stopped her. "Turn the hell around, lady. There's nothing to see here."

The woman looked at Cameron, who nodded slightly. With obvious reluctance, the woman did as Yancey said.

Morning traffic lurched along. The route became more clogged with every stop. Cameron counted eleven in total before Hendricks called them back.

"You two alone?" he asked.

Hendricks was off speaker now since there were civilians around. Yancey held the phone to Cameron's ear and tilted it so he could hear as well. When Cameron hesitated, Yancey elbowed her in the ribs. "Y-yes," she said.

"Good. Get off the bus at the intersection of Clay and Van Ness. Then cross the street and hop the northbound bus toward Fisherman's Wharf."

Once Hendricks hung up, Yancey put a finger to his

earpiece and said, "You get all that? Good. Were you able to get a lock on him this time? You're kidding me. What the fuck am I paying you for?" As he spoke, his voice rose to a shout. The other passengers turned and stared. Yancey reddened and fell silent.

When the bus reached the specified intersection, they got off and jogged across the street. They had to wait five agonizing minutes for the next bus to arrive, during which time the Caddy slid into a metered parking space nearby. The Humvee carrying the StingRay was too big to park curbside, so it was forced to circle the block. Cameron was relieved when it vanished from sight.

The second bus ride felt far longer. All the seats were taken, so they had to stand. Cameron scanned the faces of their fellow passengers and saw Yancey doing the same. She didn't recognize any of them, though, and apparently, neither did he.

Rush-hour traffic congealed around them. Passengers slammed into one another with every tap of gas or brake. Nerves jangled. Tempers flared. The breaking news of heightened threat levels had people on edge. Cameron spotted blurry pictures of Hendricks on every smartphone screen and tablet.

Half a block ahead, a Prius jetted through a red light and got clipped by a delivery van. The gunshot crack as their fenders met made pedestrians shriek and sent ripples of unease through the bus. Even Yancey, who'd sown the current unrest, seemed affected by the crowd's mood. He grew more agitated by the minute and hissed a steady stream of orders at his men.

When Hendricks called back, he told them to get off at North Point and Mason, and he stayed on the line while they complied. Cameron—who could see the Humvee's cabin peeking out over the traffic a few blocks away, the StingRay's oversize antenna bobbing atop it—wanted to shout at him to hang up, but she didn't dare. This time, the Caddy was nowhere to be seen.

"Okay, fucko. We're off the bus. What next?"

"There's a shopping center to your right. Enter the parking garage and head south. Remain on the first level and move quickly."

Hendricks hung up, and Yancey and Cameron headed for the parking garage. Yancey led her by the arm. The zip-tie bit into her wrists beneath the plastic poncho.

"Do you goddamn have him yet?" Yancey barked into his earpiece. "I don't want your fucking excuses, what I *want* is his location!" His face was blotchy, his eyes manic. As he shoved Cameron through the open door of the garage, her emotions teetered queasily between anxiety and hope.

A man in workout gear spotted them on their way through the garage and cocked his head. Late thirties or early forties. Well muscled and damp with sweat. When they neared, he stepped into their path to block their way.

"Excuse me, miss, are you all right?"

"She's fine," Yancey replied.

"Sorry, Tex, but I was asking her, not you."

Yancey tightened his grip on Cameron's arm. "Tell the man you're fine, darlin'."

Cameron winced. "I—I'm fine."

"Forgive me for saying so, but you don't *look* fine."

"Relax, asshole," Yancey said, his temper flaring. "I'm a cop."

"Good," the man replied. "Then you won't mind me

311

calling 911 to confirm that." He took his cell phone from his pocket and began to dial.

"You know what?" Yancey said, tapping the button on his Bluetooth earpiece to terminate the link to his men. "We don't have time for this shit."

He drew his gun and pulled the trigger.

The shot echoed through the concrete structure. The man dropped, his chest a bloody mess. Cameron wailed, and her knees buckled, but Yancey's grip kept her from falling.

Yancey's phone rang. He answered it. "Weirdest fucking thing," he said. "My signal dropped out for a second. Seems fine now, though." Then he dragged Cameron—sobbing, hysterical—through the parking structure.

Hendricks called again. Cameron could barely speak. Her breath came in ragged gasps. Pinpricks of light danced at the edges of her vision. He asked her what was wrong, but Yancey yanked the phone away before she could reply. "Maybe she just misses you," he said.

Hendricks told them to take a right onto Bay Street. They passed a darkened sushi joint, a Starbucks, a Trader Joe's. Yancey peered suspiciously at all the passersby, but Cameron, terrified though she was, knew the city well and grew less convinced by the moment that Hendricks might be hiding around some corner. In her mind's eye, she could see him peering intently at the BART app she'd installed on his phone, trying to yank the two of them around hard enough to shake their tail. The thought calmed her. She had a feeling she knew where he was directing them next.

Her phone rang. "Can you see Taylor Street yet?"

"Yes," Cameron managed. "We're right on top of it."

"Good. Take a left, and be quick about it. There should be a cable car waiting." The line went dead once more.

The trolley car was empty. The city was somber and fearful, and its streets uncharacteristically devoid of sightseers. They rode until the track ran out. Yancey spent most of the trip shouting at his men.

"What do you mean, where am I? Shouldn't you *know?*" A pause. "Oh, good. We're out of range now too. That's just fucking *perfect.*"

He hung up. Threw his earpiece in a rage. Sat fuming as the trolley car clattered down the hill.

When they reached the end of Powell Street, they disembarked. Usually, looky-loos would crowd around three-deep to watch the rickety old turntable turn the trolley car around, but today the only people on the sidewalk hurried nervously past, eager to get where they were going. Yancey's head swiveled like a nervous bird's as he tried to take in everything at once. A blood vessel throbbed in the center of his forehead. Their Bellum escorts were nowhere to be seen.

Cameron's burner phone trilled. Yancey answered it. "Listen, motherfucker, I'm getting sick and tired of being jerked around. You keep this up much longer, I might just put a bullet in this bitch and hunt you down at my leisure."

"Relax," Hendricks said. "You're almost done. There's an escalator across Market Street. Take it."

They did as Hendricks instructed, Yancey's left hand holding Cameron's right triceps in a death grip. Once they stepped onto the escalator, Yancey thumbed the button to put the phone on speaker. "Where are you, asshole? I'm running out of patience."

The line crackled, the signal weakening. Two bars dwindled to one as they descended. Cameron worried the call would get dropped. Hendricks drew the moment out by taking forever to respond.

"I'm in Oakland. Take the Richmond/Daly City line. And if I were you, I'd hurry. The train leaves in ninety seconds."

Hope fluttered in Cameron's chest. So *that's* why the StingRay couldn't get close enough to track his call. He wasn't in San Francisco anymore—he was across the bay.

Yancey balked. "That's not enough time!"

"If you want Segreti, it had better be," Hendricks replied.

"But—" Yancey began. They'd reached the bottom of the escalator.

The signal vanished.

The call was dropped.

Yancey stuffed Cameron's phone into his pocket. Checked his own phone for a signal and swore. Then he pushed her toward the ticketing machines.

Cameron realized this must have been Hendricks's plan all along. Even if Yancey *could* tip his buddies to their destination, it'd take them forever to get there. And if his fancy-pants encrypted phone didn't have a signal here, it was a safe bet it wouldn't have one on the train: it remained underground until it hit the Transbay Tube, three-odd miles of track that ran forty meters beneath the churning surface of San Francisco Bay.

40.

H ENDRICKS, FEVERISH AND edgy from adrenaline, bounced
lightly on the balls of his feet at the center of the busy
platform as the train from San Francisco pulled into the
station. Brakes squealed. Warm air buffeted his cheeks.
Loudspeaker announcements echoed off the tiles.

He knew that Yancey'd sent the body-cam images of
him to every news outlet and law enforcement agency in
the area, so he had altered his appearance as best he could.
He'd ditched the windbreaker and wore a Raiders cap low
on his head. A piece of medical tape stretched across the
bridge of his nose, as if he'd broken it. He hoped it was
enough to render him unrecognizable, but he worried his
bedraggled appearance would warrant a second look. His
navy henley was filthy, and darker where his wound had
bled through. His pants were stiff from seawater because
he'd had to hop out of the dinghy when they'd neared the

315

Oakland waterfront to drag it into the shadow of the dock. Whenever BART police walked by, he averted his eyes, and he'd taken care to position himself in a surveillance-camera blind spot.

As Hendricks scanned the crowd, he realized that—his nervous fidgeting aside—he was the only person in sight standing still. All around him, people in business attire shuffled on and off of trains. Most were tense and watchful. Others fiddled compulsively with their phones.

Hendricks's phone was in his pocket, dead and useless. He'd worn the battery down to nothing directing Cameron and Yancey around town. As it dropped into the red, he began to wonder if he'd get them here before it shut down.

But it had held on long enough—and now, their train had arrived.

Segreti was in position.

It was time.

Despite Hendricks's teasing, it turned out Cameron was a genius for putting the BART app on his phone. If this went as planned, her foresight would have played a major role in saving her life. If it didn't...best not to think about that. Given how beat up he was—his knife wound throbbing, his face flushed, his brow beaded with sweat despite the platform's relative cool—he didn't like his odds if this meet went south.

Yancey stepped off the train, eyes darting everywhere. He pushed Cameron ahead of him as he walked, his left hand gripping her shoulder so tightly, his knuckles were white. His right hand was obscured by his sport coat, which was draped to conceal the gun pressed to her side. Hendricks put his right hand on the butt of the SIG Sauer he'd taken from Reyes; it was tucked into the waistband of his pants, his shirt pulled down to cover it.

When Yancey's eyes lit on Hendricks, Hendricks gave him a nod, scarcely more than a subtle raise of his hat brim. Yancey smiled wolfishly and maneuvered Cameron toward Hendricks, the morning commuters oblivious around them.

She had a poncho slung over her bound wrists, a silly hat on her head and sunglasses on her face. Despite the getup, it was clear to Hendricks she'd been viciously beaten. Her shoulders hitched slightly as she struggled not to cry.

"Where the fuck's Segreti?"

"Let the girl go and I'll tell you."

"You're outta your goddamn mind if you think that's how this is gonna go down. You're a wanted man. I'm law. If you force me to, I'll gun you both down here and now."

"Easy," Hendricks said. "Just keep cool and we can all get what we want."

Yancey laughed. "No chance of that," he said. "That ship sailed for me when Segreti resurfaced. All I wanted was that fucker to stay dead when I killed him."

"As I understand it, he's not the only one who died that day."

"Which makes his resurfacing all the more regrettable. Now those people died for nothing."

An announcement blared. Hendricks cocked his head and listened.

"I'm sorry," Yancey said, "am I boring you?"

"Not at all," Hendricks replied. "It's just, that announcement was for your train. If I were you, I'd hurry up and catch it."

Yancey squinted in puzzlement at Hendricks, then followed Hendricks's gaze toward the train departing for San Francisco on the other side of the platform. And in the nearest car, he spotted Segreti slumped across two seats, his eyes closed, one wrist cuffed to the metal grip on the seat beside the aisle.

Cameron saw him too and said, "Michael, no, you can't—" but Yancey silenced her with a jab of his gun barrel to her ribs.

"He alive?" Yancey asked.

"Last I checked," Hendricks replied. "But he was… uncooperative… when I told him about our deal, so I had to drug him."

Yancey snorted. "That sounds like the Segreti I know."

Hendricks took a small silver key out of his pocket and extended it to Yancey. A handcuff key. Yancey had to let go of either Cameron or the gun to take it. He elected for the former and snatched the key out of Hendricks's hand. Then he grabbed Cameron once more and tried to yank her backward, toward the train. Whether he intended to use her as cover until the last second or bring her with him was unclear, but either way, it wasn't going to happen. Hendricks had a hold of her.

They played tug-of-war for a moment with the scared young woman caught between them. The train hissed. The doors began to slide shut. Yancey was forced to make a choice.

He released Cameron. She fell forward into Hendricks's arms.

Yancey turned and ran. The doors nearly closed on him as he leaped through.

Hendricks watched him go and held Cameron close

while she trembled in his arms, tears spilling down her cheeks. Then, at once, she tensed. Over Hendricks's shoulder, she thought she caught a glimpse of a familiar face in the crowd. Familiar, but unwelcome. One of Yancey's men. But as soon as she thought she saw him, he was gone.

"I—I think they followed us," Cameron managed through her sobs. "Yancey's men, I mean. I don't know how they could've, but they did. We need to move."

"It's all right," Hendricks told her. "You're safe now."

"You don't understand," she protested.

"Believe me, kid. I do. You're scared. Rattled. No one followed you, I promise. Now c'mon, let's get out of here."

He cut her free of her zip-tie with the X-Acto knife, took her hand, and tried to lead her to the up escalator and the street. But Cameron remained fixed in place and didn't move until the train pulled out of the station, sending Yancey through the Transbay Tube once more.

41.

THE HARDEST PART wasn't the fear of dying, Segreti thought. It wasn't the uncertainty. It was pretending to be asleep.

Segreti's mouth was open, his muscles relaxed. He watched through his eyelashes as Yancey leaped through the closing doors onto the train car and slammed into its unsuspecting passengers.

"Watch it, asshole!" A wiry punk in a Dead Kennedys T-shirt wheeled on Yancey and shoved him. Yancey pistol-whipped him in the face, and he went down bleeding.

The passengers recoiled, shouting and pushing toward the exits, but it was too late; the platform doors were closed. The train shuddered and began to move.

"Listen up!" Yancey yelled, holding his government-issued credentials in the air like a badge. "I'm a federal investigator, and I have reason to believe there's a bomb on this train car! For your safety, I'm gonna need you all to proceed to the adjacent cars immediately!"

Panic rippled through the crowd. People scrabbled over one another as everyone attempted to squeeze through the narrow doors at once. Soon, the car was quiet save for the clatter of the tracks.

Yancey strolled down the aisle toward Segreti. As he approached, Segreti closed his eyes completely, worried that parted lids would give the ruse away. Yancey reeked of cigarettes and aftershave. His shadow painted the backs of Segreti's eyelids a deeper black.

Yancey backhanded Segreti across the face. Segreti's lips split against his teeth and began to bleed. It took a supreme force of will for Segreti to keep his eyes closed and allow his head to loll, but he knew he had only one shot of leaving the train alive, and he had to make it count.

"Wake up, shithead," Yancey said. "I want you to look at me and know that, after all these years, I've got you. That there's no one coming to save you this time. That there's nowhere left for you to run."

Yancey leaned in close and punched Segreti in the gut. Segreti doubled over but failed to open his eyes, so Yancey slid into the row of seats behind him, yanked him upright by his hair, and rested the barrel of his gun against the nape of Segreti's neck.

"Aw, c'mon, Segreti," Yancey continued. "Killing you won't be as satisfying if you're not awake when I do it. I confess, this setting ain't my first choice for an execution, but lucky for me, one of my company's subsidiaries operates the security cameras for the entire fucking BART system, including the ones in this train. All our surveillance systems are equipped with an emergency backdoor, so it'll be a breeze for me to wipe the hard drive before anyone's the wiser—once I send a copy to your buddies at the Council, that is. Which means I get the pleasure of painting this train car with your brains, and there'll be nobody to dispute my version of events. I'm thinking of going with *When I tried to bring him in for questioning, the crazy bastard went for my gun*, but I'm open to suggestions."

"Yancey!"

The call came from the front of the train car. Segreti peeked through slit eyelids once more and struggled not to flinch. Reyes stood just inside the doorway to the adjacent car, his left pant leg caught on his empty ankle holster, a compact Remington R51 nine-millimeter in his hand.

"Christ, Reyes," Yancey said, "I thought I lost you miles back. You can lower your weapon—this fucker's unconscious."

"How about you lower yours?" Reyes said.

Yancey didn't. "I don't know how much you heard just now, but this ain't what it looks like."

"Good. Because it looks like you were about to kill an unconscious man in cold blood. You told me this guy was a person of interest in the bridge attack, but this seems more like a personal vendetta to me."

"You know, son, I'm starting to get the impression you don't like me very much."

"Not particularly, no."

"Then tell me what I need to do to, uh, rebuild our relationship."

"How about you start by letting me turn this man over to the FBI?"

"Sure thing," Yancey said. "In fact, I'll deliver him myself."

"There's no need," Reyes replied. "I called them from the station. They'll be waiting for us on the other side of the tunnel when we arrive."

Yancey sighed. "I really wish you hadn't done that."

"Why's that?"

"Because, whether you believe me or not, I promise you, Segreti's a lowlife piece of shit. You, on the other hand, may be a dick, but you're still one of the good guys. And now I can't let either of you walk out of here."

Yancey grabbed Segreti's collar. Yanked him backward in his seat. Ducked behind him. And aimed his gun at Reyes.

With Segreti in the way, Reyes didn't have a shot—and at this distance, Yancey couldn't miss.

Reyes watched helplessly as Yancey's finger tightened on the trigger. Then Segreti opened his eyes, slipped his hand free of its cuff, and twisted in his seat. He drove an open palm into Yancey's shooting arm as Yancey's gun roared and stuck his other hand into the pocket of his sweatshirt. Reyes tensed for impact, but the shot went wide and blew a hole in a nearby window. Wind, cold and metallic, whistled through it.

Three more gunshots quickly followed. Yancey jerked upright in his seat. Then he swayed a moment and slumped into the aisle, the revolver falling from his hand.

His eyes were wide. His face was pained. His stomach blossomed red.

Segreti rose from his seat, the .45 Hendricks had given him trained on Yancey. In his seat back were three bullet holes, their edges scorched by muzzle flash.

Yancey cupped his hands over his stomach, trying in vain to keep his blood where it belonged. It bubbled up between his fingers when he pressed down. Yancey's face paled, then slackened. His hands fell away. His sightless eyes stared vaguely toward the ceiling. He was gone.

Segreti aimed his gun at Yancey for thirty seconds longer, making sure, and then he lowered it.

"Thanks," said Reyes, his gun still aimed in Segreti's general direction. "You saved my life."

"No problem," Segreti replied.

Reyes nodded toward the handcuffs dangling from the metal handgrip on the seat back. "How'd you manage to slip those things?"

"They're not real—they're plastic toys. Got a hidden release button on the side. Buddy of mine broke into a fetish shop on our way here and stole 'em."

"The same buddy who sprung you from our custody at the Broussard house?"

Sadness flitted across Segreti's features at the mention of Lois's last name. "That's the one."

"You didn't have anything to do with what happened at the bridge, did you?"

"No, I didn't."

"Then how about you put the gun down and tell me why Yancey wanted you dead?"

"It's a long story," Segreti said. He kept his weapon pointed at the floor but didn't drop it. Reyes slowly lowered his.

Reyes looked out the window at the darkness blurring by outside. The car rattled down the tracks, empty but for the two of them, Yancey's bleeding corpse sprawled in the aisle between. "Seems like we've got time."

"Hey," Segreti said, "did you mean what you said about the Feds or were you bluffing?"

"I wasn't bluffing. I gave 'em a ring when I began to suspect that Yancey wasn't what he seemed. They'll be waiting for us at the station."

"Goddamn it. I can't let them take me."

"Why not?"

"The people Yancey worked for won't stop coming for me until I'm dead. And if I'm in custody, they'll know right where to find me."

"I don't get it—what does Bellum want with you?"

"Not Bellum," Segreti said. "The other ones."

"What other ones?"

Segreti frowned. "You got anybody in your life you care about? Friends, family, pets, whatever?"

"Sure. Doesn't everybody?"

"The lucky ones do. And if you count yourself among them, you're better off not knowing."

"Fine. Don't tell me who's after you, but you should tell the Feds, at least. I'm sure they can protect you."

"You have no idea how fucking wrong you are," Segreti said. "The worst part is, I actually thought I'd gotten clear of all this shit. Now I realize there's no escaping your past—anywhere you go, it's always right behind you. Hey, you ever hear of a guy named Heraclitus?"

"Who?"

"Never mind. It's not important. What *is* important is, I'm sick of this life—it ain't mine anymore. And the truth is, I'd rather go out on my own terms than wait around for the fuckers Yancey worked for to catch up with me."

"Don't talk like that," Reyes said. "You and me are

walking out of here together, okay? The rest will sort itself out. You have my word."

"Your word," Segreti echoed. "I've heard that one before. Even, once, from him." He nudged Yancey's body with his foot. "For what it's worth, I'm sorry you're gonna hafta see this—but if it makes you feel any better, I'm sick. The Big C. I didn't have long left anyway."

"Whatever you're thinking about doing—" Reyes said, but by the time the words cleared his lips, it was too late.

Segreti inhaled sharply. Raised the .45 to his head. As Reyes screamed for him to stop, he pulled the trigger. His head snapped back, and his body fell to the floor.

42.

CAMERON AND HENDRICKS watched Segreti die on the nightly news as they sat holed up in a shitty hotel room. The train's surveillance cameras captured the whole thing. It was a somber, horrifying affair, traumatic enough that Cameron had to look away. Hendricks watched every second of the footage, though. He felt he owed Segreti that much.

The train was halted soon after. The passengers were forced to hike single file down the tunnel's narrow service walkway to the nearest station—still Oakland, at that point. The tunnel was shut down for hours afterward so it could be inspected for damage and so the crime-scene techs could do their thing, and BART service between the cities was suspended.

The news identified Segreti by name and peddled a slanted version of the whole sordid tale. A gangster in hiding. A retired federal agent recognizing him and making it his mission to track him down, hell-bent on bringing in the one who got away. A bloody altercation leaving both men dead. One was painted a two-bit lowlife, the other a hero.

If you asked Hendricks, that wasn't far off—only they had it backward which was which.

Segreti's death didn't dominate the news cycle for long. Later that evening, the White House announced that government operatives had raided a body shop in South San Francisco and—after what was described as a protracted gun battle—had killed two members of the True Islamic Caliphate, one of them the man from the video. Inside, they found handguns, assault rifles, and a pair of partially assembled explosive vests, as well as a map of San Francisco on which the Federal Building and several targets in the Castro District were marked.

The statement never mentioned Bellum by name, but come Wall Street's morning bell, their stock soared nonetheless.

Hendricks's memories of the next sixteen hours or so were spotty. His wound was in bad shape, and a brutal fever had taken hold of him. He slathered it with antibiotic ointment and popped aspirin like Tic Tacs until his fever broke. Cameron was so worried about him, she refused to get checked out at the nearby urgent care clinic until he threatened to go off his meds. It turned out she needed stitches and a tetanus shot, but thankfully, Yancey and the assholes at the hospital hadn't broken any bones.

When Hendricks was feeling well enough to move, he and Cameron parted ways. She seemed bummed but didn't argue. "Guess it was silly of me, thinking I could help you ... do what you do," she said.

"I don't know," he said. "You did all right out there. And I may still need a favor from time to time. IDs. Aliases. A little background work, maybe. You know—the kind you can manage from your dorm room, well out of the line of fire."

"Deal," she said. "But I'm not going back to college, not until I decide what for."

"What are you going to do in the meantime?"

She shrugged. "There's a lot of advocacy groups out there that need volunteers. I think I'll try to do some good while I figure out what's next."

"Something tells me you'll do plenty."

They hugged. She squeezed him so tight, his stitches hurt. When she finally let him go, tears brimmed in her eyes. "Do me a favor out there, would you?"

"What's that?"

"Don't die."

Hendricks smiled, but said nothing.

He didn't want to make a promise he couldn't keep.

43.

CHARLIE THOMPSON STOOD in an apartment full of boxes and wondered where the hell she'd put her keys.

Officially, she'd moved out of O'Brien's house four days ago, once her transfer had come through. That's when the movers picked up her boxes and drove them here. But unofficially, she'd been sleeping at a hotel every night since the shit went down in San Francisco. Hard to believe that less than three weeks ago, she and Kate were engaged. Now she was single, living in a condo with a partial view of Lake Michigan, and working out of the Milwaukee field office.

She'd never seen a transfer go through so quickly. But O'Brien had been motivated. "You're lucky you're keeping your badge," she'd said. "If it were up to me, you'd be leaving here in chains."

Thompson spotted her keys atop the mantel. Snatched them up and headed for the door. She was late. Halfway out, she doubled back and grabbed the manila folder on the counter. She'd brought it home from the office yesterday and needed it today. If she'd forgotten it, she would have had to turn around.

Once she was on the road, she let her car's GPS guide her through the unfamiliar streets to I-43. She headed not south toward the field office, but north toward a small town called Grafton. Toward her new assignment.

The sky was clear and bright, the Saturday-morning traffic sparse. The September air was just crisp enough to remind her of summer's passing. She drove with the windows down, the radio off, her hair blowing, enjoying the roar of the wind in her ears, and the sun's warming glow through the windshield.

The drive was flat and green, the highway divided by a strip of grass and lined with trees on either side. Occasionally, the trees would fall away, and farmland would peek through.

She exited the highway and headed west on a commercial stretch. Best Buy, Costco, Home Depot. Eventually, a town sprung up around her.

Ever smaller streets, ever more residential, until finally she stopped outside a modest ranch in a nondescript suburban neighborhood. The house was white with red shingles. Arched windows and doorways lent it an almost Spanish air, making it something of an oddity on this block.

Thompson strode up the short walkway onto the porch and rapped twice on the front door. An agent peeked through the narrow window to the side of it. He unlocked the door—bolts clunking, chains rattling—and let her in. "Where is he?" she asked.

"Kitchen," the agent replied.

He was eating breakfast when she walked in. Half a grapefruit. A cup of coffee. A pill organizer sat beside his plate, the kind with a compartment for every day of the week. A tan ball of fur snored quietly on his bony lap. "Agent Thompson," he said, smiling.

"Morning, Frank," she said.

She hadn't liked Hendricks's plan one bit when he'd called to read her in. It was too dangerous, she thought, and there were too many opportunities for it to go wrong.

Honestly, it *had* gone wrong. The deal had been that Yancey would be delivered alive and made to answer for what he'd done. But in the end, he'd given Segreti no choice. Thompson wouldn't lose any sleep over it. Yancey was a bad man. The bomb blast that leveled Segreti's safe house killed nine federal employees, some of them her friends. And then there was that poor bastard who Yancey shot dead in the parking garage—a case that officially remained unsolved because Cameron could never testify without compromising the Bureau's case against the Council.

Thompson knew nothing about Yancey's role in bringing the members of the True Islamic Caliphate into the country. Bellum made sure anything that could implicate them in the bombing of the Golden Gate was buried.

Segreti's apparent suicide, which was supposed to happen once Yancey was safely neutralized and removed from the train car, was another sticking point for her. She thought it reckless and unnecessary. But Segreti refused to testify against the Council unless the world thought him dead—not to protect himself, he insisted, but because he couldn't stand another Albuquerque on his conscience—so it was unavoidable.

Staging it had been easy enough. Every BART train is

equipped with between eight and twelve cameras; they simply leaked the most convincing angle to the press and had Hendricks's Bellum contact, Reyes, delete any footage that made it clear Segreti shot six inches past his own left ear.

Enlisting Reyes in the effort, however, had taken some work. Hendricks reached out to him a few hours before he was supposed to exchange Segreti for Cameron, using the number from the texts Cameron had intercepted. At first, Reyes was furious—Hendricks had assaulted him, after all, and put several of his men in the hospital. Hendricks let him vent. When Reyes finally ran out of steam, Hendricks told him what he knew of Yancey's interest in Segreti.

"You really expect me to take your word for it that Yancey's in the pocket of some vast criminal conspiracy?" Reyes had asked.

"No," Hendricks had replied. "That's why I need you to get in contact with Special Agent Charlotte Thompson of the FBI."

Hendricks provided him with no contact information, instead insisting Reyes do the legwork, so he would know she wasn't fake. In the time it took for him to track down her phone number, Hendricks filled her in on his exchange with Reyes and gave her a rough outline of his plan. Once Reyes was onboard, it was simply a matter of moving the pieces into place and everyone playing his or her respective part.

In a way, she thought, Segreti's apparent demise was fitting. He'd been resurrected on camera and killed again the same way. This time, the FBI wasn't leaving anything to chance—aside from Charlie and her handpicked detail, the only people in the Bureau who knew Segreti was still alive were O'Brien and the director himself.

"How'd your appointment with the doc go?" Thompson asked. Segreti looked like he'd lost weight since she'd last seen him—which seemed impossible, since it was only days ago—and he'd developed a sickly pallor.

"Good," Segreti said. "He says the cancer's responding to treatment. I might have another year in me after all. And he gave me something for the nausea, so food's been staying down a little better."

"Glad to hear it."

The dog, Ella, stirred and looked at Thompson. Then she yawned and went back to sleep.

"How's she been doing?" Thompson asked.

"A little better every day, but the agents tell me she still whines something fierce whenever I leave." He smiled again. "Whatcha got there?"

Thompson opened the manila folder. Handed him the top page. When Segreti saw it, he laughed. It was a death certificate with his name on it.

"Thought you might get a kick out of that. In the eyes of the U.S. government, you're officially a dead man."

"Twice over now. You got anything else in there for me?"

She handed him the second document. "That's a copy of your immunity agreement. Everything's exactly as we discussed, and as you can see, the attorney general has signed off on it."

Segreti read it carefully, nodding when he reached the section that ensured that Cameron and Hendricks could not be prosecuted for what went down in San Francisco. Then he set the document aside.

"So," Thompson said, "what now?"

Segreti smiled. "Now you pull up a chair and I tell you everything I know about the Council."

44.

HEADLIGHTS SPLASHED ACROSS Sal Lombino's living-room window and cast a diamond pattern that slid leftward up the wall. As Sal's ex backed her Mercedes out of the driveway, his daughter, Izzie, waved from the backseat. Sal, watching through the window, waved back, a smile pasted on his face for Izzie's benefit. As soon as the car slid out of sight, he frowned and said, "That fucking whore."

It was Sal's weekend with Izzie. He was supposed to have her until tomorrow night, but an hour ago, Vanessa called to say she'd just won tickets to tonight's performance of *Disney on Ice*. If he'd picked up the call, he would've put the kibosh on his ex's bullshit, but like an idiot, he'd let Izzie answer, and once she heard about the tickets, she could barely contain her excitement. Sal couldn't bring himself to break her heart, so he agreed to let her go.

It was just one weekend, he told himself—and Vanessa had better relish it. One of these days she'd push him too far, and he'd be forced to have her taken care of. Then every weekend would be his weekend with Izzie.

At least the empty house gave him a chance to make a phone call. He'd been planning on doing it first thing Monday, but with Izzie gone, there was no point in putting it off.

He headed to the guest bedroom, activated the audio jammer, and dialed the number for the chairman's latest burner.

"Hello, Sal."

"Mr. Chairman," Sal replied.

"Please. I'm at home. The room's been swept, and active countermeasures are in place. You can speak freely."

"Thank God. That makes this conversation a whole lot easier. I have good news."

"Let's hear it, then."

"Those photos of the junior senator from Texas worked like a charm. He agrees that his constituents are unlikely to reelect someone of his...proclivities...and assures me that, come Wednesday, we can count on his vote—provided he can count on our discretion."

"He was the final holdout, wasn't he?"

"Yeah, which means the legislation's gonna pass. Bellum stands to make billions in domestic contracts. Their stock is already through the roof—it's gonna hit the stratosphere once the news breaks. The Council should see a thousand-fold return on its investment, at least."

The majority of Bellum stock was owned by Council front companies, and had been since Bellum's initial public offering five years ago.

"That *is* good news! Any updates on the investigation?"

"It's winding down, and based on everything my sources tell me, we're in the clear. As far as the Feds are concerned, Yancey died a hero. Bellum thinks he was a reckless idiot whose poor judgment made them inadvertently complicit in a terrorist attack on U.S. soil, so they've worked hard to bury any evidence of their dealings with the True Islamic Caliphate. Even the Council has no idea you and I maneuvered Yancey into place and ensured that the boat and bomb schematics found their way into the proper hands. They made it clear when we started down this path they didn't want to know how the sausage was made."

"That's a relief. I won't lie, this high-wire act has done a number on my stomach. If Bellum had been connected to the attack in any way—"

"—we would have scapegoated the living fuck outta Yancey to limit the exposure and shorted all our Bellum stock before the news broke, like we discussed. Relax, Wentworth. The plan worked like a charm. We made the FBI and Homeland Security look like chumps. Sent Bellum in on a white horse to save the day. Turned playing cops and robbers into a multibillion-dollar industry. Now that we control both sides of the equation, there's no limit to the money we can make. And as an added bonus, we managed to smoke Segreti out and kill him too."

"That was a happy accident."

"Maybe," Sal replied, "or maybe it was, you know, poetical. If it weren't for him, I mighta never picked the Golden Gate to hit."

"How's that?"

"Frank was always going on about how he'd retire out there one day. Got the idea from some boring-ass old movie. After he tried to drop a dime on us, I figured what better fuck-you? Turns out, the guy was serious. Guess he shoulda moved to Boca instead."

"Anyone ever tell you that you're a vindictive mother-fucker?"

"Yeah, my bitch ex-wife, every day for five years."

By the time Sal hung up, he was feeling good. Went-worth, it seemed, had forgiven him—and why shouldn't he? Together, they'd delivered on a promise to the Council seven years in the making.

He felt so good, in fact, that when he saw the stranger standing in the bedroom doorway with a gun, he shook his head and laughed.

"Something funny?" the man asked.

"Yeah," Sal replied. "You're one unlucky son of a bitch, that's what. If I were you, pal, I'd turn and walk away right now, because, believe me, you picked the wrong house to break into."

"No," he said. "I didn't. But I caught the tail end of your phone call, Sal, and I've gotta say, you should really show the mother of your child a little more respect."

"Wait—did *Vanessa* put you up to this? It'd explain the bullshit with the tickets. So, what, she thought she'd get Izzie out of the house and send some dumbfuck goon to rough me up?"

"Your ex has no idea I'm here. As far as she knows, she won those tickets fair and square."

"What the fuck is this about, then?"

"I have some questions for you. You're going to answer them."

"Is that so." Sal's eyebrows raised in disbelief.

"You might not believe it, but yes."

"Who the hell do you think you are?"

"Last year, you and your people sent a man to kill me. I took it personally—and I'm not the kind to turn the other cheek. Call it a character flaw."

Sal went pale. His heart thudded in his chest. Suddenly, he wished to hell he kept a piece in the guest room, but he didn't, because that might tip anyone who searched it that there was more to this room than there appeared.

"I don't...how did you find me?"

"It's a long story."

"Bottom-line it for me, then."

"Okay." Hendricks smiled. "Frank Segreti says hello."

ACKNOWLEDGMENTS

I'm incredibly fortunate to have some of the finest folks in publishing in my corner. Chief among them are my agent, David Gernert, and my editor, Joshua Kendall, who helped shape this book into the best version of itself. Thanks, gents. I owe you big-time.

Special thanks to Ellen Goodson, Anna Worrall, and the rest of the Gernert Company team; Pamela Brown, Sabrina Callahan, Betsy Uhrig, and everyone at Mulholland/Little, Brown; Sylvie Rabineau of RWSG Literary Agency; and Tracy Roe.

Thanks also to Steve Weddle, at whose urging Michael Hendricks was created; my family—Burns, Holm, and Niidas—for foisting my books on anyone within reach; and the crime-fiction community, who've embraced me as their own at every turn.

My deepest gratitude is reserved for my wife, Katrina. Without her unwavering love and support, Lord knows where—or who—I'd be.

ABOUT THE AUTHOR

Chris Holm is the author of *The Killing Kind*, the first novel to feature Michael Hendricks, and of the Collector trilogy, which blends fantasy with old-fashioned crime pulp. He is also an award-winning short-story writer whose work has appeared in a number of magazines and anthologies. Holm lives in Portland, Maine.

You've turned the last page.

But it doesn't have to end there . . .